# LETHAL
# EXPERIMENT

John Locke is a *New York Times* bestselling author, and was the first self-published author in history to hit the number 1 spot on Kindle. He is the author of the Donovan Creed and Emmett Love series. He lives in Kentucky.

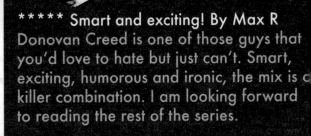

JOHN LOCKE

***** Smart and exciting! By Max R
Donovan Creed is one of those guys that
you'd love to hate but just can't. Smart,
exciting, humorous and ironic, the mix is a
killer combination. I am looking forward
to reading the rest of the series.

***** I love this book. By Madeleine
Labitan This novel is chock-full of surprising plot twists and turns from beginning to
end. It grips you from page one. I read it
in an evening.

***** Bingo! Cool. Read this book and
you're hooked on Locke. By Karin
Locke keeps the story moving and in such
an effortless way. I'm passing it on to my
husband. It's been awhile since I've read
something sexy: this fits the bill.

***** So Entertaining I just went
and downloaded another one.
By Patti Roberts
I read this book over a period of 2 days
on my kindle and loved it! So I have
just downloaded another one. I hereby
declare that I am a John Locke fan. Do
yourself a favor....

***** Outstanding. By Coolfire
An outstanding read. A roller coaster of
action and stunning surprises.

***** 10 stars. By Ally
A wonderful mystery thriller. I love all of
them but I think this is just my favorite.

customer reviews from
AMAZON.COM

# LETHAL
# EXPERIMENT
## JOHN LOCKE

HEAD
of ZEUS

First published in the UK in 2012 by Head of Zeus Ltd.

9 7 5 3 1 2 4 6 8

A CIP catalogue record for this book is available from
the British Library.

ISBN (Paperback): 9781781852323
ISBN (eBook): 9781781852330

Printed and bound by CPI Group (UK) Ltd,
Croydon, CR0 4YY

Head of Zeus Ltd
Clerkenwell House
45-47 Clerkenwell Green
London EC1R 0HT


www.headofzeus.com

# PROLOGUE

THE SMALL HOUSE was old and cramped by furniture that seemed even older. A transaction was taking place at the kitchen table, where the three of them sat. A slightly foul odor seeped in from the living room. Trish didn't know it yet, but the next few minutes would change her life. She cleared her throat.

"We were hoping to get eighteen thousand dollars," she said to the loan officer.

The young blond loan officer wore her hair combed back with a part midway above her left eye. "No offense," she said, "but it took more than eighteen thousand dollars of stress to put those dark circles under your eyes. Not to mention the car in your driveway, the condition of your home, the fact you've been turned down by every lender in town…"

Trish swallowed, seemed about to cry.

The loan officer's face was visually stunning, with flawless skin, impossibly high cheekbones, and sandy blond eyebrows that arched naturally over electric, palegray eyes. Her name was Callie Carpenter, and she was wearing driving gloves.

Trish's husband Rob wasn't looking at the gloves. His eyes had found a home in Callie Carpenter's perfectly-proportioned cleavage.

"You know the vibe I'm getting?" said Callie. "Pain. Frustration. Desperation. There's love in this home, I can feel it. But it's being tested. I look at you guys and I see the vultures circling your marriage."

Trish and Rob exchanged a look that seemed to confirm her words.

Trish said, "This sounds all New Age to me. I'm not sure what this has to do with our loan application."

Callie looked at the chipped coffee cup in front of her from which she'd declined to drink. She sighed. "Let me put it another way: how much money would it take to remove the stress from your lives, allow you to sleep at night and help you remember that the important thing is not other people and what you owe them, but rather the two of you, and what you mean to each other?"

Trish had been quietly wringing her hands in her lap, and now she looked down at them as though they belonged to a stranger. "I'm afraid we have no collateral."

Rob said, "The banks got us on one of those adjustable rate mortgages that turned south on us. Then I lost my job. Next thing you know?"

Callie held up a hand. "Stop," she said. "Would a hundred thousand dollars get you through the bad times?"

"Oh, hell yeah!" said Rob.

Trish eyed Callie suspiciously. "We could never qualify for that type of unsecured credit."

"This wouldn't be a conventional loan," said Callie, getting to her favorite part of the story. "It's what I call a Rumpelstiltskin Loan."

Trish's voice grew sharp. "You're mocking us. Look, Ms…"

"Carpenter."

"…I don't particularly care for your sense of humor. Or your personal assessment of our marriage."

"You think I'm playing with you?" Callie opened her

2

briefcase, spun it around to face them.

Rob's eyes grew wide as saucers. "Holy shit!" he said. "Is that a hundred grand?"

"It is."

"This is ridiculous," Trish said. "How could we possibly pay that back?"

"It's not so much a loan as it is a social experiment," Callie said. "The millionaire I represent will donate up to one hundred thousand dollars to any person I deem worthy, with one stipulation."

"What's that?" Rob said.

Trish's lips curled into a sneer. She spoke the word with contempt. "Rumpelstiltskin."

Callie nodded.

Rob said, "Rumpel—whatever you're saying, what's it mean?"

Trish said, "The fairy tale. She wants our first born unless we can guess the name of her boss."

"What?" Rob said. "That's crazy. We're not even pregnant."

Callie laughed. "Trish, you're right about there being a catch. But it has nothing to do with naming a gnome or giving up future children."

"Then what, you want us to rob a bank for you? Kill someone?"

Callie shook her head.

"So what's the catch?" Trish said.

"If you accept the contents of this suitcase," Callie said, "someone will die."

Trish said, "All right, that's enough. This is obviously some type of TV show, but it's the cruelest way to punk someone I've ever seen. Here's an idea for the next one: get a normal-looking woman instead of a beautiful model. And don't use

3

all the flowery New Age language. Who's going to buy that bullshit? Okay, so where's the camera—in the suitcase?"

The suitcase.

From the moment Callie lifted the lid, Rob had been transfixed. He'd finally found something more compelling to stare at than Callie's chest. Even now he couldn't take his eyes off the cash. "Do we get some sort of fee if you put this on TV?"

Callie shook her head. "Sorry, no TV, no hidden cameras."

"Then it doesn't make sense."

"Like I said, it's a social experiment. My boss is fed up with the criminal justice system in this country. He's tired of seeing murderers set free due to sloppy police work, slick attorneys, and stupid jurors. So, like a vigilante, he goes after murderers who remain unpunished. He feels he's doing society a favor. But society loses when any person dies, no matter how evil, so my boss wants to pay something forward for the life he takes."

"That's a crock of shit," Trish said. "If he really believed that, he'd pay the victims' families instead of total strangers."

"Too risky. The police could establish a pattern. So my boss does the next best thing, he helps anonymous members of society. Each time my boss kills a murderer he pays society up to one hundred thousand dollars. And today you get to be society."

Trish was about to comment, but Rob got there first. He was definitely getting more intrigued. "Why us?"

"A loan officer forwarded your application to my boss and said you were decent people, about to lose everything."

Trish said, "You represented yourself as a loan officer."

"I did."

"And you're not."

"I'm a different type of loan officer."

4

"And what type is that?"

"The type that brings cash to the table," Callie said.

"In a suitcase," Trish said.

Trish looked at the cash as if seeing the possibilities for the first time. She said, "If what you're saying is true, and your boss is paying all this money to benefit society, why tell us about the killing at all? Why not just pay us?"

"He thinks it's only fair that you know where the money comes from and why it's being paid."

Rob and Trish digested this information without speaking, but their expressions spoke volumes. Rob, thinking this could be his big chance in life, Trish, dissecting the details, trying to allow herself to believe. This was a family in crisis, Callie knew, and she had just thrown them the mother of all lifelines.

Finally Trish said, "These murderers you speak of. Is your boss going to kill them anyway?"

"Yes. But not until the money is paid."

"And if we refuse to accept it?"

"No problem. I'll ask the next family on my list."

Rob said, "The person your boss is going to kill—is there any possibility it's someone we know?"

"You know any murderers?"

Callie could practically hear the wheels turning as Rob and Trish stared at the open suitcase. Callie loved this part, the way they always struggled with it at first. But she knew where this would go. They'd turn it every way they could, but in the end, they'd take the money.

"This sounds like one of those specials, like 'What Would You Do?'" Trish said, unable to let go of her feeling this was all an elaborate hoax.

Callie glanced at her watch. "Look, I don't have all day. You've heard the deal, I've answered your questions, it's time to give me your answer."

Her deadline brought all their emotions to a head.

Trish's face blanched. She lowered her head and pressed her hands to either side of her temples as though experiencing a migraine. When she looked up her eyes had tears in them. It was clear she was waging a war with her conscience.

Rob was jittery, in a panic. No question what he wanted to do—his eyes were pleading with Trish.

Callie knew she had them.

"I'll give you ten minutes," she said briskly." I'll put my headphones on so you can talk privately, but you'll have to remain in my sight at all times."

"How do you know we won't contact the police after you leave?" Trish said, wearily.

Callie laughed. "I'd love to hear that conversation."

"What do you mean?"

"You think the police would believe you? Or let you keep a suitcase full of cash under these circumstances?"

Rob said, "Are we the first, or have you done this before?"

"This is my eighth suitcase."

Again they looked at each other. Then Rob reached over, as though he wanted to stroke the bills.

Callie smiled and closed the top. "Nuh uh."

"How many people actually took the money?" he asked. There was a sheen of sweat on his upper lip.

"I can't tell you that."

"Why not?" Trish asked.

"It could influence your decision and impact the social experiment. Look. Here's what you need to know: when someone takes the money, my boss feels he's gotten the blessing of a member of society to end the life of a murderer."

"This is crazy. This is just crazy," Trish whispered, as if

6

daring herself to believe.

"People die every day," Rob said. "And they're going to die whether we get the money or someone else does."

Trish looked at him absently, her mind a million miles away.

"They're giving this money to someone," Rob explained, "so why not us?"

"It's too crazy," Trish repeated. "Isn't it?"

"Maybe," Callie said, putting on the headphones. "But the money—and the offer—are for real."

# 1.

"AND YOU, MR. Creed," she said.

I looked up from my mixing bowl. "Ma'am?"

"What do you do for a living?"

"Apart from making brownies? I'm with Homeland Security."

Her name was Patty Feldson and she was conducting a home study as part of the adoption process. My significant other, Kathleen Gray, was hoping to adopt a six-year-old burn victim named Addie Dawes. Addie was the sole survivor of a home fire that claimed the lives of her parents and twin sister. Ms. Feldson had been watching Addie and Kathleen play dolls on the living room floor. Satisfied with the quality of their interaction, she turned her attention to me.

"Do you have a business card?" Patty said.

"I do." I took my wallet from my hip pocket and removed a card that had been freshly printed for this very occasion. I handed it over.

Patty read aloud: "Donovan Creed, Special Agent, Homeland Security." She smiled. "Well that doesn't reveal much. But it certainly sounds mysterious and exciting. Do you travel much, Agent Creed?"

I wondered how well we'd get along if I told her I was a government assassin who occasionally performs freelance hits for the mob and for an angry, homicidal midget named Victor.

"I do travel. But I'm afraid my job falls short of being mysterious or exciting. Mostly, I interview people."

"Suspected terrorists?"

I layered the batter into Kathleen's brownie pan with a silicone spatula and swirled Addie's name on top before placing the pan in the oven.

"Apartment owners, business managers, that sort of thing." I closed the oven door and set the timer for forty minutes.

"What's in the brownies?" she said.

I felt like saying marijuana, but Kathleen had warned me not to joke with these people. She was in the home stretch of the adoption process and I intended to do all I could to help her.

"You remember the actress, Katharine Hepburn?" I said.

"Excuse me?"

"This is her recipe. I found it in an old issue of the *Saturday Evening Post.*"

"Oh," she said. "I'd love to have it!"

"Then you shall."

A home study is a series of meetings you have to go through as part of the approval process for adopting a child. Kathleen had provided all her personal documents, passed the criminal background check, made it through all the appointments and provided personal references. But at least one meeting is required to be in your home, and all who live there (Kathleen) or spend nights there (me) had to be in attendance.

Patty Feldson wasn't here to do a "white glove" interview. She'd already made a positive determination about Kathleen's ability to parent. All that remained was to see what sort of person the boyfriend was. She knew, for example, that I had a daughter of my own, who lived with my ex in Darnell, West Virginia. If she'd done any digging she also knew that while

I've always been emotionally and financially supportive, I hadn't spent as much father-daughter time with Kimberly as I should have.

Patty moved closer and locked her eyes on mine. Lowering her voice, she said, "There's a big difference between being a father and a dad."

*Right*, I thought. *She's done her research*.

"I had to learn that lesson the hard way in my own life," I said. "And this might sound funny, but Addie's the one who inspired me to build bridges with Kimberly. We're closer now than ever before."

Patty nodded. We were both silent a moment, waiting to see who would speak first. In case you're keeping score, she did.

"Addie has become a special needs child," Patty said. "She's been traumatized physically and mentally and she's going to need a lot of nurturing."

"I understand."

"I hope so, Mr. Creed, because it's going to put a lot of stress on your relationship with Kathleen. Have you thought about your role in all this—I mean, *really* thought about it?"

Addie was an amazing kid. Funny, affectionate, brave — over the past few months she'd become special to both of us. Special wasn't the right word, she was more than that. Addie had become essential to our lives.

"I love Addie," I said.

She nodded and paused a few seconds. "I felt you must, Mr. Creed. What you've done for her and Kathleen speaks volumes."

Patty knew I'd recently given Kathleen a million dollars and put another ten million into a trust for Addie. What she didn't know is that I'd stolen all that money and more, from a West Coast crime boss named Joe DeMeo.

After witnessing another hour of unparalleled domestic harmony, Patty Feldson gathered Addie, the recipe, and half a pan of brownies.

"You're a shoo-in!" she gushed to Kathleen.

"I'll see you again tomorrow, darling," Kathleen said to Addie. Addie swallowed before speaking, to lubricate her throat. We had grown accustomed to the procedure, the result of her vocal chords being permanently damaged by the fire that nearly took her life.

"At the hospital?" Addie finally said in her raspy, whisper of a voice.

"Uh huh."

Another round of hugs was in order and then they were gone. I looked at the lovely creature that had defied all the odds and fallen for me.

"This might be the last time she'll have to leave you," I said.

Kathleen dabbed at the tears on her cheeks. "Thank you, Donovan." She put her hand in mine and kissed me gently on the mouth. "For everything," she added.

Life was good.

An hour later Victor called me on my cell phone. A quadriplegic little person on a ventilator, Victor's metallic voice was singularly creepy.

"Mis…ter Creed…they took…the…money," he said.

"The couple from Nashville?"

"Yes, Rob and…Trish."

"Big surprise, right?"

"When you get…a chance I…would like you to…kill the …Peterson…sis…ters."

I paused a minute, trying to place them. "They're in

12

Pennsylvania, right?"

"Yes, in…Camp…town."

I assumed my best minstrel voice and said, "You mean De Camptown Ladies?"

Victor sighed. "Really…Mis…ter Creed."

"Hey, show some appreciation! In France I'm considered a comedic genius."

"You and…Jerry Lewis… So, will you…go to … Camptown and…kill the…Petersons?"

"Doo Dah!" I said.

## 2.

THERE ARE NO racetracks in Camptown, Pennsylvania, population four hundred seventeen. Nor are there any bars. You want a drink, you head fourteen miles west to Towan-da. Closest nightlife is Scranton, fifty miles away.

The little town became famous throughout the world in 1850 after Stephen Foster published his famous song, "De Camptown Races." The horse race Foster immortalized started in Camptown, ended in Wyalusing, and yes, it was about "five miles long."

By the time I got my rental car and hit the road I was so hungry I took a chance on a beef burrito at the Horse Head Grill in Factoryville. I should have known better. You want a burrito, go to El Paso, not Factoryville. My lunch tasted like something you'd ladle out of an outhouse pit and serve to the finalists on *Survivor*.

But I digress.

Camptown is located in Bradford County, where the most recent crime stats showed 248 burglaries, 39 assaults, 24 rapes and two murders. If all went well, the Peterson sisters would double the murder tally in time to make the six o'clock news.

Which I intended to watch.

On a TV.

In a bar.

In Scranton.

"Your destination is one hundred feet on the right," said the sexy lady's voice on my navigation system. She led me to a long, white-gravel driveway that I purposely overshot. After driving a couple hundred yards, I turned and approached from the opposite direction, checking for witnesses. Once comfortable with the general layout, I pulled my rental car into the driveway and followed it to the concrete pad where a green 1995 Toyota Corolla was parked.

The Petersons were living in a white doublewide trailer with a brown metal roof. To that they'd added a screened porch that overlooked about two acres of front yard that was few trees and mostly dirt. I parked, cut the power and sat, waiting for dogs. None showed, but I used the time to wonder what the hell I was doing. Years ago I'd been a government assassin for the CIA, and the people I killed had been a threat to national security. When I retired, I took a short break and then began killing terrorists for Homeland Security. But those jobs were infrequent, so I began killing people for mob boss Sal Bonadello on the side. Sal's victims were always criminals and often murderers, so justifying their deaths hadn't been a problem.

But at some point I drifted into doing freelance work for Victor, and the types of jobs he was giving me were becoming more and more questionable. This latest series of killings were the result of a proposal Victor had made to my boss at Homeland, to see how far everyday Americans could be trusted. For example, would a couple like Rob and Trish be willing to house a terrorist in return for a specific amount of cash?

The initial results said no.

But would they be willing to allow innocent people to die?

Still no? Hmm. Interesting.

How about anonymous, unpunished murderers?

I put a roll of sealing tape in one of my jacket pockets, and two syringes in the other. The Peterson sisters, like Rob and Trish and half-a-dozen others, had accepted "Rumpelstiltskin Loans" after being told that by taking the money, an unpunished murderer would die. In Victor's mind, that made the recipients guilty of conspiracy to murder. Hence, accepting the cash, Rob and Trish were sentencing the Peterson sisters to death by execution. When Callie placed the next suitcase, Rob and Trish would have to die. It was, in all respects, a lethal experiment, and it would continue to be one until the day an applicant refused the money.

I exited the car and climbed the three preformed concrete steps in front of the Peterson trailer, thinking, *I've come a long way from the guy who used to kill to preserve our nation's freedom.*

The Peterson sisters had a tempered glass front door that offered a partial view of the living room. When I knocked on it, the entire front of the trailer shook. Soon a young lady came to the door and peered at me through the glass.

"Elaine?"

"Yes?"

"I'm Donovan Creed, with Homeland Security. May I come in?" I showed her my badge. She had no reason to know that Homeland agents don't carry badges.

A look of concern crossed her face as she slowly opened the door.

"What is this about, Mr. Creed?"

*What, indeed?* I wondered. *Is this what I've been reduced to, a guy who kills civilian men and women who didn't realize they'd become accessories to murder simply by accepting a sum of money they desperately needed? Was it really a fair experiment?*

Elaine Peterson was an attractive, thirty-two-year-old brunette in the first stage of weight gain. She wore black sweat pants and an oversized Pittsburgh Steelers tshirt that probably belonged to her estranged husband, Grady.

"It would save time if I could talk to both of you," I said. "Is Amber here?"

Not that Amber and Elaine were the most innocent people in town. They had used the bulk of their loan proceeds to buy drugs to resell to local high school kids.

Elaine started to turn her head toward the hallway but caught herself. "What's this about?" she repeated firmly.

"Please," I said. "Have a seat." As she started to sit I bolted past her and raced down the hall. She managed to get off a loud scream, but by then I'd opened the master bedroom door and caught the very large Amber cocking a pistol. I lunged at her and managed to knock her off balance. As she struggled to keep from falling, I snatched the gun from her hand and spun around just in time to avoid Elaine's flying fists. Elaine was too small to hurt me, but I smacked her in the nose anyway, in order to concentrate on Amber. I heard Elaine fall to the floor and figured that was a good place for her to stay while I dealt with her sister.

"What the fuck do you want?" Amber shouted, trying to make her voice bigger than it was.

She was handy, an accomplished bar brawler. At fiveten, two hundred forty pounds, she had some power. But her money punch was thrown in haste, before she'd got her feet under her. I jumped out of the way, set my feet and launched a hard back fist that caught her squarely on the temple. Amber shuddered a moment, then crashed to the floor. Moments later I had both girls face down on the master bedroom floor with their hands taped behind their backs. I rolled them over with my foot and taped their mouths shut.

Then I had a heart attack.

# 3.

"THERE ARE TWO types of chest pain to worry about," Dr. Webber said.

"Hang on a second, Doc," I said. "I'm putting you on speaker."

I pressed the button on my cell phone and forced myself to a standing position.

"Okay, go ahead," I said.

"You sound terrible."

I felt terrible. Moments earlier I'd crashed to the floor clutching my chest. Amber took that opportunity to flip and flop her enormous body, attempting to cross the floor and crush me like a beached whale flattens a sand castle. Luckily, the crushing pain had already begun to subside, but I was still weak and hurting, and it was a question of multitask or face lethal consequences. I rolled out of her path while removing the syringe from my pocket. I flicked off the protective plastic and hurled myself toward the fat girl. I had to stretch to reach her, but I made the effort and managed to jab her neck. I don't know if I had the strength to push in the plunger at that moment, but I didn't have the angle. Either way, it's a moot point, because Amber shook her head violently, and the hypodermic dislodged and skittered across the floor.

She tried to make the adjustment to flipflop back to me, but I climbed on her back and rode her like the wild hog she was. Elaine flailed away, attempting to help her sister, but only succeeded in kicking the syringe back to me. I picked it up and pushed it into Amber's neck and drove the liquid home.

Then I speed-dialled Darwin, my government facilitator, and asked him to get me a Homeland Security doctor. When Dr. Webber answered, I placed him on speaker phone.

Which brings us back into the moment.

"What are you doing right now?" Dr. Webber said, as Elaine shrieked in the background.

"Just tying up a few loose ends," I said.

I took the second syringe from my pocket and slammed it into Amber's sister. She stopped in midscream.

I immediately felt a stab of my own, in the center of my chest. Through clenched teeth, I said, "Now, what was that about the two kinds of pain?"

"Okay, well there's the squeezing kind that feels like you're squeezing a tube of toothpaste. Except that your heart is the toothpaste."

I staggered, but remained on my feet. I propped myself against the nearest wall to keep from falling. I still had to wipe down the scene before trying for my car.

The doc continued. "The second kind is like an elephant standing on your chest."

"Bingo."

"Okay," he said, "Don't panic. It's important that you lie still. Is anyone with you?"

I looked at the two bodies on the floor. "Only in spirit," I said.

"Okay, that's not so good. Do you have any aspirin? If you do, take one. But first, give me your location and I'll send an ambulance."

"I can't do that," I said.

I ended the call and put my hand in my pocket to feel my lucky silver dollar, the one my grandfather gave me when I was a kid.

"Don't fail me now," I said to the coin.

I called Darwin back and told him to send a chopper two miles northeast of Camptown, on 706. "And send someone to take my rental car back to Scranton."

"This isn't Sensory business. You'll have to reimburse the expenses."

"Of course."

Sensory Resources is the division of Homeland Security for which I work.

I paused.

"What else?" he said.

"Better send a couple of extra guys. I need them to clean a crime scene for me." I gave him the details.

"It's going to be very expensive. Shall I call you back with the total before you commit?"

I sighed, which caused a new round of pain to surge through my body. On the bright side, the pain seemed to be heading away from the center of my chest.

"I'll cover the costs," I said, "but let's get this thing in motion."

"You're not going to die on me, are you?"

His question caught me by surprise. The thought of dying never crossed my mind. Through all the years of being shot at and bombed and targeted by foreign death squads, and all the years I'd been testing weapons for the Army—it suddenly dawned on me that I'd never considered the possibility of dying.

And still didn't.

I forced a laugh. "I'm immortal, Darwin."

He paused, processing the comment. Paused long enough for me to wonder if he might be thinking this could be the perfect time to ambush me. I'm Darwin's top guy, I control Callie and Quinn and Lou Kelly and a halfdozen other trained killers.

On the other hand, I know a lot about the government that wouldn't look good on *60 Minutes or Dateline*.

"Anyone else know about your current situation?" Darwin said.

My best insurance against Darwin was my associates.

"Just Callie and Quinn." Figured I might as well let him think about those two hunting him down if anything happened to me.

"Camptown?" he said. "Like the song? What state?"

"Pennsylvania," I said. "Look it up."

"Doo Dah!" he said.

Victor was right. It wasn't funny.

# 4.

TRINITY HOSPITAL, NEWARK, New Jersey.

The treatment rooms in the Heart and Vascular Unit were small, but mine had a window that overlooked the freeway. I was lying semireclined in a hospital bed, wearing one of those openassed hospital gowns, watching the traffic, thinking how amazing it was that so many people had places to go. Did all these people have families and friends and jobs and people who depended on them? These thousands of people intersecting my life by passing my window at the very moment I watched them.

I focused on a single car, a cherry red Ford Mustang with a tan rag top, circa 1997. It was in my viewing range for maybe twenty seconds. I wondered if the driver was a man or woman, and if our paths had ever crossed. Maybe our paths were destined to cross in the future, and the driver of the Mustang would someday change my life. Maybe the driver has a child who will grow up to be the man or woman who eventually kills me. Or perhaps, moments from now, while attempting to exit the freeway, the driver will be sideswiped and fatally injured. Perhaps emergency rescue personnel will check his or her wallet and find a donor card, and the driver of the cherry red Mustang's heart would be harvested just in time to save my life tonight.

There was a swooshing sound in the doorway as a young

blonde with a perky smile slid the privacy curtain aside and entered the room.

"How are we doing today?" she said, in a practiced tone.

"We're hanging in there like a hair in a biscuit," I said.

She stopped a second, and then smiled.

"You're funny," she said.

She'd brought a small tray of medical items that included hypodermic needles, cotton, rubbing alcohol, and some type of rubber tubing. She placed the tray on the counter by the sink and I heard the snap of sterilized gloves being put on. Then she started swabbing the center of my forearm with alcohol.

"You'll feel a little stick when I numb the area, and then I'll set the IV," she chirped.

It had been almost three hours since Camptown, and the pain in my chest had long since subsided. I considered getting out of bed and foregoing the emergency heart cath they'd been discussing, but decided I'd rather know if my ticker was going to be an issue. I couldn't see any veins in the area the nurse had deadened, but I figured she knew what she was doing.

"Oops," she said. "I missed. That happens sometimes." She pressed a piece of gauze against the wound to stop the flow.

I nodded to show her I was a sympathetic guy.

"I'll move up your arm a bit and try this nice vein just below your muscle."

She was exceedingly young. Young enough that I felt dirty just reading her name tag, though it was nicely elevated.

Dana.

I forced my eyes to stop lingering in the area of her name tag and watched her face as she stuck me to numb the vein she thought was nice looking.

Dana's mouth twitched slightly as she gracelessly plunged the IV needle into the crook of my arm. She had a pleasant face and flawless skin, but something caused her to frown.

"Oh dear," she said.

"What now?"

"This one seems to have collapsed."

I glanced at my arm and saw that my vein had done nothing of the sort. She had in fact missed it by a full centimeter.

"You're a tough one," Dana cooed. "You didn't even flinch." She gave me a wink that, due to her age, seemed practically obscene. She pushed the IV needle into a third spot and missed.

"Don't be offended," I said. "But you're done here."

She looked at me to see if I was serious.

I was.

Her eyes welled up with tears and she packed up her needles and bloody gauze pads and ran from the room.

Before Dana had time to tell her tale to the other candystripers, a disheveled young man in a wrinkled lab coat came in. He appeared to be exhausted. Dana was practically a child, but this guy could have been her kid brother.

"Mr. Creed, I'm Dr. Hedgepeth."

"Your parents know you stole that lab coat?"

He sighed. "Don't start with me. I'm a fully-qualified, first-year resident in Internal Medicine."

"Of course you are," I said, thinking, *I wouldn't trust this kid to set up my Xbox.*

Dr. Hedgepeth looked at my arm. "Sorry about that," he said. "Dana's new on the job."

"What happened to the old nurse?"

"Mary? She was great. Best needle nurse I ever had. It broke my heart to let her go."

I shook my head at the absurdity of his comment. This so-called doctor couldn't possibly be in charge of hiring and firing staff. He couldn't possibly be out of junior high school, for that matter. But I was committed to the conversation, so I forged ahead.

"If Mary was your best needle nurse, why'd you fire her?" I said.

"The patients kept complaining she was too young."

"Of course they did." I locked my eyes on his face. This had to be a joke. I can usually break a man's resolve just by staring at him. This kid was about to crack. I could feel it.

"So what made you choose Dana?" I said.

"Dana's the oldest nurse on the ward."

"Is she," I said, thinking, *any nurse younger than Dana would have to be wearing a training bra.*

"Dana will be just fine," Dr. Hedgepeth said, "but there's a learning curve, you see."

I decided to move things along.

"Are you doing the heart cath or shall I look forward to meeting your grandson, the Chief of Surgery?"

"No need to be contentious," he said.

"Contentious," I said, wondering if that had been one of his spelling bee words.

"Performing a heart catheterization would be premature at this point," he said. "You're relatively young, you're in great physical shape, your blood pressure's excellent, your EKG is perfect, and the tests we've done showed none of the classic heart attack symptoms."

"So what happens now?"

"We do a Cardiolite stress test. If that comes back normal, I'd advise you to get the hell out of here as soon as possible."

"Why's that?"

"You can get sick faster in a hospital than almost anyplace on earth."

I was beginning to like Dr. Hedgepeth. "So I don't need a heart cath?"

"I don't think so. What you probably need is a couple of hours and a bathroom."

"A bathroom."

"Your problem could be acute heartburn, a precursor of food poisoning. Did you eat something of questionable origin recently?"

I thought about the beef burrito I'd choked down at the Horse Head Inn a few hours ago. And realized "beef" didn't necessarily mean cow.

"Could you have eaten something truly vile and shortly thereafter engaged in some form of physical activity?"

I thought about the Peterson sisters.

"Look," I said. "I've had heartburn before. But this pain was severe, and emanated from the center of my chest."

"Hey, we can always do the heart cath if you want. I mean, the hospital would love to pick up another thirty grand today. Ten times that, if we manage to poke a hole in your artery while performing the procedure."

I frowned. "Is that type of complication likely?"

"How to put this delicately," Dr. Hedgepeth said. "Our cath guy seems to be a cardiologist, but according to law he doesn't have to be a surgeon. He's from India and appears very bright, but he's quite young and his experience with heart caths is limited."

"How limited?"

"You'd be his cherry."

"Uh huh. Heartburn, you say?"

"Acute heartburn, yes. That, coupled with physical stress,

could certainly produce the types of symptoms you've experienced."

I understood why he'd said it, but I've always had a castiron stomach. In years of testing weapons for the Army, I've had to swallow pills that made Horse Head burritos seem like Saltines.

"If the stress test comes back clean, what should I do?" I said.

"Go home and spend some quality time bonding with your toilet."

"And if that doesn't work?"

Dr. Hedgepeth hesitated. "Do you currently see a psychiatrist?"

I frowned. "You think I'm imagining this pain?"

"I believe the pain is very real. But you appear to be the sort of man who can handle a great deal of pain."

*If you only knew*, I thought, wondering if I should tell Hedgepeth that I'd been testing torture weapons for the Army for years. In the end I decided to just say, "I've certainly never had a problem handling heartburn in the past."

"Well, the pain's coming from someplace," he said, "and I'm almost certain it's not the heart. But the heart is what I do, so we'll test that first. Then the toilet, then the brain."

"Okay, I'm sold," I said. "What's the first step to this Cardiolite thing?"

Dr. Hedgepeth, without the slightest trace of a smirk, said: "We need to get an IV started."

Then he walked to the doorway and yelled for Dana.

# 5.

I WAS STILL in the hospital, back in my street clothes, awaiting the results of the stress test. With time on my hands, I decided to break hospital rules and make a call on my cell phone. Kimberly answered on the first ring.

"*Daddy*!" she squealed.

"You sound almost *too* happy," I said.

"Does it show?"

*Oh oh*, I thought. *She's in love*. "Does what show?"

"I'm in love!"

"You're too young," I said, instinctively.

"Oh, Father," she said. "I'm a junior in high school."

"That's young. Anyway, you're not a junior until next semester."

"A technicality," she said, "seeing as how school starts in ten days."

I sighed.

"His name's Charlie," she said.

"Please tell me it's not Charlie Manson."

On the other end of the phone, in Darnell, West Virginia, my daughter giggled.

We spent the next fifteen minutes talking about books we'd read, music we liked, and summer vacations we hoped to take someday. I asked her how serious her relationship with Charlie was, and she changed the subject.

"Has Mom called you?" she said.

"Not recently."

"She will."

I groaned. "What now?"

"She found out about Kathleen. Her friend, Amy, told her."

I knew it had to happen. Several months ago, my ex-wife, Janet, had been engaged to the former wife beater, Ken Chapman. In the course of discouraging Janet from marrying the jerk, I met and fell in love with Ken's former wife, Kathleen.

"Dad?"

"Still here, Kitten."

I wondered how much Janet knew about Kathleen. Did she know only that I was dating the ex-wife of her former fiancé? Or had she somehow learned that the woman who came to Janet's home and identified herself as Ken's ex was actually a hooker I'd hired to pose as Kathleen; a hooker who lied about being beaten up by Ken Chapman.

Whatever Janet knew, however angry she might be, it had been worth it. I'd prevented the marriage. I knew firsthand about Janet's ability to push a man's buttons. With his history of violence, Ken Chapman probably would have killed her.

Kimberly sensed I was distracted. "Did you hear what I said?"

"You said Mom knows about Kathleen and she's going to call me."

"That was earlier. Just now I asked if you and Kathleen were living together."

"It's complicated."

"Dad, why is it that when you talk about Charlie it's all cut and dried, but when I talk about Kathleen it's 'complicated?'"

I paused a moment before saying, "I wish I had a better answer, but the truth is, that's a good point."

"Damn right, it is! I'm your kid after all."

"You are that," I said. "Okay, here's the scoop."

Over the next few minutes I told her about my feelings for Kathleen, and how I stay with her whenever I'm in New York. I told her about Addie Dawes, and about Kathleen's adoption efforts. When I finished there was a brief silence on the line.

"You okay?" I said.

"Are you aware this is the first time in my life you've treated me like a grown-up?"

"How could I not? You're a junior in high school."

"Try to remember that, next time you start worrying about me and Charlie."

"Ugh," I said. "Speaking of Charlie, how much do you know about this kid?"

Kimberly said something about him being twenty-one, but I was distracted by the curtain being pulled aside as Dr. Hedgepeth entered my cubicle. I motioned for him to give me a second. He frowned at my use of a cell phone in the emergency room, but waited respectfully.

"I'm sorry, Kitten. What did you just say?"

"I said, 'Don't even go there, Dad.' Don't go all crazy and run a credit check or background report on Charlie. He's a good kid. His father's a bigtime attorney."

"Attorney? I'd rather have you date Charlie Manson than an attorney."

She sighed. "He's not an attorney, his father is. Look, just promise you won't run his records."

"I promise."

"Good," she said. "Now go spend some quality time with Addie. She sounds adorable. And, Dad?"

"Yes?"

"I'm happy for you. And I love you."

"I love you too, Kitten."

I clicked the phone off and Dr. Hedgepeth said, "As I suspected, you've got the heart of a lion."

I nodded.

"Any pain since the test?"

"None."

"Any stomach discomfort?"

I shook my head. "Not yet."

"Food poisoning can take up to forty-eight hours to hit," he said.

"What's the average?"

"Six to eight."

"So it could still be that," I said.

"Yes, but we pushed you pretty hard on the treadmill. And you aced it. Even in the early stages of food poisoning I would have expected some abdominal cramping. Makes me think it's not food poisoning."

He handed me a piece of paper with a name and phone number.

"A shrink?" I said.

"In case you want to see someone here, instead of your home town."

I pocketed the slip of paper and shook his hand. "You're young, but you're good."

He winked. "That's what they all say!"

# 6.

"YOU KNOW ANYTHING about this kid Charlie Beck? His father's a big-time attorney in Darnell."

I was on the phone with Sal Bonadello, Midwestern crime boss and my sometime employer.

"I know people who probably know him," Sal said.

Okay, so I promised Kimberly I wouldn't run a credit or background check on her new boyfriend. But I never promised not to ask around.

"Kimberly's usually a great judge of character," I said. "But something bothers me about this kid. For one thing, he's old enough to drink legally."

"That's a small town, Darnell," Sal said. "People talk. I'll make some—whatcha call—inquiries."

I thought about the way Sal might ask around. "I don't want to make a big deal about it," I said, "and I especially don't want Kimberly to find out that I'm the guy trying to get the information."

"Hey, I got a girl of my own. I'll take care of it."

"Thanks, Sal."

"You still comin'to my party?" he said.

"I wouldn't miss it for the world."

"You bringing that new girl? The one lives in New York?"

"We're going dress shopping later today," I said.

"Dress her up hot," Sal said.

"She'd look hot in a flour sack."

"Flour sack's fine. Make sure it's a small one."

"I'll keep it in mind."

"What about the blond that works with you?"

"What about her?"

"She comin'?"

"To the party? No way."

"Did you invite her?"

"I did."

"Maybe I should—whatcha call—extend a personal invite."

I thought about Callie dressing up, attending a social event. Gorgeous she is. But, "She's not a people person," I said.

"Unless it comes to killing them."

"Unless that," I said.

"If a kid's gonna get in trouble in Darnell, West Virginia, it's gonna be at the Grantline Bar & Grill."

"So?"

"So I know the bartender, Teddy Boy. He owes me, big time."

"I'm not ready to have Charlie's legs broken. Not yet, anyway."

"All I'm sayin', Teddy Boy knows what's what. If your kid's been in the bar, he'll tell me. If she goes in, he'll keep an eye on her."

"Kimberly's only sixteen," I said. "You're not going to find her in a bar."

"Darnell's Darnell," Sal said.

"Meaning?"

"You been there?"

"No."

"Nothing to do in Darnell but drink, drug and fuck."

"Excuse me?"

34

"Hey, no offense," Sal said.

I thought about what he'd said, and how parents never think their kids would take the wrong path.

"Maybe you better call Teddy Boy today," I said.

"I'm on it," he said. "Hey, you know those midgets?"

Sal could change subjects faster than a Congressman.

"Victor and Hugo?" I said.

"The same."

"What about them?"

"They're coming to my party."

"I'd heard that," I said.

"In the flesh."

"I'll try to shake off that image," I said. "You better tell your boys not to make fun of them. They're pretty formidable."

"Hey, they been warned. Those midgets brought down Joe DeMeo."

"They prefer the term little people," I said.

"I prefer big envelopes."

Sal was referring to the contribution envelopes his underbosses and special guests were expected to bring to his party.

"I been good for you," he said. "And this here, with your daughter, that's another example. Charity—whatcha call—begins at home."

"In this case, your home."

"That's what I'm sayin'. So surprise me," he said. "In a good way."

Sal's world is a rough one, where loyalty is measured in cash or body count. I make it a habit to kick back more than my share of both.

"Surprise you?" I said. "Sal, I'm going to *amaze* you!"

"All I'm askin'," he said.

# 7.

THE OFFICE OF Ms. N. Crouch, MD, was located in Newark, New Jersey, corner of Summer and Seventh, off Interstate 280. Ms. Crouch shared an office condo with a pediatric psychologist named Agnes Battle. Agnes was working the reception desk when I walked in. She pointed me to Ms. Crouch's office, and I went in.

Ms. N. Crouch stood and extended her hand to greet me. We identified ourselves and she gestured in the general direction of her seating area and said, "Please make yourself comfortable."

I did a quick survey of the office. Deep plum was the dominant color, except for the far wall, which was fauxfinished in light brown with delicate black threading, to resemble cork. On this wall hung several professional certificates, including a diploma from the University Of Pittsburgh School Of Medicine. Everything felt crisp and modern, save for the antique wooden coat rack in the entryway corner.

I chose a plush, highbacked leather throne chair and settled in.

Ms. N. Crouch said, "Dr. Hedgepeth mentioned a possible psychosomatic pain?"

If Darwin, my government facilitator, knew I was seeing a psychiatrist, he'd put an assassin on me. With that in mind, I was reticent about jumping right into things. I sat quietly and stared at her.

She had on a layered skirt, navy, with a matching jacket she wore opened. Her blouse was cream-colored silk, with a round neckline. A cablewrapped, white gold necklace dangled in two strands and rested modestly at the center of her chest.

"Mr. Creed, you can remain silent if you wish. But just so you know, I get paid either way."

With that, she went quiet and stared back at me. It has been my experience with women that they don't like to remain quiet for long periods of time. Which is why I was surprised that she allowed us to sit there in total silence, staring at each other, for the next twenty minutes.

Finally, I said, "I believe I like you, Ms. Crouch."

"I'm glad to hear it, Mr. Creed."

"Call me Donovan."

She nodded, and we remained silent until she realized it was her turn to speak.

"Donovan, in one way my profession is similar to that of a dentist."

"How's that?"

"Like your dentist, I can't begin helping you until you open your mouth."

I nodded.

She continued, "There are several chairs here, from which a patient can choose. I purposely stay out of the selection process because the chair choice tells me something about the patient."

"Uh huh."

"For example, the chair you selected tells me you're accustomed to being in control, which often indicates trust issues. You're obviously finding it difficult to let your guard down enough to discuss your personal life with a complete stranger."

"Good point," I said. "So tell me a little about yourself, and then we won't be strangers."

She smiled. "With all due respect, Donovan, this session is about you. It would be highly unprofessional of me to discuss my personal life with you. More importantly, the less you know about me, the easier it will be for you to share your feelings."

"Fine," I said. "Don't tell me. I can find out anything I need to know about you by looking around the room."

"Really, you're that perceptive?" she said.

I noted that Ms. N. Crouch was on the edge of mocking me, despite her best effort to keep all emotion out of her voice.

I stood up. "Shall I demonstrate?"

"If you feel it necessary."

"Your face tells me you've been beautiful your whole life, but you're older now, in your late fifties, and your clothes and hair style reflect your acceptance of that fact. You've aged gracefully, and you believe you're smarter than your friends, even those who have surpassed you professionally. You keep but one picture on your desk, two young boys who appear to be Japanese-American. They're your sons, but neither you nor their father is in the picture. If your husband had taken it, you'd be in the photo with your sons. If you'd taken it, he'd be in it. If your husband were dead, you'd have his picture on your desk to honor him. But there is no picture of the husband, which tells me you're divorced. Based on your current age, and the age you had to be to give birth, these pictures are at least ten years old. You haven't updated them because they remind you of a happier time."

I looked at her to see if she was impressed. If she was, she was hiding it well. But no matter, I'd only just begun.

"You struggle to remain proper at all times," I continued, pointing to her diploma. "You hide behind the name N. Crouch because you think Nadine pegs you as a hick from the sticks. You suffer from feelings of inadequacy because your contemporaries graduated from prestigious colleges while you were stuck at the University of Pittsburgh School Of Medicine. You feel you haven't lived up to your potential."

"Why's that?"

"There are no books or articles on display, which means you're unpublished. What kind of big money psychiatrist is unpublished at your age?"

N. Crouch pursed her lips. "I see," she said. "Anything else?"

"Your sons are off in college or working and they don't call as often as you'd like. To compensate, you keep two dogs as pets."

"What," she said. "Not the breed?"

I smiled. "Akitas," I said. "Japanese dogs brought to our shores by returning American servicemen, after WW2. Twin dogs from the same litter."

I bowed and sat back down on the leather throne chair. I may have smirked.

"That's amazing, Mr. Creed," she said. "Truly remarkable."

"Why thank you, Ms. Crouch."

She said, "You took all the evidence on display and managed to get every single fact wrong. Every fact but one."

I smiled and said, "Bullshit."

N. Crouch stood. "I'm in my early sixties, not fifties. I don't think I'm smarter than my friends, though none have surpassed me professionally. The pictures on the desk are my sister's adopted children. I'm not divorced because I've never been married. I'm not from the Midwest, I'm from Miami. My contemporaries didn't graduate from prestigious colleges because psychiatrists graduate from medical schools, not colleges. Speaking of which, Pittsburgh Medical happens to be the number one medical school in the country. In 2005 alone they received one hundred and eighty NIHA's—that's National Institute of Health Awards—totaling more than seventy-six million dollars.

"And by the way," she added, reaching into her lower desk drawer, "I don't hide my first name and I *am* published." She held up a book titled *Cognitive Remediation in Neuropsychological Functioning* and pointed to the author's name: Nadine Crouch, PhD.

She stopped for a minute and said, "What are you grinning at? You look like the village idiot."

Then it hit her.

"Shit," she said. "You just got me to tell you all about myself."

"Don't take it too hard," I said.

"You probably already knew about the book."

"I Googled you before setting the appointment."

"I'm going to have to keep an eye on you, Mr. Creed," she said. "You're quite the manipulator."

"Thank you."

"You take that as a compliment?"

"What's the one thing?" I said.

She looked puzzled.

"You said I was wrong about everything but one."

She smiled.

"Wait," I said, sharing the smile. "I know what it is. I was right that you've been beautiful your whole life."

She grinned, and I cocked my head at her.

"Ms. N. Crouch," I said. "Did you just wink at me?"

And thus began my professional relationship with Nadine.

# 8.

THE WORD ON Teddy Boy Turner was that the gambling bug bit him long before he scored the bartending gig at the Grantline Bar & Grill in Darnell, West Virginia. As a teenager, he mowed lawns and washed cars until he amassed enough money to start betting the sports book.

In gambling, winning early in life usually leads to financial ruin down the road, and Teddy Boy's experience was no different. His current losing streak had put his life in serious jeopardy. He was deeper in debt than his Grantline salary could ever pull him out—to Salvatore Bonadello, no less, one of the biggest and most notorious crime bosses in the country.

Teddy Boy lived in the constant fear that one day soon the goons would walk in around closing time and demand payment. He was prepared to get a broken arm or leg, maybe some cracked ribs. What he wasn't prepared for was a personal phone call from Sal Bonadello himself.

According to Sal, the call went this way:

"I been looking over your account," Sal said.

"I'm doing my best, Mr. Bonadello. I just need a little more time."

"How would you like your—whatcha call—slate cleared?"

Teddy Boy thought about that. "I can smack someone around with a baseball bat for you, but I'm not a professional," he said. "I never took a life or nothin'."

"Naw, not like that," Sal said. "I need some information and a favor. You do a good job, maybe I wipe your slate clean. How would that be?"

"It'd be like getting a new lease on life, Mr. Bonadello. Not to complain, but I'm working day and night just to pay the vig. I haven't been able to make a dent in the loan."

"You know this kid, Charlie Beck?"

"Everyone knows Charlie."

"He a friend of yours?"

Teddy Boy paused. "Not unless you say so, Mr. Bonadello."

"Good answer. You seen him in your place with any girls?"

"Yeah, sure. He gets a lot of action. Looks sort of like Tom Brady."

"Ever seen him with a high school girl? Short blond hair, name of Kimberly Creed?"

"Not that I know of," Teddy Boy said.

Sal said, "Ted, you disappoint me. I was hoping to help you out with your—whatcha call—lethal problem."

There was a long pause and then Teddy Boy cleared his voice and said, "Well, there is a rumor going around."

"Ted?"

"Yes sir?"

"Gimme something I can use."

# 9.

NED DENHOLLEN AWOKE confused and disoriented. He looked at one arm, then the other, trying to get his bearings. Ned probably remembered setting the alarm, closing up the drugstore and walking across the parking lot toward his car. Now here he was, lying on his back on the floor of a room he couldn't possibly recognize, and—could this be possible?

His wrists were in cuffs, chained to eyebolts in the floor.

He lifted his head and saw me sitting on a chair positioned above his legs.

Ned lashed out, tried to kick the chair over. And realized his feet were also chained to the floor.

He shook his head angrily, pitched his torso upward a few times in an effort to show he was a fighter, a man not easily intimidated. But in fact Ned was *not* a fighter and he *was* easily intimidated, which is why he soon gave up posturing and began to blubber and cry.

"Who are you?" Ned wailed. "What do you want? Why have you done this to me?"

I sighed. "Ned, the reason we're here, I'm worried about my daughter."

Ned abruptly stopped whimpering. No doubt he thought me a lunatic. "Excuse me?"

"I'm Donovan Creed, Kimberly's father. I'd shake your hand but..."

Yeah, of course you would, Ned must have thought, but it's chained to the floor!

Ned studied me, as if trying to place me by inventorying my facial features. For Ned, it was a given I was unstable. But was I capable of murder? He wouldn't want to find out. "Mr. Creed, I don't know your daughter and that's the God's honest truth. I'm happily married. I think you must have me mixed up with someone else.

"You're the pharmacist?"

"Yes sir, I work at Anderson's Drug Store here in Darnell."

"What makes you think we're still in Darnell?"

"Oh, sweet Jesus!"

"Ned, let me tell you what's happening here. You and I are going to put an end to what's been going on in Darnell. Before it affects my daughter, or her friends."

"Mr. Creed, I don't understand why you're doing this."

I sighed again. "If you think I'm enjoying this…" I paused. Ned began shivering.

"Are you comfortable, Ned?"

"I beg your pardon?"

"I can get you a pillow and blanket if you like."

Ned shouted, "If you wanted to make me comfortable, you shouldn't have chained my arms and legs to the floor, you son of a bitch!"

"I can't fault you for being upset," I said, "but I need to move things along. I have it on good authority that you're selling drugs."

Ned said, "I know your daughter, Kimberly. I've filled prescriptions for her. But I would never sell her any illicit drugs. You can ask her, if you don't believe me."

"I'm not talking about Kimberly," I said. Then I thought of something completely off the subject.

"Is Kimberly on the pill?"

Ned thought for a minute. "Not that I'm aware," he said.

I looked at him a long moment before saying, "It's really none of my business, but that's good to know."

"Sir," Ned said, "I do sell drugs, I'm a pharmacist. But I only sell prescription drugs."

I kept my voice steady. "My daughter's been dating a kid named Charlie Beck. Charlie's twenty-one, his dad's a local attorney, Jerry Beck. You know this kid Charlie?"

"No sir, I honestly don't." Ned said through gritted teeth as he tried to control his anger.

"Charlie's a good-looking kid, really popular with the ladies. What I'm saying, Ned: he's a *player*."

"I'm sorry to hear that, sir, I truly am. But I've got a wife. She must be worried sick about me. Please let me go! I swear I never did anything to hurt your daughter. *Please*! I don't know what you're talking about with the drug thing, I swear to God."

"You see, Ned, this is why I had to chain you up. It's why I might have to kill you."

"Wh-what?"

"Even after all this you're still not being honest with me."

"How can you *say* that?" he wailed.

"Tell me about your cousin."

"My cousin?"

"Bickham Wright."

Ned's face fell. "Oh, shit," he said.

"Oh, shit indeed," I said. "Look, I'm going to save you some trouble. I already know the facts. I'm just looking for details."

I took a syringe from my pocket, removed the cap, and tapped the plunger to remove any trapped air.

Ned's eyes went wide. "What's in that?"

"It's a lethal dose."

"Okay, stop. I'll tell you everything."

"Thought you might."

"I don't personally know any of the women they drugged," Ned said. "But I know some of the names. I'm positive they didn't drug Kimberly."

"Why's that?"

"She's underage."

There was something in his eyes.

"What aren't you telling me, Ned?"

He closed his eyes and winced. When he spoke his bottom lip quivered. "I know they killed one of the women. Erica Chastain."

"Who killed her?"

"Bickham and Charlie."

"What did they do with the body?"

"Buried it somewhere in the hills, where they like to hunt."

"They told you all this?"

"When Erica went missing, there was an investigation. A lot of people remembered seeing her at the Grantline. I told Bickham it was over."

"You cut him off?"

"Yes sir."

"But he threatened you."

"Bickham said if they got caught they'd all rat me out. I was in it deep enough to do serious time. I'd lose everything."

"They drugged a lot of girls, didn't they?"

Ned nodded.

"And all those girls have something in common. You know what it is?"

"I'm not sure what you—"

47

"They've all got fathers, Ned."

Ned paused before speaking. When he did, his voice was heavy with regret. "I'm sorry," he said. "I wish I could…" His voice trailed off. He started to cry, then swallowed back the tears. "I'm…I'm truly sorry."

I didn't know what to say, so I said nothing.

Then, trying to keep the fear out of his voice, Ned said, "So…what happens now?"

"Now you tell me exactly how it works. Leave nothing out. You can start with the names."

"Names?"

"The names of the members."

"The members of—"

"That's right, Ned. The members of Fuck Club."

Ned winced. "I never meant for this to happen," he said. "They—"

"But it *did* happen, Ned. And you let it happen."

"Okay," Ned said. His voice was weary. He'd given up the fight. "I'll tell you everything I know. And then?"

"And then I'll end your suffering." I paused a minute, then thought of something. "You have an insurance policy?"

Ned smiled ruefully. "Cashed it in. See, this whole thing was always about needing more money."

"How much insurance?"

"The death benefit would have been a hundred thousand."

I nodded. "Tell me what I want to know, I'll make sure your wife gets the hundred grand."

"You mean—"

"Yeah. I'll cover it."

"Anita."

"Excuse me?"

"My wife. Her name's Anita."

# 10.

WHEN I LOOK at her I am reminded of all that matters.

It was early afternoon and I was back in North Bergen, where Kathleen rents half a duplex that was so small, I could hear her shower running when I came in the front door. I crossed the living room to the single bedroom and noticed the pile of clothes on the bed that Kathleen had laid out for the trip. The bedroom was twice the size of a standard prison cell, which made it large enough to hold a queen bed, an end table, and a medium dresser. On the far wall was a door that led to the bathroom. I pushed it open a few inches and peeked inside. The shower door was made of ribbed glass. The steam from her shower had fogged it up pretty well, but I could make out enough of her form to get my heart pumping. I silently backed up and closed the door so I wouldn't startle her.

When she shut off the shower I called her name. A moment later she opened the door, wrapped in a towel. She glided through the bedroom, into the hall, and adjusted the thermostat to a cooler setting. Then she jumped into the bed where I'd been waiting.

Afterward, she slipped out of bed and I propped my head on one arm as I always did, to enjoy the view of her backside. Kathleen lifted her arms high above her head and stretched, arching her back, totally unaware of her sensuality. It was so Kathleen, the way she could turn a simple activity into a defining moment. Still with her back to me, she stepped into her panties and wriggled her lower body just enough to get them over her hips.

She went back to the bathroom and started drying her hair and I tried to decide what the best thing about her was. And gave up. In a word, she was spectacular, and I was confident that everyone who met her at Sal's party that night would instantly fall in love with her.

As I watched her working her hair, I thought about how completely comfortable I felt in her presence. And that's when it hit me: in the full hour I'd been home, we hadn't felt the need to exchange a single word.

By four o'clock we were wheels up in the Lear 45 I'd leased from Sensory Resources, the government agency headed by my facilitator, Darwin. I can usually wrangle free use of the agency jets, even when it's not agency business, but this flight was taking us to the birthday party of a known criminal, and Darwin wasn't taking any chances being linked to that.

At around six p.m. we checked into my favorite hotel in Cincinnati, the Cincinnatian. While I hit the mini bar, Kathleen began stripping.

"Again?" I said.

"Relax, Tiger. I'm just taking my real shower."

"What's wrong with the shower you took a few hours ago?"

"That was for you. This one's for the party."

# 11.

"WHERE ARE ALL the G-men?" Kathleen said as our stretch limo passed through the gates and headed up the long entrance to Sal's mansion.

In the old days, the FBI and local police would have been stationed at the bottom of the hill, writing down license plate numbers and snapping pictures of all the guests.

"These are happier times for organized crime," I said. "These days the feds are more interested in terrorists. As for local law enforcement, the mayor and police chief are apt to stop by for a celebratory drink."

Kathleen frowned. "No submachine guns?" she said.

I'd made the mistake of mentioning Sal's party to Kathleen a week earlier, and she insisted on coming. I had been determined to keep this part of my life a secret from her, but two days of her world-class pouting weakened my resolve. Plus, there was a part of me that wanted to see how she'd react to meeting Sal. Would she be able to handle a gangland social event?

"You might see the occasional weapon brandished," I said.

Kathleen seemed fascinated by the prospect of meeting an underworld crime boss. Over the past few days she asked a hundred questions about my relationship with Sal. I lied by omission, commission, and every other way a person can lie. In the end I led her to believe that Homeland Security had an unofficial alliance with the mob, and that they helped us identify and locate suspected terrorists. I told her that going to Sal's birthday party was good business for the government, and asked if she'd be willing to perform with a magician at Sal's party. After telling her what she'd have to do, Kathleen was delighted to be included. As evidenced by her B-movie mob speak.

"Will there be a lot of guys named Lefty?" she said.

"Don't know."

"How come criminals never call anyone Righty?"

"Don't know."

We pulled up to the front entrance and came to a stop. The driver climbed out, circled the car, and held the door open for us. Kathleen was wearing a cocktail dress, so I got out first and served as a modesty shield.

As she climbed out behind me she whispered, "Am I allowed to call anyone a dirty rat?"

I tried not to smile, but failed.

"Say it," she said.

"What's that?"

"I'm funny too."

"You are not funny."

"Am too!"

We climbed the steps and entered the house. I remembered every nook and cranny of the place from two years earlier, when I'd broken into this very same home and set up residency in Sal's attic for a week.

The party was in full swing. Some of the guests were half plastered, as evidenced by the young, up-and-comer from Dayton, who shouted, "Hey, Creed! Yeah, I'm talking to you. You think you're hot shit? You ain't nothin'!"

Beside me, I could feel Kathleen's body tensing.

I gave him the hard stare and his eyes went wild. He started moving toward me. Lucky for him, his father grabbed him by the collar and passed him off to his bodyguards.

"My son has no manners," said Sammy "The Blond" Santoro. "Please forgive him, Mr. Creed. It's the liquor talking. I shouldn't have brought him."

I looked at him without speaking. We'd made it maybe ten feet inside Sal's home and I was already on the verge of being exposed.

Sammy, a well-known killer in his own right, a city boss in Sal's organization—was visibly nervous, practically cowering. Bringing Kathleen to this party had been a mistake. I could only imagine what she must be thinking. She had to be wondering why these hardened men were terrified of me.

"Mr. Creed, I'm prepared to make this right," he said.

I moved close to him and whispered something in his ear. He bowed, thanked me profusely, and backed away.

"What on earth did you say to that man?" Kathleen said.

"I told him he and his son gave a great performance."

"What are you talking about?"

"It's all part of the show," I said. "Sal hires people to maintain the theme. It's all staged, like when you go to a Wild West town and a gunfight breaks out in the saloon."

The foyer led to the huge great room, decorated in white. We crossed the foyer and got stuck in guest traffic for a minute.

"You think a phony gunfight might break out tonight?" Kathleen said.

"If it does, just play along," I said.

Looking over her shoulder I watched Sammy "The Blond" and his goons drag Sammy's son out the front door. One goon had his meaty hand smothering the kid's mouth so I wouldn't hear the insults he was attempting to hurl at me.

I recognized Jimmy "The Pearl" Remini standing next to us.

"Hi Jimmy," I said.

He turned to see who was speaking. When he recognized me his face blanched.

"Jimmy?"

"The Pearl" had gone mute.

"Jimmy, it's okay," I said, extending my hand. "I'm just a guest here, saying hello."

Jimmy breathed a visible sigh of relief. "Jesus, you startled me," he said. "I haven't seen you since—" he stopped to consider his words.

"Since that thing," I said, helpfully.

"Yeah, right," he said "the thing."

We introduced our significant others, and Kathleen said, "What thing?"

"Take care, Jimmy," I said. "You too, Mrs. Remini."

They backed away quickly and gratefully.

"You gave a great performance, Jimmy!" Kathleen shouted.

Jimmy "The Pearl" and his wife smiled and nodded and kept backing away.

"They seemed nice," Kathleen said.

The great room was cavernous, with twenty-four foot ceilings. Up above, there was only room for a crawl space, something I knew firsthand. The week I "visited," I hung out in the areas above the bedrooms. There was standing room there, and I'd managed to fashion a relatively comfortable lifestyle. I had to remain quiet and cramped at night, of course, but when the family was out I could move around and make some noise. My first job had been to divert a portion of the heat and air to the attic. Next I hooked up a phone jack, so I could record all the landline calls that came in and went out of the house.

Kathleen looked at the ornate painting over the fireplace.

"Is that Sal's wife, Marie?" she said.

"It is."

"She seems so young. How long ago did she pose for it?"

"Maybe fifteen years ago."

A young lady was making a bee-line to us through the crowd. Kathleen squealed, "Why Donovan, she's *beautiful*!"

"Damn right, she is! Kathleen, this is Liz Bonadello, Sal's daughter."

Liz was a tall, classic Italian beauty, close to Kathleen's age, meaning mid-thirties. Watching them interact socially was a thing of beauty. Over the next two minutes they had started and discarded half a dozen topics of conversation and were now deep into an animated discussion that generated no small amount of laughter, as if they'd known each other for years.

Liz had her own place, but Sal and Marie kept her old bedroom ready for the occasional weekend visit. Liz spent the night here only once during the week I hid in the attic. After the first day, after I'd completed my noisy work, I was able to relax and enjoy their home. On those occasions, while Sal and Marie were out, I'd push down the attic stairs, climb down and raid the cupboard or fridge, take a shower, and use Liz's old computer.

Liz and Kathleen concluded their discussion and promised each other they'd stay in touch.

As Liz walked away I said, "What do you think of her?"

Kathleen said, "Classy, olive complexion, nice boobs, knows her fashion."

"Do women always size each other up that way?"

"Always. What planet are you from?"

"What do you suppose she's thinking about you right now?"

"Classy, porcelain complexion, small tits, sexy boyfriend."

"I'll drink to that," I said. "Especially the last part."

"Me too," she said. "So where's the bar?"

"There," I said, pointing to the door that led to the terrace.

Once outside I could see that Sal had really outdone himself. The terrace had been professionally decorated with lavish columns, topiaries, and hundreds of tiny white lights that made it seem like a fairyland. The tables were draped in textured, white linen, with centerpieces of fresh-cut orchids. The chairs were covered in white fabric with organza sashes in cobalt blue. The bar was at least twenty feet long, with three bartenders going at it double-time.

Despite the ample and capable staff, it took ten minutes to get our drinks. While I waited, I looked back up at the house. The curtains along the back of the house were open. All the lights were on, and I could see inside Sal and Marie's bedroom.

I'd been hiding in Sal's attic for a reason. He had been given some misinformation about me and decided to have me whacked. I figured the safest place to hide out was in his attic. I tapped his phones and bored some tiny holes in the various ceilings and fitted them with pinhole cameras. I was trying to learn which of Sal's lieutenants had lied about me. I figured I'd find him and torture a confession out of him. Barring that, I'd kill Sal. As it turned out, I didn't have to wait long. Six nights into my stay, while Sal and Marie slept in their bed, I heard two guys break into the house. Through pinhole cameras I watched them creep toward the master bedroom with their guns drawn. I positioned myself over Sal's bedroom. When they flipped on the lights, I put a gun in each hand and jumped through the space between the floorboards, came crashing through Sal's ceiling with guns blazing. I killed both the would-be assassins, and later learned they'd been sent by Artie Boots, the guy that tried to set me up.

You'd think Sal would have been grateful, but it took all this time for him to forgive me. One reason he finally began trusting me is because, with Victor and Hugo's help, I took down Joe DeMeo. I seized several of Joe's off shore accounts, worth millions of dollars, and gave Sal half of everything I stole.

Money may not buy happiness but enough of it buys loyalty.

As we stepped away from the bar, I spotted Sal and Marie holding court on the far end of the terrace. One by one, criminals approached him, kissed his cheeks, and handed him envelopes. Sal shook their hands, appeared to make some small talk, and spent a lot of time smiling. As the mugs left, Sal looked in the envelopes and said something to either T-Bone or Big Bad, his bodyguards. T-Bone seemed to be writing something in a small ledger book, probably recording the size of each man's contribution. Then Sal deposited each envelope into a large wooden box on a bar table that Big Bad was guarding.

Kathleen and I were particularly impressed with the backyard.

At the center of the terrace, eight wide steps down led to the sun deck and swimming pool, which had been covered for the occasion with an enormous dance platform. An eightpiece swing band had set up in the gazebo, next to the pool house, but hadn't started playing yet. For now, the music was provided by an unlikely pair of very old men. One, the violin player, had a shock of white hair and wore the thickest black glasses I'd ever seen. He moved through the crowd while playing, pausing occasionally to whisper something in the ear of each pretty lady he encountered. The other guy, the guitar player, squinted and scowled at the guests like a jealous lover, and did his best to keep up with the violinist, both musically and spatially.

"I love the musicians," Kathleen said. "They're so cute!"

"Cute," I said.

"Well, just look at them. They must be eighty years old."

I did look at them, in fact, I knew them. And "cute" didn't seem an appropriate description. Johnny D and Silvio Braca were a pair of octogenarians who could play a romantic ballad one minute and break your knee caps the next.

"I wonder what he's whispering to all those women," I said.

Kathleen flashed a grin at me. "Maybe I'll just walk over there and find out," she said.

# 12.

SAL CAUGHT MY eye and motioned us over. We worked our way over to him.

"This is my wife, Marie," he said to Kathleen.

"And this is Kathleen," I said.

I nodded at Big Bad and T-Bone and they each gave me a short, tight nod in return.

Sal made a great show of bowing and kissing her hand. Then he took a step back and appraised her body like a meat inspector deciding between choice and prime. Prime won.

"Ah," he said, licking his lips. "You done good with this one here, Creed."

Marie said, "Stop it Sal. You're making the poor girl uncomfortable." To Kathleen she said, "Don't pay any attention to him. He thinks he's a stallion."

Kathleen smiled.

Marie's eyes turned fierce. "I mean it," she said. "Don't pay any attention to him!"

Kathleen flashed me a look of confusion.

Sal said, "Marie, this is Creed's girlfriend." He emphasized the word by arching his eyebrows.

Marie showed skepticism.

"They're adopting a kid, for Crissake," he said.

Marie's demeanor changed instantly. "Really, Donovan?"

"It's true," I said.

Marie beamed at Kathleen. "You'll have to let me help you plan the wedding!"

Sal laughed. "Hell, they ain't gonna exchange—whatcha call—nuptials. They're going to keep living in sin like we used to do." He gave her a wink.

"We did nothing of the kind," Marie huffed. She turned to Kathleen. "That true? No marriage?"

Before Kathleen could think of a response, Marie shook her head and left us to chat with some guests.

Sal said, "You bring an envelope?"

"Better than that," I said, "but we have to go inside to get it."

"No shit?" Sal said. "Then let's go!"

He told T-Bone to guard the stash and motioned to Big Bad to follow us. We started making the journey through the crowd of well-wishers and glad handlers. As we walked I said, "How'd you know about the adoption?"

Sal smiled. "I got my—whatcha call—sources."

To Kathleen, Sal said, "You ever see this one fight?"

"I *heard* him once."

Sal said, "Heard him? What's that mean?"

She gave me a look. I said, "Nellie's Diner. Joe DeMeo's goons."

Sal said, "You was there?"

Kathleen nodded. "Sort of," she said. "I was in the restaurant, hiding under a table."

We entered the great room. Santo Mangano waved from the foyer and yelled, "Hey, Sallie!" Sal returned the wave.

"Thing of beauty," Sal said, "the way Creed—whatcha call—inflicts physical damage. We was in a place one time, some martial arts guy was drunk and comes at me for no frickin' reason. Before Big and T have a chance to react, Creed

60

goes after this guy and I swear to Christ, it looked like a cyclone fightin'a water bug!"

Kathleen squeezed my arm. "You think that's something, you should see him in the sack."

"No shit?"

"Yeah," I said. "Except in the sack, I'm the water bug."

Sal started to laugh but a thunderous voice suddenly took over all the speakers in the house. He flinched slightly, but stood his ground. All around us, gangsters hit the floor, pulling their wives down with them. Women screamed as their husbands scrambled for cover. Guns were produced from ankle and shoulder holsters. Servers brandished knives, proving me right about the brandishing.

The voice was masculine, and powerful, like the wrath of God.

The voice boomed: "The mightiest warriors are not the most physically impressive!"

The lights went out and circles of blue lasers started flashing at the far end of the foyer. The giant voice spoke again.

"Behold the mightiest warriors of all time!"

A giant cloud of smoke appeared and the lights came back on. A wheelchair stood where the smoke had been. Not an ordinary wheelchair, but one fashioned from space age materials. It was equipped with a series of roll bars, lights, and all manner of electronic equipment. Navigating the chair was a little person with enormous dreadlocks, wearing an electrified shirt.

Victor.

At Victor's side, the everpresent, always angry Hugo, "The Little General," stood guard. Hugo was Victor's aide, confidante, and advisor in all things military. Victor and Hugo were little people who dreamed of conquering the world with their midget army. If they ever succeeded it truly would be a small world, after all.

All eyes turned to Sal.

"Relax," he said. "The little guys wanted to make a—whatcha call—entrance. I told 'em, knock yourselves out."

Dozens of gangsters sheepishly holstered their weapons and dealt with their angry spouses with severe, whispered threats.

Victor made an adjustment on the arm of his chair and the loudspeaker voice softened. "Could I have the honor of Salvatore Bonadello's presence for one moment?"

Sal said, "Let's—whatcha call—indulge the little guy." We started walking toward Victor and Hugo.

"I need to check my make-up," Kathleen said, just the way we'd rehearsed. "Can you point me to your powder room?"

"Powder room?" Sal said. "Now that's class!" He pointed the way and Kathleen headed there.

"At first I thought she meant gunpowder," Sal said, studying her ass as long as he could before she disappeared from view. "That there's a winner. I envy you, wakin' up to that every morning."

Victor's speaker voice said, "Will you all please give a warm welcome to my manservant, Merlin."

No one moved to make a sound. Once again, all eyes were on Sal. He looked around the room and shouted, "He means clap your hands. Show some class here!"

Sal began clapping his hands. Others, clearly befuddled, reluctantly joined in.

From behind the assembled guests a woman screamed. Everyone spun around. Then the scream circled the room through the speakers and the guests saw that Victor had created a diversion so the magician could appear.

Merlin began approaching Sal. Big Bad produced a .357 magnum and held it at Merlin's face.

Merlin regarded the gun with more than a little trepidation. "I was told there'd be no guns?"

Sal said, "I'm gonna let the gun stay where it is. Just in case."

Merlin assembled his courage and said, "Very well, but please be careful. Can you give me a dollar please?"

"The fuck?" Sal said.

Sal looked at Victor. "It's my friggin' party," he said. "It don't set well givin'money to this guy here."

"Just one dollar," Merlin said. "I can assure you, you won't be sorry."

"I better not be."

Sal dug into his pants pocket, produced a wad of cash big enough to choke a wide-mouth frog. He flipped through the bills until he found a dollar, which he peeled off and handed to Merlin. Merlin's right hand was empty—I was watching it—then suddenly it held a felt-tip pen.

I've seen good before. Merlin was great.

"Please sign the dollar, so we'll know it's yours."

"I already know it's mine, shithead!" Sal said. But he signed it anyway.

Merlin took the bill and held it high over his head as he backed up a few steps. Sal told Big Bad, "Keep an eye on this friggin'guy."

Big Bad nodded and kept his gun sighted on the magician.

Merlin produced an envelope, again seemingly out of midair, placed the dollar in the envelope and tore it. When he did that, Big Bad cocked the trigger.

A very nervous Merlin probably never had to work under

this type of pressure, but he managed to complete the trick. He folded the envelope several times while tearing sections of it. Then he unfolded the perfectly intact envelope and held it high above his head, waiting for applause.

There was none.

Sal said, "Where's my money? These guys'll tell you, you don't want to owe me money."

Sporadic nervous chuckles broke out from various areas of the room.

Merlin handed the envelope to Sal. In it was a certified check for one hundred thousand dollars.

The guests erupted in cheerful applause, hooting and whistling. To a man, they understood what a certified check meant.

Sal wasn't grinning, but he was close. He looked like a kid who'd just inherited FAO Schwartz. He slapped Merlin on the back, shouted "Bravo!" at Victor.

Victor's speaker voice said, "Read the signature on the check."

Sal tried to read the signature, frowned, and took a pair of reading glasses from his jacket pocket. "Donovan Creed," he said. I bowed and said, "I told you I'd amaze you."

Sal gave me a body hug. "Now *that's* appreciation," he said, looking around the room. Then he stopped as if suddenly remembering something.

"Where's my dollar?" he said.

From the other end of the room, Kathleen said, "I've got your money right here, Mr. Bonadello."

She held two items high over her head while crossing through the crowd. She presented them to Sal. One was his signed dollar bill. The other was another cashier's check for a hundred thousand dollars.

Sal was way ahead of her. He went straight for his glasses and got to the bottom line quickly. He announced to the crowd, "Victor just gave me another hundred grand!"

Once again the crowd erupted into thunderous applause. I gave Victor a thumbsup, and he returned the gesture.

Sal's eyes were on Kathleen. He kissed her cheek.

"You better reel this one in," Sal said, "before she gets away. You ain't getting'any younger, you know."

Sal hugged me again and left us to mingle.

I smiled at Kathleen. "You did a good job with the magic trick," I said.

"It was fun."

We gorged ourselves on the classic Neapolitan food, which consisted of hearty, straightforward dishes, like ziti al forno, chicken cacciatore, panzerotti, steak pizzaiol, rigatoni with broccoli, lasagna, and several standing rib roasts.

We followed that with an hour of dancing, under the lights. As the night wore on, the gangsters and goons seemed more accepting of my presence at the party. The reason for that was simple. Sal had spread the lie that I was retired, and that my donation had been my buy-out from the life.

As Kathleen and I stood in the foyer, waiting for our car, I said, "Anybody hit on you tonight?"

She reached in her purse and pulled out a slip of paper and handed it to me.

"Whose number is this?"

"Some guy named Ice Pick," she said, "though I doubt that's his Christian name."

She looked around the room filled with fierce wise guys, badly healed broken noses, missing fingers, and an endless assortment of scars.

"Then again," she said.

# 13.

IT TOOK AWHILE to piece all this together, but between Ned's confession, my and Teddy Boy's observations, the video camera I'd installed in The Grantline, the wireless mike I'd hidden in Callie's purse—and Callie's firsthand experience—it went down this way, give or take:

Bickham Wright always came to the bar with high hopes, looking for gorgeous, but The Grantline was a redneck dump in West Podunk, a good forty miles from the big city action. So Bickham always hoped for gorgeous, but he was willing to settle for cute. After a couple hours and several drinks, he and his friends would forget all about cute and start fighting over what's available.

And for that, they didn't need the date rape drug.

Lately, even "available" hadn't been an option, and Bickham's friends were beginning to grumble, especially Charlie, the good-looking one. He didn't need this shit, he could get chicks on his own. Had one, in fact, a cute little cheerleader named Kimberly Creed. But Kimberly was proving to be a difficult lay, thank God, and Charlie was getting tired of playing first base.

That is not to say that Charlie had lost his respect for "The Plan." Even for Charlie there was probably something exciting and primal about doing it this way, something that linked his brain to that of his ancient forebears and satisfied the need to hunt, capture and conquer. And of course, "The Plan" provided instant gratification: he didn't have to go through all the dating bullshit just to get laid.

Still, if there *were* no chicks, the best plan in the world was useless. Where *were* the little bitches? That was the real question. Maybe word was getting around. Hell, even the best fishing holes eventually got fished out.

Three weekends in a row had yielded squat, and Bickham was the last holdout of the group. He didn't want to drive the extra forty miles across the county line to troll unfamiliar bars where he didn't know the layout. There were too many variables. One mistake and they'd be in jail with no back up. "Yeah," said Robbie, "but at least there'd be some action!"

Bickham got the boys together and sat them down. "Look," he said. "Maybe we don't always score, but you gotta admit, it's a great plan. Bickham gave it all he had, told them to put their faith in the plan. In the end he persuaded them to meet at the local dive, and once again they showed up, hoping for gorgeous.

After an hour of drinking, the main room was crowded, the band was rocking, the dance floor working, and the boys were getting so rowdy they almost missed Beauty (Callie) and the Beast, the tough-looking older guy (me, in disguise) working their way through the crowd to occupy the last vacant seats at the bar.

Bickham worked his way through the maze of good ol'boys sucking in their beer guts and jockeying their seats to get a better look at Callie. When he found a spot where he could check her out, he couldn't believe his eyes. There at the bar, their bar, sat the most beautiful girl he'd ever seen.

Bickham couldn't stop blinking as he checked out the whole package, top to bottom, slowly. Then back up. Thinking hot! Blond! *Flawless*! And sporting what had to be the most amazing tattoo he'd ever seen on a woman—it covered most of her right arm and, from a distance, looked almost like a sleeve.

Bickham looked over his shoulder, saw Charlie checking her out, salivating. Robbie and George were back at the table high-fiving and punching each other's arms. Bickham must have felt vindicated. They always came hoping for gorgeous, so why could they not, just once in their lives, hit the jackpot?

And speaking of jackpots, Callie had just slapped my face. When I pretended to protest, the bartender, Teddy Boy, pulled out a baseball bat and pretended to send me packing. I made my way to the rental car and watched the action on my video monitor.

Bickham made eye contact with Charlie, who signaled the others. Game on!

The boys had every reason to believe it was a good plan. The way it works, Bickham checks out the girl, finds out what she's drinking, and orders himself one. He drinks most of it, then pours the drug into the remainder. Bickham walks up to the girl, tries to pick her up. Of course, even ugly girls don't like Bickham, so she's thrilled when the handsome Charlie shows up from the opposite direction to protect her from the local loser.

While Charlie engages her in smooth conversation, Bickham pours the rest of his drink into hers. If anyone notices, it just looks like he's sharing his drink before ordering another. Though no one ever notices, Bickham knows it's these small details that make a plan come together.

When the girl becomes groggy, Bickham circulates loudly through the bar, diverting attention from her while Charlie escorts her out the door.

Later, no one will remember seeing Charlie and the girl leave.

The other two, George and Robbie, run interference on Teddy Boy, the bartender, and stand ready to take over in case the girl doesn't want to leave with Charlie. In that situation, George will stand up to Charlie.

Once they get her in the van, George and Robbie stand guard. Bickham does her first because it's his plan and he supplies the drug. Charlie goes second, because he's the one who does the hard work. George and Robbie work out who gets third and fourth spot. After that, the boys rotate turns doing her until their stamina runs out. If the bar starts closing down before they're done, they drive her out to the woods and hit it all night.

So the plan was foolproof and the boys are local, so there are plenty of witnesses to cover for them if a complaint surfaces later on. Plus, Charlie's dad is the top lawyer in the county, in the pocket of every judge, and no father dared face him in court, fearing for his daughter's reputation.

Bickham patted his pocket, making sure the drug was there.

GHB, gamma hydroxybutyric acid, is one of three so-called date rape drugs. Legal with a prescription, GHB is used to treat narcolepsy. Although widely available as a powder or pill, those forms can leave residue and give off a salty taste. The liquid form is Bickham's delivery system of choice. It's odorless, colorless and mixes in alcohol, which intensifies the effect dramatically.

Bickham's cousin Ned, a local pharmacist, makes the drug in his store after hours. Ned has a high-maintenance trophy wife—a fine looking young thing named Anita, whose expensive tastes would normally be hard to support on a small town druggist's income. But cousin Bickham has lots of money, so theirs is a partnership made in heaven.

Bickham has a large stash of GHB in his closet, a good thing since Ned went missing a couple of days ago. Bickham probably wondered if Ned was in some sort of trouble with drug dealers or the law, and this thought surely prompted daydreams about making it with his cousin's wife. According to Ned, Bickham still loved conjuring the visual of Ned testing the GHB on Anita before selling it to Bickham the first time.

On their "dates," when Bickham and Charlie feel the party needs to be moved to the woods due to drunks in the parking lot or because the bar is closing down, George and Robbie take a second car, since they're younger and can't stay out past two a.m.

The younger pair are unaware Bickham and Charlie had to kill and bury one of their "dates" a few months ago. The killers aren't worried about Erica's body turning up. They've hunted these woods their whole lives and know the high ground that will never be explored.

Usually, the girls were fat or worse. Tonight, if they could pull it off, they'd hit the Pussy Power Ball!

Okay, so the game was on.

Teddy Boy had just poured Callie a second drink. George and Robbie sprang into action and called Teddy Boy over to the other end of the bar to talk about liquor and sports.

Bickham took that opportunity to slide into the empty seat I had vacated. "Hey there, pretty lady," he said.

Callie rolled her eyes.

"This can be a pretty rough place," he continued. "I'd be glad to watch your back if you want, keep the flies away while you enjoy a drink or two."

"Oh goody!" she said, "my knight in shining armor."

*Typical bitch response*, he probably thought. According to Ned, Bickham seemed to elicit this attitude from all women, even what he called the OFU's (old, fat and ugly ones).

He tried again: "Drinking alone, I see…"

"Usually I drink to make men more interesting. In your case…" Callie waved her hand in a dismissive manner, as if she were casually swatting air currents at a fly. She looked at the array of whisky bottles on the bar shelf and continued, "I don't think there's enough alcohol."

She drained half her glass and set it back on the bar.

Bickham moved his hand close to her drink as Charlie approached her from the other side.

"Hey Bickham," he said, "and hello, gorgeous! I'm Charlie, what's your name?" As she turned to face him, Bickham poured the liquid into her drink, no doubt thinking, *See what I mean? Foolproof!* Callie and Charlie spoke a minute, which gave me time to check the detonator. Then he held his drink up as if to make a toast.

Callie smiled, reached for her drink, clinked his glass and paused a moment, watching Charlie drink. She waited there, glass poised in midair, as if trying to decide if she really needs this last one. She shrugged. Why not? As she moved the drink toward her perfect mouth, a small explosion rocked the back of the building.

"Shit!" Charlie screamed. "The hell was that?"

He and Bickham hit the floor. As most of the patrons ran toward the back to check out the explosion, Charlie stood up, embarrassed to see that Callie had not left her stool. She shrugged again, chugged her drink, and set it on the counter.

Over the next few minutes, confusion reigned as half the local boys ran to their trucks to retrieve squirrel guns, baseball bats and crowbars. The police were called and Teddy Boy did what he could to restore order.

Charlie regrouped, raised his eyebrows at Bickham, who knew an opportunity when he saw one.

"Sugar, we better get you out of here, get you some-where safe," Bickham said.

Callie said, "I don't think so."

Charlie said, "It'll be okay. You can trust me."

Their eyes met. His were sincere, hers had a faraway look.

"C'mon!" Charlie said.

He and Bickham began herding the brown-eyed, tat-tooed blond through the crowd, out the front door. She said, "Wait a minute, I'm feeling kind of dizzy."

And Bickham suppressed a smile.

# 14.

NOW, OUT IN the parking lot, wanting to leave before the cops arrived, Charlie said: "Climb on in, we'll drive a bit, get some air."

I started my car and turned up my radio to pick up the wireless mike in the handle of Callie's purse. I could have driven ahead, since I knew where they were going, Bickham drove and Charlie rode shotgun, trapping Callie between them on the bench seat. Above her head, the boys probably exchanged a grin, thinking, *city girls! This is too damn easy!* Callie tried to ask where they were going but slurred her words to make them think her speech was already severely impaired.

Bickham put his hand on her thigh, patted it. "I know you're sleepy. We'll stop in a couple minutes," he said in his most sincere voice. This part was important, keeping her calm till the drug took effect.

She made a half-hearted effort to swat his hand away, but seemed to lack the coordination. Charlie cupped her breast with his hand and murmured, "God, you're beautiful!"

Callie's eyes were half shut, her breathing labored. "Get your hands off me!" she was trying to say, but her voice came out as slow and lazy as ketchup from a bottle. As far as they knew, she was barely conscious.

Bickham moved his hand to her crotch, tried to feel her

through her jeans. Charlie, out of control, ripped her blouse open, lifted her bra, exposing her breasts. He stuffed one in his mouth while rubbing the nipple of the other with his thumb.

"Quit that shit!" yelled Bickham. "You know the rules! *Goddamn it Charlie, relax!*"

Bickham wasn't kidding about the rules. They were as important as the plan itself. Charlie had been a huge help in formulating them, thanks to years of experience watching his father prepare for criminal defense trials.

In all, there were seven rules in Fuck Club, as Charlie called their group, and the four friends had agreed to follow all seven faithfully, on pain of death.

The first rule is you never talk about the plan, even to each other, because you never know who might overhear you. When your friends ask how was your weekend you always tell them the same thing: you struck out again. What do you care if your friends think you can't get laid?

The second rule is you wait until she's unconscious before removing her clothes. The last thing you want is to have to explain why she's screaming if the sex is consensual.

The third rule is, undress her completely but carefully, paying attention to which buttons were buttoned and what was tucked in, and how. If she's a little heavy and doesn't button the top button of her jeans, she'll know if someone else did. She might not remember if she had too much to drink and got in your van, but she will remember she had some tissue stuffing her bra that isn't there when she gets undressed at home afterward.

Then you fold her clothes or lay them out to avoid wrinkles or stains. "Always remember," Charlie had said, "without the dress stain, Monica was a liar, a slut, and a stalker. With it, she nearly brought down the President!" Afterward, you dress her carefully, replacing every item as it had been before you unwrapped the package.

The fourth rule is, use a condom. You don't want any fluids turning up later. DNA evidence is hard to overcome if you're on record denying you had sex with her. Of course, later on you can always just say you were trying to protect her reputation, or yours, and that the sex was consensual. But in that case you're arguing after the fact, trying to play make-up. You've lost a measure of credibility and created doubt. It's better not to be in this position in the first place.

The fifth rule is you remain calm at all times. Do her gently to avoid marks or abrasions typically associated with sexual assault. You never attempt oral or anal. Oral could choke her to death because the drug constricts her breathing, and anal is something she would figure out later on.

The sixth rule is you take no pictures, videos, souvenirs or evidence of any kind. Speaking of evidence, you leave none. This means, curb the saliva. No hickies, love bites or marks of any kind. No sense giving the cops or prosecuting attorney a gift-wrapped conviction.

The final rule is you never admit to anything. If the police bring all four of you into the station and isolate you in separate interrogation rooms, you never admit anything. If the cops threaten you or tell Charlie that Bickham is cutting a deal, Charlie knows it's a lie because of rule number seven. Under no circumstances do you break rule number seven. As Charlie says, "Put your trust in the American system of justice and you'll be fine, because the rules of evidence are flawed when it comes to date rape. If no one breaks any of the seven rules, none of us will ever be convicted."

Also, as long as Charlie's involved, you inherit his high-powered father as your legal safety net.

Of course, if anyone was likely to violate the rules it would be Charlie himself—and he'd already proved it tonight by ripping Callie's blouse and getting his saliva all over her breast.

Bickham turned the van down the dirt road toward the wooded area owned by his grandfather, drove a few hundred yards before stopping, and extinguished the head-lights. I passed their turnoff and went a mile further before turning into the dirt road I knew would eventually bring me a quarter mile from Bickham's preferred banging area.

Bickham put his van in park and cut the engine. He pushed Charlie off of Callie. "Goddamn it, Charlie. Wait your fuckin' turn!"

"Jesus Christ, Bickham, check out these tits!" he gushed. "She's a fuckin' ten, man!"

"No shit," said Bickham. "Now help me get her in the back before I explode!"

The back of the van had a couple of layers of sleeping bags spread out, so the girls wouldn't have marks on their backs afterward.

Charlie opened the passenger door, climbed out, and lowered the passenger seat to create easy access to the back of the van. He figured he'd reach under Callie's arms and drag her back there. But as he leaned toward her, his face exploded.

In that small, enclosed area, the gun shot noise was deafening.

"Jesus!" screamed Bickham. He tried to scramble out the driver's side, but lacked the clarity of focus.

"I'm so glad your friend liked my tits," Callie said. "But I saved something *really* special for you!" She pointed the gun at his face.

Bickham threw his hands in the air, surrendering. "No, ma'am, please! Shit! I didn't mean nuthin', I swear! I swear to God I won't bother you! Please, Jesus, just let me go. You can have the van. Just, oh Jesus, please don't kill me! *Please*!"

She looked at his crotch. "Did you just *wet* yourself?" Christ, Bickham, you're the guy who was supposed to *protect* me!

He put his hands in front of his face, turned his head away from her, whimpering. His voice reduced to a squeak, he pleaded again. "Please, ma'am. Please don't kill me."

"You know," Callie said, "it never ceases to amaze me how much damage these prefragmented bullets can do at close range."

She pointed the gun at his crotch, pulled the trigger. He screamed in pain, started convulsing. Callie slid out the open passenger door while Bickham flayed his arms about, sobbing hysterically. The impact of the shot had knocked Charlie's body back about six feet. She dragged it around to the front of the van and kicked until it was concealed beneath the fender.

The gorgeous blonde with the wild tattoo and the dark brown eyes climbed back in the van and watched Bickham's medical condition deteriorate until she saw headlights ap-proaching from the dirt road behind the van.

"Sorry, lover boy. I'd love to stay and party with you some more, 'cos really, you're everything I look for in a man. Especially now that you've shit your pants! I can't speak for the other girls, but that's a real turnon for me. Unfortunately, I've got to mingle, greet my other guests. You know how it is when you're the one throwing the surprise party."

She put a quick one in his left eye and stuffed him as far as she could into the floorboard. She climbed into the back of the van and opened the door about an inch.

The first rule of being a good hostess is knowing how to dress for the occasion. Callie had to decide how much skin to show the boys. George and Robbie were expecting to see her naked, so she had to show something. On the other hand, she was in no mood to show them everything. Her blouse was already torn open, so that was good. She made a mental note to collect the buttons later.

To honor Charlie, she lifted her bra, exposed her breasts in the manner he seemed to favor, and slipped off her jeans. She considered sliding them down to her ankles, but decided that might hinder her ability to move quickly in the event she miscalculated the situation. Anyway, showing boobs and panties ought to be enough for these pups. She lay on her back, knees bent, and spread her legs toward the back door of the van. Her left arm lay lifeless, her eyes half-closed. By her side, her jacket covered the gun in her right hand.

Moments later Robbie brought his car to a stop behind the van. The two boys stubbed out their weed.

George laughed. "Let's mess with 'em. Turn your lights back on." Robbie did, and the boys noticed the back door of the van was ajar. They got out of the car and tentatively approached, trying not to giggle too loudly. Robbie tapped on the door.

"Yoo Hoo!" he said, "anybody home?"

George peeked first. "Oh my God," he squealed. "Check this out!"

He flung the door wide open so Robbie could see. George was starting to say, "What's that smell?" when the blond bolted up and fired twice.

George was dead before he hit the ground. Robbie was alive, but his chest wound was going to be a problem.

Callie put her outfit together, collected her belongings, and wiped the interior of the van clean. Then she walked over and sat next to Robbie.

"Wh-what are you d-doing?" he managed to say.

"Sitting here, watching you bleed out," she said.

"W-why?"

"For the fun of it."

She turned at the sound behind her.

"Hey Donovan, nice explosion," she said.

I surveyed the carnage. "Jesus, Callie."

"I know, I know," she said. She shrugged. "What can I say? Sometimes it's personal."

I walked over to the kid they called Robbie, saw him gasping, eyes bugged out, silently mouthing words no one would ever hear. I placed a round into the boy's head to end his suffering, and gave Callie a look.

"I owe you," I said.

"If you really feel that way," she said, "there's something I want you to do."

"What's that?"

"Come to Vegas with me."

# 15.

*EXCUSE ME?* I thought. *Did Callie just ask me to come with her to Vegas?*

Even sitting there on the ground with her blouse torn and her torso covered in blood spray, Callie was hotter than a habanero. To any other man her invitation would have sounded like a dream come true. But I knew her well enough to know that whatever this was about, it wasn't about us hooking up. In earlier times I'd taken my best shots to bed her and struck out every time.

Still, a little clarification wouldn't hurt.

"I'm with Kathleen now," I said. "I thought you knew."

Callie laughed and said, "Jesus, Donovan, get a grip!"

"Okay," I said. "I was just making sure."

"You have any idea how old you are?"

"I got it, Callie, it's a platonic trip. I get the picture."

"Old enough to be my father, you sick degenerate."

"I'm fourteen years older than you. Period.

"In dog years, maybe."

I sighed. "When do you want to go?"

"How's Wednesday sound?"

"I've got a meeting in Newark Wednesday morning, eight-thirty. I can meet you at the airport there around ten."

"Same Fixed Base Operator as last time?"

"Same FBO, different jet."

"I'll be waiting in the lobby," she said, "with bells on."

"Try getting bells through civilian security these days," I said.

"I appreciate it, Donovan."

I nodded.

She stood and said, "Bickham's in the driver's seat, Charlie's under the front wheel, right side, these two you've seen. We done here?"

I handed Callie a small flashlight.

"Can you hold this on the dash for me?" I said.

Through the driver's window, she focused enough light for me to work. I took a small plastic baggie out of my pocket and leaned into the van through the passenger seat door. I took some fingerprint tape out of the baggie and transferred several partials onto the dashboard and a perfect palm print for the side of the seat that Charlie had lowered. Then I took three strands of blond hair from the bag and put one on the seat, one on the floor, and one on the sleeve of Bickham's shirt, near the cuff.

"You left the shells where they landed, right?" I said, going through my mental checklist.

Callie didn't bother to answer. She was the consummate pro.

I looked around a bit longer, making sure I didn't miss anything. I put the plastic baggie back in my pocket and took two gallon-sized plastic bags out of my duffel bag.

"Ready for the guns," I said.

I wiped mine down and placed it carefully into one of the plastic bags and put it in the duffel. Callie handed me hers and I cleaned and packed it with the other one.

"Crime scene's okay," I said.

"What about the video camera?"

"Sal didn't trust Teddy to remove it, so he put a guy in the bar. He won't leave without it."

"You think Sal will try to use it against us someday?"

"Nah. Our people can discredit any type of evidence."

I took a windbreaker out of the duffel and handed it to her.

"Put this on to cover your arm," I said. "We'll drive awhile before removing that tattoo."

"I'll do it after you drop me off. I've got some polish remover that works pretty well, but a job like this will take some time."

"You still wearing the brown contacts?" I said.

She turned the flashlight onto her face.

"You like? You saw them earlier."

"Huge difference," I said. Callie's natural palegray eyes were hypnotic. These were normal.

"I guess we're ready," I said. "Still, I'd feel better if we were doing the body double instead of Sal."

Callie shrugged. "This is Goober Town, Donovan, not *Miami CSI*."

Part of the plan was to have Teddy Boy take a picture of Callie at the restaurant with his cell phone camera, from a distance, but making sure he got at least a hazy shot of the outrageous tattoo on her right arm. When the local detectives come to the bar to interview people, Teddy Boy would remember taking the picture.

Sal already had a victim lined up that matched the tat-too, a dancer named Shawna. It was Shawna's hair that I'd placed in the van. Shawna only vaguely resembled Callie, but Sal didn't intend for much to be identifiable beyond the hair and tattoo. She was a dancer in one of Sal's clubs in Cleveland, and had recently committed the unpardonable sin of threatening one of Sal's lieutenants with exposure. Sal's guy was preparing to kill her when Sal forced him to hide her instead, and keep her alive until he gave the word. I hoped the angry lieutenant would refrain from killing her until I could get Callie's gun to Sal, so he could get the dancer's prints on it. I hadn't intended to use my gun tonight, but I did, so now I'd have to take it apart and scatter it, piece by piece, over a wide area.

"How long will we be in Vegas?" I asked.

Callie smirked at me. "Gotta check in with the ol' ball and chain?"

I shrugged. "When you're in a committed relationship, there are certain rules of protocol."

"So you'll tell her we're going to Vegas, just you and me?"

"Full disclosure is not one of the rules."

"One night."

"Excuse me?"

"We'll be in Vegas one night."

I assumed she had a tricky freelance killing to do that required a second person. If so, I'd need to know a few details before we left.

"What type of equipment should I bring?" I asked.

"A nice suit."

"That's it?"

"We're just going to a show. At the Bellagio."

"Oh."

"That's right."

"What's right?"

"'O'."

"Oh, what?" I said.

"The show is called 'O.'"

"In that case," I said, "who's on first?"

"Does that work for Kathleen?"

"What, humor?"

She looked at me and rolled her eyes.

"Not really," I said.

We sat there a moment, Callie staring straight ahead, thinking of one thing but talking about another.

"She probably thinks you're funny," Callie said. "It's early in the relationship."

"That'll change soon, though, huh Dr. Phil?"

"You're probably wondering why I want you to see this particular show this particular week," she said.

"Hey, I'm honored. The reason doesn't matter."

"It might, later on."

"Why's that?"

"Because after the show you're going to have to make a life and death decision."

"My life and death?"

"No," she said. "Mine."

# 16.

SUNDAY MORNING. I was heading to Kathleen's house when my cell phone rang. I checked the display, saw my daughter was calling, and had my driver raise the privacy partition. Before I clicked on, I reminded myself to start off cheerfully.

"Hi Kitten, what's up?"

"*Oh my God, Daddy, someone's killed Charlie!*"

"What? *Who's* been killed?" I said.

"Charlie! My boyfriend! *Oh, my God! Someone's killed Charlie!*" Kimberly started sobbing. "Oh, my *God!*" she screamed.

With each sob I felt a stab of guilt. But also relief. That son-of-a-bitch might be hurting her in death, but he would have hurt her far worse by living.

"Kimberly, try to calm down. Tell me what happened."

"They found a van this morning, in a field. Four boys were shot. One of them is Charlie. Oh, God, Daddy!" She started sobbing again. "How can this have happened? Who could possibly want to hurt Charlie? He was the greatest guy ever."

"Are you absolutely sure it was Charlie? Has anyone identified the body?"

She was having trouble catching her breath.

"It's him, Dad. All four boys were killed."

"I'm so sorry, Kitten," I said. "I'm so very sorry."

We went on like that awhile. Somewhere in there she said, "I wish you could have met him. You would have liked him."

"I know I would have," I lied.

She cried some more and I remained on the phone until she was all cried out. I asked if there was anything I could do.

She said, "Is there any way you'd consider coming to the funeral?"

"Of course I will," I said. "Just tell me when and where."

I wasn't worried about being recognized as Callie's date from the Grantline Bar & Grill the night before. For one thing, all eyes were on Callie. For another, I'd worn elevator shoes that added three inches to my height, a brown wig, glasses and a full beard. The beard covered the scar on my face, and the clothes I wore are long gone. The guns were cleaned and currently in Sal's possession. There was nothing to tie me to the scene.

Kathleen and I spent the day quietly, commiserating about Kimberly. I had to bite my lip a dozen times as Kathleen kept asking the same questions Kimberly had posed about poor, sweet, wonderful Charlie. It pissed me off that Kathleen assumed the kid she'd never met had been a choirboy. I mean, when four boys are murdered gangland style, wouldn't you naturally assume there might be something amiss? I kept reminding myself that Kathleen was a civilian. She had no instincts or training that would lead her to suspect that Charlie had murdered one woman and raped a dozen others. I remained neutral on the subject of Charlie, knowing that in the days to come most of the sordid details would be revealed in the news. But I knew I could never tell Kathleen about my involvement in his death, despite the fact that by killing Charlie, Callie and I had saved Kimberly and countless other women. No matter how deep Kathleen and my relationship grew, this would be yet another terrible secret I'd have to keep from her.

"Donovan, is there anything you can do?" she said.

"You mean like trying to find out who did it?"

"Or at least get some updated information for Kimberly. I'm sure it would make her feel better."

"That's a good idea," I said. "I'll put Lou Kelly on it."

Lou is my right-hand man, the guy that heads up my support team for Sensory Resources. Lou's geek squad would be able to provide me with up-to-the-minute information from the sheriff's department.

All afternoon the calls went back and forth between Lou and me. By eight p.m. the investigation had made enough progress to give Kimberly a credible report.

"I know you're hurting honey, but I called in some favors and did some checking. You can't tell anyone about this, because it's privileged, but I've got some information about the shooting."

"Thank you, Daddy." She sounded painfully subdued.

"I've got to warn you, you're probably not going to like what I have to say."

"Then it's probably a pack of lies."

Well, at least there was still a spark there. "It might be, Honey, but the evidence they've gathered is pretty strong against the boys."

She was quiet, bristling a little.

"It's up to you, Kimberly."

"I want to hear it," she said. "I'll find out eventually, so I may as well know now."

"All right, then. I'll start talking, and if it gets to be too much, just tell me and I'll stop. Here goes: all four of the boys were from Darnell. Two of them were shot execution style with a single shot between the eyes. Charlie was one of them, the other was a boy named George Rawlins."

I paused to let her finish crying.

"Go ahead, Dad. I'm sorry."

"I know, Baby. It's hard. Maybe this isn't the best time."

"No Dad, really. I want to hear."

"Okay. I'm reading from a memorandum now: 'The other two, Bickham Wright and Robbie Milford, were wounded first; then finished off with head shots. The driver of the van, Bickham Wright, was shot in the groin. Robbie Milford was shot in the lower chest. Police on the scene speculated the shootings may have been gang related, and likely involved drugs; a conclusion they reached in an effort to tie the crime to the recent disappearance of Bickham Wright's cousin, Ned Denhollen, also from Darnell.'"

Kimberly said, "Mr. Denhollen was our pharmacist. There's been a rumor he left his wife. Has he been found?"

"There's nothing in the report about it," I said. "Here, I'll read you what I have: 'Denhollen is or was a Darnell pharmacist. Friends and neighbors interviewed considered Ned and his wife Anita to be living beyond their means, suggesting possible after-hours drug sales. The kill shots appeared to be professional in nature, suggesting a gangland-style murder or underworld execution.'"

"So far, none of this makes any sense," Kimberly said. "If Mr. Denhollen was selling drugs, they would have shot *him*, not Charlie and the others."

"Let me keep reading," I said. "It starts to come together: 'Madison Park police discovered the four bodies Sunday morning. Because the area where the bodies were found encompasses both jurisdictions, police officers from Madison Park and Darnell have joined forces to create a task force to investigate the shootings. All four victims were known to police at the scene and therefore identified simultaneously. At 1:25 p.m. today the task force began a thorough search of the victims'homes, personal belongings, and computers. They discovered several clear, odorless vials of liquid in a box on the top shelf of Bickham Wright's bedroom closet, which they turned over to a local medical lab for testing. Riley Cobb, a local computer expert, was able to access Robby Milford's computer. He was able to uncover hundreds of pornographic downloads, as well as a folder named 'Fuck Club.'"

I waited to see if she had a comment about that. She didn't.

"Sorry about the language," I said.

"Its okay, Daddy," she said. "I've heard the word a million times."

"There's a lot of stuff about this," I said. "Rather than read it, I'll summarize. The task force found several files in the Fuck Club folder on Robbie's computer, including seven rules for participating in the club, and photographs of three local girls, all nude, all apparently unconscious."

"Who were they, Dad?"

"I don't have their names yet, but the task force has identified them as local girls, meaning either Darnell or Madison Park, or both."

"Why were they unconscious? Were they drunk? I don't understand."

"This is the part you're not going to like. The task force is almost certain that the test results on the vials found in Bickham's closet will reveal GHB, the date rape drug. Based on the files and photographs they uncovered from Robbie's computer, and the vials found in Bickham's closet, it looks like the boys had a club where they were drugging girls and having sex with them."

"That's ridiculous!" Kimberly shouted. "I don't know the others. I mean, I know of them, but I don't know them. But I do know Charlie. He was *gorgeous*, Dad. He could've had *any* girl. He didn't need to drug anyone. If there actually *was* such a club, Charlie couldn't possibly have been a part of it."

I had to bite my tongue not to speak. Because not only was Charlie part of it, he was the worst part of it.

"I'm sure you're right, Kitten. By the time they finish the investigation maybe they'll conclude it was the other three, not Charlie."

"I can guarantee it," she said.

"Well, you certainly knew him better than me," I said, "so I'm sure you're right."

"Did they find any evidence when they searched the van?"

*That's my daughter*, I thought.

"In fact, they have. In addition to blood evidence, they've found five shell casings that are almost certainly related to the shooting, hundreds of fingerprints, and they've collected dozens of hair and fiber samples. They've also found numerous semen stains and other bodily fluid stains on sleeping bags found in the back of the van."

"They'll test the semen against the boys, won't they?" she said.

"They will."

"And if they find a match to Charlie, they'll think he was in on it."

"Not necessarily."

"What do you mean?"

"From what I understand, Charlie's father is an outstanding criminal lawyer. I'm sure if Charlie is innocent, his father will be able to make a compelling argument to prove it."

"You believe me, don't you Dad? About Charlie?"

"I do, Honey."

"Good. I couldn't bear it if you didn't."

"I understand there's going to be a vigil tonight," I said. "At the high school."

"It starts at nine. We're all going."

"Well, you be safe, okay?"

"I will. And thanks for trusting me with all this. I won't tell anyone."

"No problem. I love you, Kimberly."

"I love you too, Dad. And..."

"Yes?"

"I loved Charlie."

I winced. "I know you did, Honey."

# 17.

"DONOVAN, LET'S CUT to the chase," said Dr. Nadine Crouch. "This is our third visit, and so far you've refused to talk about your parents or your childhood, you've refused to talk about your job, or even what you were doing in the moments before the chest pain occurred. So I have to assume you were doing something illegal or immoral."

She paused to see if her words stirred a reaction in me.

"Do you deny it?" she said.

"Would it bother you?"

She said, "Suppose you found a bird with a broken wing that needs your help. Is it really important how its wing got broken?"

I paused a moment, trying to follow her train of thought. Giving up, I said, "Maybe you should just tell me what you're trying to say."

"It's not my job to judge you."

"In that case, I don't deny it."

"Very well," she said. "So you were doing something immoral or illegal when the pain began. Is this an activity you've engaged in previously?"

"Hypothetically?"

"Of course."

"Yes."

"Would I be right in assuming you haven't suffered chest

pains while performing this activity in the past?"

"You would."

She pursed her lips. "Normally I wouldn't make a rush to judgment, but you're not a typical patient. By helping you, I might be protecting others."

"I appreciate that," I said. "So what's the verdict?"

"We haven't spent enough time together for me to pronounce this with a high degree of certainty. But at first blush, this seems to be a classic example."

"Of?"

"Psychologically Induced Pain Syndrome. PIPS, for short."

"PIPS? I've got PIPS? Boy, won't Gladys Knight be jealous!"

"Psychological pain syndromes are defense mechanisms created by your subconscious mind to cover up unresolved emotional issues. In short, whatever your body was doing the day of the chest pains, your mind wanted no part of it. Your mind fought back the only way it could: by creating pain."

"Are you being serious?" I said.

"Completely. Your mind creates an intense pain to try to force you to stop doing whatever it is you're doing. It forces you to focus on the pain. If you don't, the pain gets worse. Your mind is determined to make you stop doing whatever it is that is so distasteful. If you don't come to grips with it, it can shut you down altogether."

I thought about that for a minute. "Is this a common thing?"

"It is, but it typically manifests in back pain."

"Then why the heart this time?"

"Look at you," she said. "You're strong as an ox. I'm guessing you've never had the slightest back pain, am I right?"

"You are."

"So your mind knows you wouldn't believe a back pain.

The subconscious mind is very clever. It won't create a pain that can be ignored or put off. It takes advantage of you by creating something so convincing, you have to focus on it. In your case I'm going to go out on a limb and guess your father, or someone close to you, died of a heart attack."

I could feel her looking at me, hoping for a reaction.

"So you're saying the pain is only a smokescreen, something my subconscious mind created to distract me from what I was doing at the time."

"That's correct. Be glad it wasn't colitis."

"Colitis?"

"That's the worst of the psychosomatic pains."

"Worse than the heart?"

"Far worse."

"Fair enough," I said. "But as we discussed, what I was doing at the time is something I've done many times before."

"Think it through, Donovan. I'll bet there was something different about that particular time."

So she was saying that my mind didn't want me to kill the Peterson sisters. No, it was more than that. My mind tried to prevent me from killing them. But why? I'd killed dozens—okay, more than a hundred—people before. What made the Petersons different? It couldn't be that they were women. I've killed women before, with no pains or afterthoughts. It couldn't be that I'm going soft, because I'd recently killed Ned Denhollen without the first sign of chest pains.

So what made the Peterson sisters different from all the rest?

The answer was somewhere in the back of my mind, hiding in a place I couldn't quite access. I was probably trying too hard to make sense of something my mind was trying to repress. Best thing to do was put it on hold and come back to it later. I stood.

She stood.

We shook hands.

"Will you come back?" she said.

"You've given me a lot to think about."

"You need this," she said.

"I'll let you know."

For a moment it seemed as though she wanted to say something else. The thought seemed to flit about her face like a scrap of paper caught on a wind current. In the end, she chose not to say it, whatever it was, and I was left to wonder what it could have been.

And realized that's probably how she gets her patients to return.

# 18.

SENSORY RESOURCES HAD a Gulfstream in a hangar in Trenton that needed to get back to LA, so Callie and I caught it as far west as Vegas. With a ride like that, you grab while you can. In a perfect world it would have been a round-tripper, but hey, I couldn't complain. I'd just have to charter something on my own dime to get us back home Thursday. I'd keep it Thursday night and use it to fly Kathleen and me to Charlie's funeral on Friday.

In a G4, Trenton to Vegas runs about four hours. A lot of time to chat, but we were quiet most of the trip. I couldn't stop thinking about what Dr. Crouch had said about the psychological pain. Until I got a handle on its cause, I'd be susceptible to severe chest pains at the worst possible times. That type of physical disability could prove deadly in my line of work.

"Cirque du Soleil," I said.

Callie looked up at me. "What about it?"

"I didn't know you were such a big fan of performance art."

"There's a lot you don't know about me," she said.

*True*, I thought. And a lot I did know.

This is how you get to be Callie: you're eight years old, you watch TV, you play in the yard, you go to school, and you've got the brightest smile and bubbliest laugh in town. Except that one day you're playing outside at your friend's house and the sky has gotten dark and you decide if you run you can beat the rain, because it's only a couple of blocks.

So you start running and you get about half-way home before the rain comes hard and you do something that changes your life.

You hesitate.

You stop running and wonder what to do. Should you keep heading home, or go back to your friend's house and call your mom to pick you up.

At that precise moment of indecision, you're tackled, punched, and dragged into the bushes.

The man is large and powerfully built. He smells of garlic and moldy cheese. He's got you face down in the mud and he doesn't have to hit you in the back of the head, but he does, and he hits you again and again. And each time he hits you, you start to black out, and you wish you could scream, but when you try, nothing comes out but a hiss.

The smelly man pulls your panties down to your ankles and hits you again. He starts touching you in a certain way—you know the word: *inappropriately*. At first you don't worry so much because what you wanted more than anything was for him to stop punching the back of your head. But then, when he starts talking to you with a love voice, and calls you his sexy little girl you want to vomit. When his words turn really dirty and he starts calling you names, you start wishing he'd stop saying those things and go back to hitting you.

Then, just when you think it can't get any worse, it gets much worse. The pain is unlike anything you've ever experienced, or ever imagined. It numbs you and your mind can't tolerate it, so it just shuts down.

The man leaves you lying there to die, face down in a

muddy field. You nearly drown in the muck but someone finds you and brings you home and for the next six months you're in and out of hospitals and you can't speak, can't feel, can't think. You sit in a chair facing a window and everyone thinks you're looking out the window, but you're actually staring *at* the window, and your mind is trying to work out the way the wooden pieces intersect, the slats that hold the window panes. Something about how they intersect. If you can figure that out, well, it's not much, but it's something to hold on to; a place from which to reclaim your sanity.

And then one day it's fall and the wind is blowing the leaves off the trees and one errant leaf snags on the window pane next to the wooden slats and when it does, you focus on the leaf. For the first time in months, you see there's something on the other side of the window, and if there's something beyond that window, then maybe it's something big enough to live for.

You begin the process of building your life from scratch. But you're not building the life you were meant to live, you're building something else altogether.

You realize you're alive and not dead or dreaming. But you also realize that while you're alive on the outside, on the inside you're dead. A few months pass and they send you back to school, but something's different. All the kids know what happened to you. They taunt you, hit you, but when they do, you feel no pain. That's because none of them can hit you like the man hit you. And yet, you want to be hit, so you taunt them back. They hit you and you laugh. They hit you some more and you laugh harder. You love the feel of your own blood in your mouth. The taste and texture makes you feel almost alive.

You're fifteen now, and you keep growing more and more

beautiful, but you could care less. You start taking drugs, you flirt with the fathers of your former friends, and you get some of them to sleep with you in return for money you use to buy more drugs.

You eventually get busted for prostitution and you're sent to a state hospital for evaluation. You're coming off your drugs cold turkey and you freak out and they give you an injection and put you in restraints. The first time you wake up you find your arms, waist and ankles strapped to a bed. The next time you wake up, two orderlies are molesting you. You scream and wail and they run away and you think you know how to beat them, but all you've done was teach them to give you a stronger dose next time.

You spend a few weeks in the ward and by the time you're clean you learn you have an IQ of 182, which is a hundred points more than you need for the life you're willing to accept.

So you're back home and back to other things, as well, like buying drugs and selling your body. And by the time you're eighteen, you're doing some new things, too, like stealing cars. You love the cars, love boosting them, love driving them fast, with the windows down and the radio up and the bass line thumping strong and steady.

Like a beating heart.

One night you're driving a tweaked out Super Bee and you're blitzed enough to wonder what it feels like to slam into the car that's parked near the bushes where it all changed for you. You hit it hard, but you survive, and then it's back to the ward, back to the knockout drugs that make the late night rape sessions possible for the otherwise undateable orderlies.

And you go on like that for a number of weeks or months until something happens: for the second time in your life, a man shows up and changes your life. Except that this man

99

understands you and knows what you need. His name is Donovan Creed and yeah, he knows exactly what you need.

You need a reason.

You don't get to be like eighteen-year-old Callie without experiencing soul-crushing trauma. And you don't become the empty, broken, killing machine Callie of today unless you have a reason.

So yeah, I gave Callie a reason. I took her under my wing and trained her. She was an easy study because she was indefatigable, and because she flat didn't give a shit.

Callie's reason is revenge.

That's why it's easy for her to put a bullet into a total stranger, or kill date raping young men in cold blood. That's why sometimes, for Callie, it's personal.

I looked at her in the Gulfstream, sitting across the aisle, facing me, reclining, eyes closed. And God help her, she was and is the most exquisitely beautiful woman to ever walk the earth.

And the most deadly.

I couldn't fathom this request of hers to see a Vegas show, but if Callie's heart had opened to the point that she could appreciate theater, then I wanted to be there to experience it with her.

Still, I wondered what she meant by the life and death part.

# 19.

THE CIRQUE DU Soleil stage production of "O" was considered so important to the success of the Bellagio Hotel, they actually built the stage first, and then built the hotel and casino around it. And what a stage it is! It houses a pool containing one-point-five million gallons of water! There is a platform in the pool filled with thousands of tiny holes that allows it to rise and fall in seconds, without creating a wake. This enables cast members to perform high dives into the pool one minute, and skip across the surface the next.

Tickets are sold out months in advance. I didn't ask Callie how she obtained our front-row balcony seats, and didn't need to. Callie gets what Callie wants.

The show itself is hard to explain, but in general, it's a celebration of water. There is no real plot, per se, nor is one necessary. "O" is a stunning display of athletes, acrobats, synchronized swimmers, divers and mythical characters, all of who perform on a constantly changing liquid stage.

The program described the music as "haunting and lyrical, upbeat and melancholy"—and they weren't lying, it was superb. For me, the blend of music and choreography enhanced the beauty and spectacle of the experience. Sure, I'd seen other circus acts that impressed me. But I'd never made an emotional connection with the performers before. But here, sitting beside Callie, watching "O," I found myself caught up in the performers'world of grace, strength and art. And loving every minute of it.

There are seventeen acts in the show, no intermissions. I glanced out of the corner of my eye at Callie several times, but each time her face showed less expression than Joan Rivers after a Botox treatment.

Until the seventeenth act: "Solo Trapeze."

That's when I saw Callie's right hand tense, ever so slightly. I turned to look at her and saw her—not crying, but tearing up. Then, amazingly, a single tear spilled over the edge of her eyelashes and traced halfway down her cheek. She didn't notice me staring, didn't make a move to wipe it dry. More than nine million people have seen "O" in this theater, but none were moved more than Callie. I know, because I've seen her in dozens of situations that would have made the toughest guys cry. Add all those events to this and you get a total of one tear.

I opened my program and noticed the girl on the trapeze was the alternate. There was something familiar about the name.

And then it hit me.

It was Eva LeSage.

I'd never met Eva, but Callie used to guard her back in Atlanta for Sensory Resources. You get attached to the people you guard, and you like to see them succeed in life. Callie was proving to be far more sentimental than I'd ever known her to be. On the other hand, she hadn't so much as frowned while killing Charlie and his friends a few nights ago, so it was unlikely she'd be mistaken for Mother Teresa anytime soon.

After the show I said, "There are six Cirque du Soleil shows playing Vegas."

"So?"

"So that means tonight, five hundred performers will be walking the Strip—all of them limber enough to have sex without a partner."

She gave me a curious look. "Anyone can have sex without a partner."

"Not *that* kind of sex," I said.

"Thanks for the visual."

We climbed into our waiting limo and headed to the Encore Hotel. We had dinner reservations at Switch.

"Did you get anything else out of the show?" Callie said, "aside from the sexual dexterity of the performers?"

"It's probably the best show I've ever seen: synchronized swimmers, acrobats, Red coated soldiers with powdered wigs riding on flying carousel horses, world-class high divers, contortionists, a man so deeply involved with his newspaper he continues reading it after bursting into flames…"

"Anything else?"

I smiled. "I was particularly impressed by the solo trapeze artist who made her debut tonight. The understudy from Atlanta. Eva LeSage."

Callie studied me a moment before saying, "When did you figure it out?"

"Not till the very end."

"You think she's good enough to get the lead?"

I shrugged. "I'm not qualified to say."

I looked at Callie and sensed she needed to hear some type of personal validation from me. Something honest, from the heart. I dug deep.

"For me, Eva had a delicate, ballet quality that went beyond special. She wowed me tonight. It was like watching poetry in motion."

"Poetry in motion," Callie repeated. Her voice had a

wistful quality about it.

After a moment she said, "Did you make that up?"

"It's an old sixties song."

She grinned. "Eighteen sixties?"

"Nineteen, smartass. Johnny Tillotson."

"Donovan, seriously. How do you *know* that—you weren't even *alive* in the sixties."

"Some things are worth learning about."

"Sixties music being one of them?"

"Music was better back then."

"Song titles, maybe."

We sat awhile in silence, feeling the tires adjust to the uneven pavement.

The driver turned his head in our general direction and said, "Sorry about the construction."

"No problem," I said. Of course there's construction. It's Vegas. There's *always* construction going on.

"You hungry?" I said.

I'd wanted to try Switch because I heard they had a lobster salad appetizer and great steaks. What makes the restaurant unique, every twenty minutes the lights dim, eerie music plays, and the walls and ceilings change their theme. I heard that sometimes the waiters quick-change into totally different outfits. Touristy, I know, but it would give me something to tell Kathleen and Addie about when I got back.

"I'm not a foodie," she said, "but I'll find something to nibble on while we talk about this…situation."

"There's a situation?" I said. "With Eva?"

"There's about to be," she said.

# 20.

SWITCH DID NOT disappoint. This high-energy restaurant was all about vibrant colors, Venetian glass murals, and wild, stylish fabrics. More to the point: they had a bourbon bar that featured, among other timeless classics, my favorite spirit: Pappy Van Winkle's twenty-year Family Reserve. I ordered us each a shot of the Pappy, straight up.

"I'll have a chardonnay," Callie said.

The waiter hesitated. "Bring her a shot of Pappy," I said, "and a glass of your house chardonnay, just in case."

After he left to fetch the drinks, I said, "You remember Burt Lancaster?"

"The actor?" Callie said. She looked around. "He's here?"

"Only in spirit," I said.

"Oh." She thought a moment, and said, "I liked him in that Kevin Costner movie, the one about the baseball field."

"*Field of Dreams*," I said, "his last performance."

"What about him?"

"When he was sixteen, Burt Lancaster ran away from home and joined the circus, wanted to be a trapeze artist."

Callie looked interested. "And did he become one?"

"He did."

The waiter brought our drinks.

"Take a sip of the bourbon," I said. "You won't be disappointed."

Callie sighed. "Fine," she said. "Cheers."

We clinked glasses, and I said, "Let it sit on your tongue a few seconds, until you taste the caramel."

Callie did as she was instructed, but quickly made a face and spit a mouthful of bourbon into her water glass.

"How can you *stand* that?" she said. "Tastes like gasoline!"

I looked at the hazy, amber liquid in her water glass, and frowned.

"I can't believe you just did that," I said. "It's like spitting in church."

I picked up her tumbler and placed it next to mine.

Callie grabbed my water glass and drank furiously. When she regained her composure, she took a sip of chardonnay.

I lifted my tumbler and took another pull.

"'We make a fine whiskey,'" I recited. "'At a profit if we can, at a loss if we must, but always fine whiskey.'"

"What's that from?" Callie said.

"Pappy Van Winkle's motto."

"I wonder if I'll ever get the taste out of my mouth," she said.

"We were talking about Burt Lancaster," I said.

"Right. Why would he quit trapeze to become an actor?"

"World War II broke out, he enlisted, became an elite soldier, Army Special Services. From there, he sort of backed into the motion picture industry, using his trapeze training to become one of the greatest stuntmen in Hollywood."

Callie picked up her napkin, placed it in her lap and seemed to study it.

"I used to watch Eva practice every night," she said.

"Back in Atlanta when you were guarding her?"

Callie nodded. "At first she had trouble being upside down. It made her dizzy and gave her headaches. I figured she'd give up, but she kept at it, forcing herself to face her fear."

"Takes a lot of guts," I said, waiting to see where this was heading.

The waiter asked if we'd like an appetizer. I ordered the lobster salad. Callie deferred.

"Each trapeze artist has a unique style," she said. "Some are highly structured, almost mechanical. Emotionless. Like Chris Evert playing tennis. Others, like Eva, seem to dance on air."

She'd said that last part as if talking to herself. I had one last factoid rolling around in my head and figured to use it.

"He said he never lost his love for the trapeze," I said.

She looked at me absently, so I continued: "Burt Lancaster. He worked out on trapeze swings until he was almost seventy."

I looked at Callie and noticed her eyes had brimmed with tears. In the years I'd known and worked with her, I'd never seen this side of her.

"You okay?" I said.

"I can't let her die, Donovan."

"It's been arranged. She's Tara Siegel's body double. You have to step aside."

"I can't. I won't."

I frowned. "We need to talk about this."

"Fine," she said. "Talk."

Body doubles are disposable people we use to cover our tracks or fake our deaths if our covers get blown. By strategically killing a lookalike—as Sal was about to do to cover Callie's tracks back in Darnell—we can buy time to eliminate paper trails or change our appearance and get back to the business of killing terrorists for the government. Of course, the body doubles have no idea their lives are owned by Sensory Resources. The way it works, one of us notices a civilian who strongly resembles one of our top operatives. If my facilitator, Darwin, accepts that person as a match, he assigns a trainee to monitor and protect the civilian until he or she is needed. When I first left the CIA I protected a body double for almost a year. Callie guarded someone a year and a half before being promoted to my team of assassins.

The civilian Callie guarded was Eva LeSage.

"Who's guarding Eva now?" I asked.

"Chavez."

"He moved to Vegas to guard her?"

Callie nodded. "He's the one gave me the tickets," she said.

Eva was just twenty-two when someone spotted her at a gymnastics meet and did a double-take. That's how it happens. We're out in the world, we see someone who looks like one of our agents. Eva happened to look like Tara Siegel, who works out of Boston.

You don't have to be a perfect match to be selected as a body double. You do need to be the approximate age, same height, weight, and body style, with the same cheekbones, facial features and skin tone. When we need you, we fix you up well enough to pass for our agent, then we make the switch. Of course, it's a fatal switch.

When Callie moved up to assassin, Eva was passed off to Antonio Chavez.

"All these years Antonio never got promoted?"

"He'd rather guard," she said. "Plus, I think he's too stable to kill people."

When Eva moved to Vegas to pursue her career, Chavez could have passed her on to someone else, but according to Callie, he hadn't. He'd chosen to follow her there instead. I wondered if Chavez had an ulterior motive. It's pretty common to get attached to the people you guard.

"You think he's fallen for her?"

"Not a chance," Callie said.

"You seem pretty certain."

"Chavez is company, all the way."

"You have any reason to think Eva is about to be pressed into service?"

Callie glared at me. "You don't have to sugar coat it, Donovan," she said. "We don't press people into service. We murder them."

"The question stands," I said.

She curled her lip in disgust. "Tara Siegel's a loose cannon," she said. "It's only a matter of time before she fucks the pooch. Eva LeSage is not some every day, run-of-the-mill suburban housewife soccer mom, Donovan. She's magic. I don't care how down I am, whenever I see her, I come away happy. A person like that, who inspires so much and entertains so many doesn't deserve to die."

"None of them deserve to die, Callie. It's about the greater good. We sacrifice one to save many. Look, you already *know* this."

Now I understood why Callie had said that after seeing the show it would be a matter of *her* life and death. She didn't want this body double to die, which put me in a tough spot. If I sided with Darwin, I'd have to kill Callie. And if I sided with Callie, both our lives would be on the line.

"First of all, she looks nothing like Tara. She's half her size!" Callie said.

"Darwin must've seen something in her."

"He's a moron. They need to find someone else. *I'll* find someone else."

"Callie, there's no way. They've invested *years*…"

"I'm serious, Donovan."

This was so unlike Callie that I was having trouble wrapping my head around the conversation. I understood what she was trying to say, but she knew how the system worked. Sure, Eva's an artist, a gifted entertainer. But that doesn't make her life any more valuable than the literature professor I guarded, or the dozen other civilians who are going through life, completely oblivious that we're monitoring their every move. I could see no reason why Callie should care one way or other about Eva.

Unless…

"Are you sleeping with her?" I said.

Callie took a deep breath, held it a moment, and slowly exhaled. She looked away.

"Holy shit!" I said.

## 21.

CALLIE SUDDENLY HAD the slightest smile going. I guessed it probably felt good to share the secret.

"I can't let her die," she said.

"Give me a sec," I said. "I'm trying to visualize the two of you doing it."

"What? Oh, grow up, Creed!"

"Every man's fantasy, Cal. Bear with me."

"Are you...*oh, my God, you're checking me out! Jesus, Donovan!*"

"Relax," I said. "I'm always checking you out. You just never noticed before."

"Oh yeah, well, men are pigs."

"True."

"And you're the king pig."

"Oink."

She took another deep breath.

"I hate myself for saying this," she said, "but I need your help."

"Yes you do."

Just then I noticed an elderly lady standing by the seafood tower. I took out my phone, handed it to Callie and nodded in the direction of the lady.

"For Kathleen," I said.

"You're kidding."

"C'mon, you know the drill."

"Are you wearing panties, Creed? It starts with the panties, you know."

"Relax. I just don't want Kathleen to stress, okay? She's got trust issues."

"I think you need a spine implant."

"I'll keep it in mind. Now come with me and do your part, okay?"

We walked across the floor to the lady.

"Pardon me," I said, "but would you do me the honor of taking a picture with me?"

"Why on earth would you want my picture?" she said. "Your lady friend is gorgeous. I should take a picture of the two of you."

Jumping right in as if it had been rehearsed, Callie said, "You look like his mother."

"What?"

"Where are you from?" Callie said. "Really, you could be her sister."

"I'm from Seattle," she said. "And you?"

"Atlanta," Callie said. "By the way, I'm Julie. This is Joe."

"Nice to meet you, Julie and Joe, I'm Mildred." She pointed to an older man who was watching us from a distance. "That's my husband. He's also a Joe."

"A good man, I'm sure," I said, "judging strictly by the name."

Mildred laughed.

"Now you two scrunch in together and smile," Callie said. She pointed my cell phone at us and snapped a picture. Afterward, we walked Mildred back to her husband. We all shook hands.

"We just saw "O" at the Bellagio," Callie said. "Have you

guys ever seen it?"

"We have," Joe said.

"About two years ago," Mildred added.

"Did you love it?" Callie said.

They agreed it was remarkable. Then we told Joe how Mildred looked just like my mother. He asked if we knew anyone in Seattle and I told him I knew a fire chief from Montclair, New Jersey, named Blaunert who had plans to retire on Portage Bay.

"That's a beautiful spot," Joe said.

We wrapped up our conversation. On the way back to our table I flagged down our waiter and asked him to deliver a bottle of champagne to Joe and Mildred. Then we took our seats and looked at each other.

"Well, *that* was fun," Callie said, dryly.

"You were great back there, by the way."

"Whatever. It's not my first rodeo. So," she said, "will you talk to Darwin for me?"

"I think not," I said. "He'll want to know why I'm asking, and believe me, he'll find out. When he does, he'll end your affair with a bullet. So if you want to keep this going—and you obviously do—you can't let Darwin know you're involved with her. By the way," I added, "how were you able to keep the affair going without Chavez finding out?"

"Easier than you might think. Remember, he's following Eva. Since I know where she's going before he does, I'm already there."

"So if Eva's going to a party at someone's house you're already there?"

"A better example is when she goes out of town to visit her parents, and stays at a hotel room that happens to adjoin mine."

I thought about the logistics of Callie falling for her, approaching her, wooing her, the time involved to build this type of relationship.

"You couldn't have set this up after you passed her off to Chavez," I said.

Callie said nothing.

"This had to have started years ago, when you were guarding her."

Callie remained silent.

"And it's continued all this time," I said. "So why now?"

"What do you mean?"

"You've always known her life was in danger. Why the sudden urgency?"

"I think Tara's in the middle of an operation that could turn sour."

"What makes you think so?"

"Chavez got a call. Darwin told him to be ready, just in case."

"And you know this because?"

"Chavez and I talk sometimes."

"You've been keeping him on a string to see what he knows?"

"Something like that."

I had a sudden thought.

"You're not sleeping with Chavez, too, are you?"

"Fuck you!"

"All right, simmer down," I said. "I'm just trying to figure out how complicated this is."

"As far as Chavez is concerned, he and I are colleagues, nothing more. When he worked Atlanta, we met twice a year for drinks. I was careful when asking about Eva."

"I believe you. Otherwise, she'd be dead."

Callie eyed me carefully, as if trying to read something in my face. Finally, she said, "If you can't talk to Darwin, what's left?"

"I can try to talk Tara into quitting."

"What?"

"Like you said, she's a mess. Maybe she's had enough."

"If she has, she'd already be retired."

"Sometimes people need a nudge."

"Would you even know how to find her without Darwin's help?"

"I think so," I said. "We've got some history."

"I heard that ended badly," Callie said, lifting her index finger to the side of her cheek to mimic the angry scar that runs from the top of my cheek to the middle of my neck.

I shrugged. "Some people wear tattoos."

Callie laughed. "Boston's a pretty big city," she said.

"It is."

"But you know something about Tara, something you learned when you were sleeping with her?"

I nodded.

Callie mulled that over. "What if she says no?"

"Then we go to plan B," I said.

"Which is?"

"Kill her."

Callie leaned over and kissed me on the cheek. The one with the scar.

"Thanks, Donovan," she said. "Once again, you've saved my life."

*Such as it is*, I thought.

## 22

"THE WALLS MOVED?" Kathleen said. "How?"

"It was like a Hollywood movie set," I said. "There are five different scenes, with three sets of walls and two ceilings. One of the ceilings has crystal chandeliers."

"But how does everything switch?" she said.

"They just quietly slide into place."

"And dinner was good?" she said.

"You'd love it!" I said. "I'll take you there sometime."

"Tell me about it now, though."

"Okay. There was a seafood tower with a sculpture of a seahorse. There were three levels of oysters on the half shell, and some of the display shells had real pearls in them!"

"And the lady you had dinner with?"

*Oh oh*, I thought. "What about her?"

"How old is she?"

I scrunched up my face. "Hard to tell."

This was one of those times you had to weigh the benefits of honesty versus happiness. There wasn't much incentive to tell the truth, since first of all, I wasn't having an affair, and secondly, Callie and Kathleen would probably never meet. And even if they did meet, Callie would never rat me out. Our secrets were safe. We had each others' backs.

I looked Kathleen right in the eye, the way President Clinton taught me, and I said, "Honey, Mrs. Calloway has to be at least sixty."

"Sixty," she said.

"At least. Maybe sixty-five."

"And why did she need you to fly all the way to Vegas to take her to dinner and a show?"

"I told you that already. Her husband got sick. They had tickets for the show and dinner reservations. He's one of my bosses. I felt obligated."

"Hmm," she said. "But it does sound as though you had a good time."

"I put on a brave face," I said.

Kathleen had trust issues, courtesy of her first husband, Ken Chapman. I could tell she was struggling with my explanation. I figured it was time to put her out of her misery.

I slapped my forehead with my hand.

"What," she said, "you could have had a V-8?"

"I just remembered. I have a picture of me and Mildred."

"Mildred?"

"Mildred Calloway. Our waiter took a picture of us on my cell phone."

"At Switch?"

"Uh huh."

"Why?"

"This is sort of embarrassing," I said, working it shamelessly, "but Mildred thinks I'm cute. She wanted to forward a picture of us to her girlfriend in Seattle, so she could pretend she had a hot date with a younger man."

"Gimme the phone," Kathleen said. "I want to see the picture of you and the babe."

I clicked through some images on my phone and passed it to her.

"Here you go," I said.

When Kathleen saw the photo her face lit up.

"Aww," she said. "Mildred's *adorable*!"

"You're cuter," I said, just to prove there was no depth to which I wouldn't sink.

"Look at that smile," she said. "You can tell she's having a ball. Aww, you're a good sport, honey."

"Thank you."

"Is that the seafood tower in the background?"

"It is. I should have gotten a close up for you."

Before giving me the camera back she clicked the advance button to see if there were any additional pictures. There weren't.

Then she clicked back one, to check the previous picture, which happened to be a shot of her and Addie playing during the inhome visit with the adoption lady, Patty Feldson.

"I didn't know you took this picture," Kathleen said.

"I couldn't help myself," I said. "It was a great moment for us."

She smiled the most wonderful smile and said, "I love the way you said that: us."

Kathleen looked sad for a moment.

"What's wrong?"

"I'm so sorry," she said. "I thought maybe you'd been cheating on me."

"With Mildred?"

"No, honey. With some hot babe from Vegas. And all the time you were just being a nice guy. Can you believe I wouldn't trust you? How crazy is that?" she said.

*Compared to all the shit I've done?* I thought. *Not so crazy.*

"So," I said, looking at the door that led to her bedroom. "You think maybe we could…"

"I don't know," she said.

"Why not?"

"I'm worried you might be thinking of Mildred while making love to me."

"What?"

She burst into laughter and dragged me to bed.

At the most appropriate point thereafter, I murmured "Mildred, *oh, Mildred*!"

Kathleen laughed and said, "Maybe you *should* do it with Mildred. If you do, make sure she's on top."

"Why's that?"

"So you can see what it feels like to have old age creeping up on you."

# 23.

THE HUNTINGTON, WEST Virginia sky was dark and menacing, like an angry panther pacing its cage. Mourners kept a wary eye on the rumbling thunderheads, with good reason: lightning had already killed one golfer the day before, less than a mile from this very spot. Which meant some of these people would have a second chance to wear their black suits this week.

Jerry Beck, father of Charlie and devoted alumnus of Marshall University, had years ago purchased several prime burial plots under a giant, black-barked chestnut oak tree in Spring Hill Cemetery near the Marshall Memorial.

Jerry had been proud to score such elegant eternal accommodations at the time, only he didn't figure to need them so soon.

The Marshall Memorial honors the football team, coaches and supporters who perished in the famous plane crash of 1970. Like the Memorial and the oak tree, Charlie's grave site was located on the highest point of the cemetery, overlooking the City of Huntington and the Marshall University campus. Kimberly, Kathleen and I followed the mourners up the hill. As we passed the Memorial I noticed six unmarked graves commemorating the plane crash victims whose remains were never identified.

I wondered how many of Charlie's victims had never come

forward to be identified. I wondered if Kimberly might have been the next. I gave her hand a squeeze.

More than two hundred people showed up for the burial, making it the largest turnout I'd ever seen. Had the weather been better, twice as many might have shown. Kimberly attributed the large numbers to Charlie's popularity, but I suspected it was something else. I mean, you don't have to be a local to figure out which way the shit rolled in this part of the country. In West-by-God-Virginia, it rolled downhill, starting with the governor and Jerry Beck.

I was appropriately somber for the occasion, but it didn't keep me from noticing things. Like how many people had shown up, how many kept glancing at the sky and how many men were holding purses.

I wore a dark suit and black aviator sunglasses, and held my arm around Kimberly and did my best to comfort her. Kimberly was having a rough time. She kept sobbing and burying her face into my side. The wind whipped the women's dresses mercilessly, and those who wore hats needed both hands to keep hat and dress in place—which explained why so many husbands held their wives' purses.

My ex-wife, Janet, stood brooding a few yards away. On the few occasions we happened to catch each others' eyes I saw storms in her face that could have scared the shit out of Katrina.

If my being at the funeral upset Janet—and it did—Kathleen's presence infuriated her. Janet didn't have to stare long at my girlfriend to realize this was not the woman who met her months ago, claiming to have been brutally beaten by Ken Chapman, Janet's fiancé at the time. It was that meeting that ended Janet's relationship with Chapman. Janet always suspected I played a small part in her break up, but only now realized I'd orchestrated the whole thing.

I looked at her small, patent leather purse and wondered what secrets might lie within. Specifically, I wondered if she was still carrying the Taurus 85 Ultra Lite .38 special I'd bought her years ago. If so, I might need my own burial plot by the end of today's service.

The group closed in around the grave site and the local pastor made some remarks about life and death and doorways, and healing and belief and loved ones and the hereafter. Family members placed roses on the casket as it was lowered into the ground. Once in place, the preacher took a small shovel and scattered some dirt onto it. A few words were exchanged between the parents and the cemetery director. The director pointed at the sky and then at the two men standing in the distance holding shovels. Jerry Beck spoke quietly to the preacher and the decision was made to begin filling in the hole before the storm broke. I thought they did this sort of thing with a backhoe, and figured they would, as soon as the funeral party left.

Jerry and Jennifer Beck stood beside the grave and prayed a few minutes before walking over to the Marshall Memorial, where they planned to accept condolences from friends and family. The air had a stillness, as if all hell was about to break loose above us.

Kimberly had never met Charlie's parents, so she wanted to introduce herself. She needed a hug, as she put it, and needed to be hugged. In her mind, but for Charlie's death, she would have someday been Jerry and Jennifer's daughter-in-law. Kimberly, Kathleen and I watched the mourners form a long line that began moving quickly. Janet did not budge from her dark place, content to cast baleful looks at me and Kathleen. I kept an eye on her hand and purse. Twenty yards behind us the grave diggers were moving dirt faster than I would have thought possible. I watched them work a few minutes, until the Bobcat backhoe appeared, looked at the Becks and wondered how they felt about the grave being filled in at this point. They probably realized it was the prudent thing to do.

As the line of well-wishers dwindled, Kimberly said, "Come with me, Daddy. I need to say something to them."

I glanced at Janet and said, "What about your mother?"

"She'll be fine."

I was concerned that if I moved away, Janet might confront Kathleen and make a scene. Then again, my reason for being there was Kimberly, and if she wanted me at her side when meeting the Becks, that's where I needed to be. I whispered to Kathleen to wait for us down the hill. Kimberly gave her a quick hug and glanced at her mother. Kathleen followed her glance, felt the tension, and excused herself. Kimberly and I watched her navigate the terrain down to the driveway. Then we made our way over to the parents.

"Mr. and Mrs. Beck?" Kimberly said. Her voice sounded small in the swirling wind.

"Yes?" said Jennifer Beck.

"I'm Kimberly."

"Hello, Kimberly," Jerry Beck said, extending his hand. "Were you a former classmate of Charlie's?"

"Oh Jerry, she's too young for that!" Jennifer Beck scolded. Then she said, "Nice to meet you, Kimberly. How did your know our son?"

"I'm Kimberly Creed," said Kimberly. "I should have said."

The Becks looked at each other, clearly confused.

"Well, it's a pleasure to meet you, Kimberly," Jerry finally said. "I'm sure Charlie would be very gratified to know you that you came to pay your respects."

Jerry Beck turned to look at me. "And you are?"

"Donovan Creed," I said. "Kimberly's father. Kimberly and Charlie were dating."

They looked at Kimberly, and my daughter nodded.

"I loved your son," Kimberly said. "Very much."

Jennifer's eyes softened a bit. "How old are you dear?"

"Sixteen."

No one spoke for a few seconds.

"This is very awkward," Jennifer said. "Charlie was very popular with…well, I'm sure he intended to introduce you to us someday. I'm just sorry it never happened before this."

"He—he never mentioned my name?"

"I'm sorry," Jerry Beck said. "It wouldn't be fair to pretend he did."

Kimberly's face fell as she realized that the love of her life hadn't considered their relationship significant enough to mention to his parents.

"Sorry for your loss," Kimberly said.

She took my arm. As we walked down the hill and stepped onto the circular driveway below, Kimberly cussed a blue streak, expressing herself less like a teenage girl who'd lost her first love, and more like a woman scorned.

The shift in Kimberly's attitude warmed my heart. Once again, everything was turning out for the best. Charlie and the other rapists had paid for their crimes with their lives. Kimberly learned she was nothing more than Charlie's current flavor of the month. And Kimberly learned a valuable lesson about men.

My work in Darnell was done. Now if only I could sneak Kathleen out of there without having to deal with Janet…

"Donovan?"

It was Janet.

# 24.

"HOW MANY KATHLEEN Chapmans are there in the world, do you suppose?" Janet said.

"Hypothetically?" I said.

Out of the corner of my eye I saw Kathleen heading to-ward us. She'd be here in seconds.

"*Mom!*" Kimberly said with a severe whisper, "this is *not* the time or place."

Janet glared at me, her face twisted with fury. "We *will* talk about this again. *Count on it!*"

Kathleen arrived and put her hand out. "You must be Janet," she said.

"Oh, fuck you!" Janet said, and stormed off.

"What a delightful creature," Kathleen said. "How could you possibly have let her get away?"

Kimberly mouthed the word "*Sorry!*" to Kathleen, then "Thank you!" to me. She turned and sprinted after Janet. I didn't envy her ride home.

A flash of lightning electrified the blackened sky, followed immediately by a loud bang of thunder. The remaining mourners moved quickly toward their cars, leaving Kathleen and me standing alone on the circular driveway. We watched Janet wagging her finger in Kimberly's face as they headed to their car. You could tell Janet was shouting, but it was quiet shouting, like an angry woman ripping on her husband in a crowded restaurant. Behind us the backhoe and grave diggers had finished up. Kathleen and I remained where we stood.

"We simply must have Janet over for dinner sometime," I said. "Give you girls a chance to chat."

"That would be lovely," Kathleen said. "I'll bring my Urban Dictionary so I'll be sure to understand the references."

The sky seemed to age six hours in the blink of an eye. We watched the cars lined up, lights on, fighting to get out of the cemetery. All around us, lightning flashed like giant strobe lights. The thunder clapped and rumbled loudly. A few fat raindrops hit us, and a sudden gust of wind caused Kathleen to shiver.

"Here it comes!" I said.

She took my hand just as the driving rain began pelting us.

"Kiss me!" she yelled.

"What? Here? You think it's appropriate?"

We could barely hear each other over the din. The rain had become torrential.

"Who's going to know?" she shouted.

I looked at her rainplastered hair and drenched dress.

"You're fun," I yelled. I kissed her.

"I told you I was!" she shouted, and kissed me back.

We hugged each other in the pouring rain, two soaked, broken people clinging to their soul mates. We ended the hug and I held her at arm's length and looked her over.

"Well, check it out!" I said.

"What?"

"You look like you just won a wet T-shirt contest!"

She followed my gaze downward. "Wow! I should stand in the rain more often!"

Some people love a beautiful sunset. Others prefer an ocean view. I guess everyone gets a thrill from viewing something they consider spectacular. I know I do.

She lifted my chin with her index finger until my eyes were back on hers.

"Spoilsport," I said.

We kissed again.

"I love you," she said.

She suddenly pushed back out of the kiss, her eyes wide. "Oh, Donovan, I'm so sorry! I didn't mean that!"

"You didn't?"

"I did, I mean I do—but...I didn't mean to *say* it!"

"Why not?"

"I don't want to scare you off."

"But you *do* love me, yes?"

She tucked a thick rope of wet hair behind her ear.

"I do."

I placed the palm of my hand against the side of her face. She looked into my eyes expectantly. A roar of thunder made her jump.

"Holy shit, Donovan! Hurry up and tell me you love me! Before we get killed!"

I laughed. "I love you!"

She threw her arms around me and hugged me as though her life depended on it.

She leaned her mouth into my ear and when she spoke, her voice was husky: "I've never been this happy in my whole life."

I felt the same way, but I wasn't ready to start wearing a dress over it. I said, "This isn't premarital talk, is it?"

"Don't spoil the mood, shithead!"

"I'm just saying..."

"Hush!"

She kissed me full on the mouth while I wondered if

"hush!" meant yes or no regarding her marital expectations. Thankfully, Kathleen cleared things up.

"Relax," she said. "I love you far too much to marry you."

I let that comment rattle around in my brain a few seconds and decided I liked the sound of it.

"Then, yes. I'm happier than I have any right to be. Happier than I ever thought I could be. Happy as…"

"No need for a speech," Kathleen said. "I get it."

I brushed some of the rain from her forehead, then held her again. As we embraced, I looked over her shoulder, up the hill, at the Memorial and the chestnut oak and the newly-packed mound where, once again, Charlie's parents stood praying.

Jerry and Jennifer Beck's son had been a rotten, no good, son-of-a-bitch who drugged and gang-raped women. He probably helped kill one of them, if the rumor was to be trusted. On the other hand, Charlie had been blessed with good looks and an abundance of charm and the ability to make my precious daughter fall in love with him. At the funeral numerous stories had been told of the generous and loving things he'd done for others, so he must have had some good qualities to go with the bad.

Standing there in the rain, watching the Becks, holding the woman I'd fallen in love with, I realized I'd never met a perfect person, and only a few that were one hundred percent evil. All of us fall to one side or the other of the line dividing the two extremes, and who could argue but that I fall farther on the wrong side than Charlie? After all, I don't expect an abundance of warmhearted stories told at my funeral, and if you tried to match my crimes against Charlie's, he'd come out looking like an altar boy. And yet here we both were, in Springhill Cemetery, on opposite sides of the dirt. Charlie's mistake had been getting too close to my daughter. If that hadn't happened, he'd be alive today.

I'd just professed my love to Kathleen. Somehow she'd been placed in my life at the perfect time to give me a chance to become a better man. I wondered if Kimberly had been placed in Charlie's life by the same hand for the same reason. If so, had I interfered with some type of cosmic plan?

There on the hill, Jerry and Jennifer Beck stood ramrod straight, their bodies riddled with rain. Hand-in-hand, with heads bowed, they stared at the mound of dirt that marked the grave of the boy they'd raised and loved and lost.

# 25.

"WHAT'S THE SCARIEST thing you've ever done?" Kathleen said.

"Excuse me?"

It was night, New York City, dry clothes, The Spotted Pig gastropub, 11th Street. The menu features casual pub fare with an Italian accent. We'd been enjoying the slow-roasted king salmon.

"The scariest thing you've ever done," she repeated.

A newsreel of horror began playing in my head.

"I don't know what brought this up," I said, "but the short answer is, trust me, you don't want to know."

"Oh, stop being such a tough guy. How bad could it be? I mean, I know you get information from gangsters and you work for Homeland Security. But you're basically an interviewer, right?"

For obvious reasons, I'd given Kathleen a highly sanitized explanation of my role with Homeland—more of a Clark Kent version of my job description. While I do conduct interviews for the government and other shady people, they're either long, drawn out affairs involving pain and torture, or short, one-question events that end with bullets or lethal injections.

*What's the scariest thing I've ever done*, I thought to myself. I wondered if Kathleen had forgotten about the time I killed three men during one of our lunch dates a few months ago.

"You go first," I said.

"Okay." Kathleen works for an ad agency. By her smile I knew this was going to be good.

"On Monday I'm getting full custody of Addie."

"What? That's terrific!"

We touched glasses together to mark the occasion.

"That's not so scary, though," I said. "You're going to be a great mom."

"That's not the scary part," she said.

I waited.

"I gave my notice yesterday."

"Excuse me? You're quitting your job?"

She nodded.

"But why?"

"I'm going to buy a proper house for Addie. Nothing fancy," she added. "I mean, I'm not going to squander all the money you so generously gave me. But I want Addie to have her own bedroom and bath."

"Makes sense to me," I said. "But why do you have to quit your job?"

"The house I want isn't in New York."

"It's not?"

"It's in Virginia."

"Virginia."

"We're going to move to Virginia."

"Virginia," I said. "Why?"

"To be near you, silly!"

She was beaming.

"Well, say something," she said. "Are you surprised?"

To say the least.

At that precise moment, my cell phone rang. Darwin.

131

Darwin said, "How's it shakin', Cosmo?"

"Excuse me?"

"Your traveling name. Cosmo Burlap." He laughed. "You like it?"

I covered the mouthpiece and whispered "Business call, be right back" to Kathleen. I hurried away from the table and found a semiquiet corner outside the bar.

"You're catching a commercial light from Denver to Dallas."

"What? When?"

"Tomorrow afternoon."

"That's no good for me. I've got some things going."

"Don't even start with me, Creed. You haven't had a fucking assignment since I can't remember when. But you need a staff of geeks for one of your ridiculous research projects, or a chopper in West Bumfuck to take you to a hospital? Who's the guy you call?"

I sighed. "You."

"Who always comes through for you? Say it!"

"You do."

"Damn right I do. You need a drone to drive your car? You need your non-Homeland crime scene sterilized by midnight? You need a fucking Hummer-mounted, pulsed energy weapon flown to California on two hours' notice?"

"You made your point," I said.

"Goddamn right I did. You want to keep your cushy lifestyle?"

"I think 'cushy'might be a stretch."

"Get your ass to Denver tonight!"

"Can I use the Gulfstream?"

"Lear 60."

"Nice equipment," I said. "What's with the Cosmo?"

"Cosmo Burlap. The name you're lying under in first class."

"That your idea of a joke?" I said.

"Yeah, that's right."

"Pretty sad, you ask me."

"Hey, you want to switch jobs? Any fucking day, my friend. How about this: *I* fuck the accountant and *you* deal with Donovan Creed, the nut job. The day we switch jobs *you* get to make up the funny names."

"Uh huh."

"This a bad time for you? Interferes with your love life? Prevents you from making an extra million bucks? Gee, that's too bad. Fuck *you*!"

It was a bad time. Callie was counting on me to track down Tara Siegel in Boston, something I'd planned to do tomorrow after getting a good night's sleep. I'd had a long day, what with the funeral, Kimberly, the rainstorm, the flights, the late dinner with Kathleen. Last thing I felt like doing tonight was pulling a four-hour flight to Denver with a turn-around to Dallas.

I said, "What do you mean, 'fuck the accountant'?"

# 26.

THE GIRL SITTING next to me kept glancing at my jewelry. We'd just gotten settled into our seats when—there, she did it again.

"Business or pleasure?" I said.

The corners of her mouth turned slightly upward. Not a smile, exactly, but not a frown either.

"Business, I'm afraid. You?"

"The same. By the way, I'm Cosmo."

She gave up a quick laugh that made her eyelids crinkle at the corners. Then looked up and saw me not laughing. "Oh," she said. "You're serious."

I showed her a wan smile. "I curse my parents daily. How about you?"

She giggled. "I don't even know your parents," she said.

I shared the smile. "Good one."

"Thanks. I'm Alison. Alison Cilice."

"Cilice with an S?"

"With a C," she said, and spelled it for me.

It never ceases to amaze me how much personal information total strangers reveal about themselves in casual conversations on an airplane. In less than three minutes I can get almost anyone to tell me where, when and how to kill them.

"Nice to meet you, Alison. What sort of work do you do?"

"Oh, Gawd. It's so boring!"

I laughed. "Try me!"

"Okay. You know the Park 'N Fly's?"

"The parking lots by the airports? That's you?"

She laughed. "How old do I look? No, I don't own them. I'm their internal auditor."

Alison was about thirty, had an easy manner with men. Darwin probably had all the sexual details in a file on his desk.

"You must travel a lot," I said.

"Every other week."

"How many locations?"

"We've got nineteen lots across the country," she said, "so I stay pretty busy."

"I bet a lot of managers hate to see you coming."

"Serves them right if they do," she said.

"Do you always find irregularities?"

"Always."

"That means you're good at what you do."

She smiled.

I looked away a moment and stretched my hands in front of me so she could get a closer look at my sparkles.

"Nice jewelry," she said.

I looked back and watched her eyes take it all in: the Presidential Rolex on my left wrist, the fourcarat diamond ring on my right hand, the lack of jewelry on my left ring finger.

I said, "Let me guess: the company parks you at one of the airport hotels, and expects you to stay put the whole week."

She looked surprised. "How'd you guess?"

"We're living the same life. This is my first trip to Dallas, so naturally they've stuck me at the Airport Marriott."

"For real? Me too!" she said.

"Not such a huge coincidence. The pilots and flight attendants will probably be there too, along with half the salesmen on the plane."

She thought a minute. "Now that you mention it, I have seen a lot of the same people where I stay."

Alison had great hair, a pretty face, and a flirtatious personality. She dressed well enough to hide most of the extra thirty pounds she carried, though her use of jewelry was a bit over-the-top. She wore rings on her fingers, numerous bracelets on each wrist, diamond studs in her ears—and probably elsewhere. I wondered how long it took to get all that shit off before going through the metal detector.

Neither of us spoke until we were wheels-up and had to answer the flight attendant about our drink orders. I asked for a cabernet, Alison wanted a Diet Coke.

"You ever get to see much of the cities you visit?" I said.

"I'm usually too tired for night life," she said. "But I might hit the hotel bar for a quick drink once in awhile."

"Let me guess: mojito?"

She laughed. "Yuk, no. I'm a cosmo girl all the way."

I gave her a look. "Are you making fun of me?"

She put it together. "Oh, Gawd no!" she said, giggling. "But your name and my favorite drink: now *there's* a coincidence!"

This had been no coincidence. Darwin hadn't just saddled me with a ridiculous name out of spite or boredom. He'd been showing off, trying to impress me with the depth of his preparation. I wondered about the surname he'd given me: Burlap. I slipped my credit card into the slot and waited for an internet connection. It took me a couple tries to make it work, but when it did I plugged in my phone and typed "burlap" into the search engine. I learned that burlap is a

136

breathable fabric made from jute and vegetable fibers. I learned that its resistance to condensation protects its contents from spoilage. I read a little further and discovered that burlap is sometimes used in a religious ceremony called "mortification of the flesh," during which believers wear an abrasive shirt called a cilice.

As in Alison Cilice.

For the hundredth time I made a mental note never to fuck with Darwin.

Alison said, "You doing some research?"

"Part of the job," I said.

"Which is?"

"I'm a jewelry salesman."

"For Rolex?" she said, drawing out the word.

"Among other top brands," I said.

I slid my watch off my wrist and handed it to her and wondered if she could tell it was the real thing. Judging by her eyes, my guess was she could.

"It's really heavy," she said.

"Much bulkier than the Piaget in my case," I said. Her smile grew wider than I would have thought possible. Her eyes took on a dreamy glaze and she held the tip of her tongue against the bottom of her upper lip and tapped it in a way that seemed sexually suggestive.

"I wonder if we'll run into each other in the bar one night this week," she said.

Completely in love with Kathleen, I had no intention of bedding this plus-sized jewelry whore. Still, I had a part to play on behalf of national security.

"I'm positive we'll not only meet, but share a drink as well," I said.

# 27.

HERE'S THE STORY on Alison Cilice:

Several days before I shared a flight with her to Dallas, Alison Cilice's image was captured by a Denver Airport parking lot surveillance camera in the company of a suspected terrorist named Adnan Afaya. This, according to Darwin.

"And guess who Afaya has been linked to?" Darwin said.

At the time I was in a hurry to get back to my dinner with Kathleen at The Spotted Pig. I said, "Just tell me, okay?"

"Fathi."

That got my attention. "Father or son?" I said. The father, being the UAE diplomat, was virtually untouchable. The son, on the other hand…"

"Abdulazi," he said. "The son."

"I'm on it."

"Thought you might be."

Last Valentine's Day, Callie and I thought we'd killed a woman named Monica Childers by giving her a lethal dose of botulinam toxin. This was a contract hit ordered by Victor. As it turned out, Victor had two reasons for killing Monica: first, he wanted to test his army's ability to divert a spy satellite, which he used to view the hit, and second, he wanted to see if his antidote for botulinam toxin would work. His people found Monica's body and managed to resuscitate her. Then, having no further use for Monica, Victor sold her to the

Fathis, to be, as he put it—their sex slave. I asked Victor if Monica was still in country and he basically said that the Fathis had fucked her to death.

And that has stuck in my craw ever since.

I can just imagine my psychiatrist, Ms. Nadine Crouch, asking, "Since you tried to kill her, why do you care how she died?"

It would be a good question, and I'm not sure I'd be able to supply a credible answer. But for whatever reason, it pisses me off. Maybe it's because I'm a counterterrorist and I don't like the idea of terrorists raping American women to death. Maybe it's because I felt used by Victor, or because Monica turned out to be a decent person who didn't deserve to die that way. In the final analysis my subconscious reasons aren't important. What's important is that I made a decision to punish the Fathis, father and son, for what they did to Monica. And maybe this link to Alison Cilice could put me in a position to do just that.

Of course, Darwin wasn't interested in punishing the Fathis. He's all about destroying terror cells before they have a chance to mount attacks on domestic soil. Not that he'd shed a tear if I managed to kill either or both of the Fathis. At any rate, Darwin believed Alison and Afaya were having an affair, and that Afaya was planning to use Alison to infiltrate some of the Park 'N Flys.

"In three months it'll be Thanksgiving," Darwin said, "One of the busiest times of the year."

"So?"

"If the terrorists get a driver into the Park 'N Fly trucks, they can load them up with explosives and crash them right into baggage claim."

"What can I do?"

"Get close to her, find out what she knows."

"You want me to sleep with her," I said, trying to sound indignant.

"Sleep with her, torture her, what do I care?"

"What if she doesn't know anything about it?"

"That's my guess, by the way," Darwin said. "And if that's the case, you can hang out with her and keep your eyes open, because sooner or later, someone's going to make a move."

"I'm not going to be able to shadow her. Not after she's met me."

"Creed, you're missing the point. I believe she's already being shadowed. If they see her getting close to you, they're going to come after you."

"So I'm the bait."

"If Alison doesn't know anything, then yes, you're the bait."

"So who's going to come to my rescue when the bad guys strike?"

"That's up to you. Maybe you can call your midget army, hide them under your bed."

"Little people," I said.

"Whatever. The bottom line is, if you need backup, make the phone calls."

"Fine," I said. "What's my cover story?"

"Jewelry salesman."

"You're joking."

"I'm not. So dress sharp and wear some expensive jewelry."

"I don't own any."

Darwin paused a moment, trying to decide if what I'd said could possibly be true.

"You're hopeless," he said. He sighed. "I'll have something appropriate waiting for you in a box on the Lear jet. And

Creed—"

"Yeah?"

"I want it back."

I said nothing, choosing to ignore the implication that I might steal his jewelry. A lesser man might feel compelled to point out specific examples to certify his unparalleled honesty. But I'm a bigger man than that. Plus, Darwin might think to remind me that I was still living off the millions of dollars I'd stolen from Joe DeMeo, after having killed most of his crew.

"A jewelry salesman," I said, again, trying to make my voice sound as skeptical as possible.

Darwin jumped to defend his decision: "Pun notwithstanding, this jewelry salesman cover is pure gold. I've had a team on Alison two full days, which means I know more about her than her own mother. Trust me, Creed: you tell her you've got jewelry in your overnight bag and she'll be all over you like Octo-Mom in a sperm bank."

"That's a nice visual."

We hung up and I made a quick call before rejoining my slightly miffed girlfriend. I gave her my best stuff and managed to salvage the evening—until I explained I had to take her home and repack my bags and fly to Denver.

I slept on the Learjet and got to Denver in plenty of time to catch Alison's flight. We chatted all the way to Dallas, landed, got our luggage, and caught the shuttle to the Marriott.

Inside the lobby, the guest registration line moved quickly between two velvet ropes. After Alison checked in she motioned me to join her at the front desk. I did so, trying to guess what she was hoping to learn by watching me check in. Did she want to see if my legal name was really Cosmo Burlap? Did she want to see what type of credit card I'd use to secure the bill? Could she possibly be waiting to find out my room number so she could call or visit me later? Maybe she was just being polite. I asked the clerk to give me the room adjoining Alison's.

She looked at Alison and said, "Is that okay with you, Miss?"

"Oh, Gawd, yes!" Alison purred, displaying not the slightest trace of embarrassment. To me, she said: "This handsome jewelry salesman just made my day!"

As we rode the elevator to our rooms I said, "I've got to make a few calls. You want to get together in an hour, have some dinner?"

She said, "That sounds great. I'll freshen up. Just knock on the door whenever you're ready."

Dinner with Alison had to be someplace other than the Marriott because of the terrifying man in the lobby she thought was staring at her. We hustled past the scary man and caught a cab to I Fratelli's.

Though I like Italian food, I generally prefer a more upscale dining experience. Still, this family-friendly restaurant was good food at great prices. Their wine tasting hig-hlighted a wide selection of Italian coastal varietals. That, along with flatbread and antipasto would have made a meal for me, but I kicked in for their specialty, a large, handmade, thincrust pepperoni pizza, which I shared with Alison.

As often happens on a first date that's going well, our conversation focused on a wide range of safe subjects, and only a couple of suggestive ones, such as the loneliness of road travel, which she mentioned several times. Since we were eating finger food, there wasn't much physical contact during dinner. But there was no question where I stood: between her sultry facial expressions, winks and sensual lip licking, Alison was throwing more signals at me than a third base coach in the bottom of the ninth.

In other words, Darwin had nailed her on the cover story.

For a dedicated auditor, Alison possessed a surprising tolerance for liquor. In addition to three glasses of wine, she polished off one of her trademark cosmopolitans and was deep into her second when her face suddenly turned white.

"There he is again!" she whispered.

I started to turn, but she grabbed my arm. "Don't look!" she said.

"Who are we talking about?"

"The big, creepy guy from the hotel lobby."

I took a minute to process. "The one that scared you? Are you sure?"

"Yes!" she whispered. "I just saw him through the window."

"Maybe it was the lighting or a reflection off the glass."

"Cosmo, I swear it was him." She was visibly fright-ened. Shaking. She tightened her grip on my arm. "Thank God you're here," she said.

"What do you think he's up to?"

"I think he's following us."

## 28

I GOT THE waiter's attention, gave him a credit card and asked I him to call us a cab. I stood and said, "I'm going to check out front, make sure he's gone."

Alison said, "Please don't go out there. You might get hurt."

"I'll be fine. I'll just have a quick look around."

"Wait," she said. "Log in my cell phone number. If something happens, just press send."

She gave me her number and I punched it into my phone. Then I went out the front door and circled the restaurant, looking for darkened areas where a big guy might be able to hide. When I turned the second corner I found myself face to face with him. He pointed a finger at my face with his thumb up, as if it were a gun. He let the thumb fall. "Bang," he said.

The horrifically deformed giant had indeed been following us, just as I'd asked him to do when I called him from The Spotted Pig after talking to Darwin.

His job was to meet us in Dallas, follow us around and scare the shit out of Alison. His name is Augustus Quinn, and, like Callie, he's an integral part of my team, which is to say, he knows where most of the bodies are buried.

Literally.

"She hasn't mentioned Afaya," I said. "Then again, I wouldn't expect her to."

"Doesn't matter. Darwin was right about her."

"In what way?"

"She's robbing you."

"No shit?"

He chuckled. "After you guys left I used the key you put in the planter, got your suitcase like we planned. I took it down the hall to my room—I'm in three twenty-six by the way—and when I came out I saw two guys enter your room."

"With a key?"

He nodded.

"Must have worked a deal with the girl at the front desk."

"Bellman," Quinn said.

"You sure?"

"Positive. I went back to the lobby and waited for them. They got off the elevator and went straight to the bell desk and had a loud argument with the bellman. There was enough arm waving for me to spot a prison tat on one of the guys trying to rob you."

We were quiet a moment.

"You sure Alison's in on it?" I said.

"Otherwise, why would the bellman think you had something in the suitcase worth stealing?"

"So she flirts me into a dinner date, calls the bellman, he calls the thugs."

"That's my guess," Quinn said.

"Seems pretty risky for an auditor."

"Auditors look at other people's money all day long," Quinn said.

"Good point."

"Be interesting to see how she plays it tonight," he said, "when she finds out the robbery was a bust."

"You think she won't be able to let it go?"

"Exactly what I'm thinking."

"So you think the plan will work?"

Augustus Quinn nodded. "Only I think we'll catch convicts instead of terrorists."

"Maybe the convicts and terrorists are connected."

"One way to find out."

"I better get back," I said. "Make sure you beat us back to the hotel."

"Give me a five-minute head start," he said.

# 29.

BACK IN THE restaurant Alison seemed frantic.

"Thank God you're okay!" she said. "I was so worried about you!"

I had to admit, she was a natural con artist. But I also had to agree with Quinn: the true test would come later that night, when she had to cobble together a plan B. At the time I was thinking if she could pull it off convincingly, I'd probably offer her a job when this whole thing was over.

"Did you see him?" she said.

"I did. But he ran away."

"You think he'll come back to the hotel?"

I shook my head. "I doubt it."

The cab came and we got in and rode quietly to the hotel. I asked if she wanted to grab a coffee before going up to the room and she declined. As we walked through the lobby I watched her carefully to see if she made eye contact with the bellman. She did not. Again, I thought, very impressive. A natural.

We got to the elevators and I pressed the button. "So," I said, "you want to raid my mini bar, maybe have a glass of wine?"

She smiled. "What a lovely offer," she said. "But it's been a long day. I think I'll turn in early. Can I get a rain check on the nightcap?"

"Any time," I said.

The elevator doors opened. She gave me her best little-girl-lost look and said, "Will you walk me to my room?"

I bowed. "It would be an honor," I said.

"Cosmo Burlap—my knight in shining armor!"

She let me kiss her on the cheek before retiring. I slid the key card into the lock on my room, entered, and went straight for the mini bar.

"Already poured you a wine," Quinn whispered, gesturing to the two glasses on the table.

"Thanks," I whispered back. "But you know the rules." I opened the mini bar and rummaged around for another bottle of wine.

"They only had the one bottle," he said. Then he sighed and added, "How long have we known each other?"

"Not the point," I said.

"Sooner or later you're going to have to break down and trust someone."

"Maybe so," I said, "but not today."

"Fine," Quinn said. He took a sip from each glass and waited for me to select one. Quinn watched with amusement as I waited a full five minutes before picking up one of the glasses. Finally, I took a sip.

"Marriott stocks a good house wine," I said.

Quinn picked up the remaining glass of wine and held it up in a silent toast. I did the same. We sat and sipped quietly until we heard the light tap on the connecting door to Alison's room.

"Showtime," Quinn said, silently mouthing the word.

He took his wine with him to the bathroom and closed the door. I waited for him to get settled, and she tapped again. I crossed the room and opened the connecting door.

"I can't sleep," Alison said. "I'm scared that guy might have followed us back to the hotel."

She had freshened up and put on a red flannel nightshirt that had pink Vicky Secret hearts all over it. She showed as much leg as she could without revealing her own secrets. Normally I'd have made it easy on her and let her lure me into her bedroom so her goons could try to make good on the robbery. But I wanted to test her improv skills, since I was still considering her as a possible employee.

"You want to spend the night with me?" I said.

"No," she said. "I want you to spend the night with me."

"What's the difference?" I said.

"I've already got all my girly stuff laid out in my bathroom," she said. "Plus, I've got my iPod hooked up to some speakers. To set the mood."

"I thought you were tired."

"I am," she said. "But not *that* tired."

"And you're scared," I said.

"Without my knight in shining armor I'd be terrified," she said.

"I should probably bring my jewelry cases," I said, "just to be safe."

She raised her arms over her head and clasped her hands together, arched her back, and pretended to yawn. Which of course caused her nightshirt to rise exactly ten inches—I know because I'm a trained observer, and have developed an eye for detail.

"I have to compliment you on your grooming," I said.

"Oh, Gawd," she said. And, bless her heart, she managed to blush without pinching her cheeks.

Alison tilted her face and put some huskiness in her voice and said, "Come here, Cosmo."

150

I followed her into her room. She closed the door behind me and turned the lock. Then she stepped to the nightstand, dimmed the lights, and turned on her iPod to mask the sounds of the robbery that would soon take place in my room.

She swayed to the music a bit and peeled off her night-shirt. "Cosmo, you know what I'd like to do right now?" she purred.

"What's that?"

"I'd like to give you a blow job."

"Of course you would," I said. "But what's in it for me?"

# 30.

TO BORROW A phrase from my former Commander In Chief, I did not have sexual relations with that woman, Alison Cilice.

In fact, I didn't even engage in the type of relations that would cause a stain or force me to define the word "is." I thought about it, wondering if I could find a way to justify it in the name of national security. After all, the mission started out as a national security issue, right? Unfortunately, it quickly made a left turn into this hotel robbery ring. Alison was certainly a thief. But was she a terrorist sympathizer as well? I didn't think so. If the guy from Denver—Adnan Afaya—was trying to infiltrate the Park 'N Fly's, as Darwin believed, I didn't think he'd made the pitch to Alison yet. My guess was the cameras caught them on a first or second date. I also didn't think Afaya was tied to the hotel robberies, so I didn't see any way to justify making stains with Alison. But I was in a spot: I didn't feel comfortable having sex with her, but I also couldn't leave yet, since I had to let things run their course next door.

Which is why, after initially rebuking Alison's advances, I agreed to lie in her bed awhile, fully clothed. I routinely test weapons and torture devices for the military, so I wasn't worried about succumbing to her advances. But she came at me from a different place than the military. Where the weapons relied on pain, Alison nibbled my ear and gently blew warm air into it. This part wasn't cheating, I told myself. But it wasn't torture, either, and she was making progress. I knew I had to put a stop to it. But before I could make that announcement, Alison started moving her hands in a practiced manner all over my body. This still wasn't cheating, but it had some of the earmarks of torture. She quickly got to the area of my body that *would* constitute cheating, and it was finally time to draw the line. I managed to find my voice.

"Sometime later tonight I'm going to regret that I said this now—but you need to stop doing that," I said.

"Can't hear you," she said, playfully. She grabbed my hand and thrust it between her legs and held it there while she bucked her hips. Thinking back on it now, I probably could have muscled my hand out of there a few seconds quicker than I did.

"You're hired!" I said.

"What?"

"What I meant to say was, I can't do this."

"Why not?"

"It's that time of the month."

"Not funny," she said.

"I have a headache. I'm tired. The kids might come in."

"Is it me? Is it because I'm fat?"

"Of course not," I said. "You're beautiful."

"What, I'm not sexy enough for you?"

"You're definitely sexy enough."

"Then really," she said. "What's wrong?"

"I'm sort of involved with someone."

"Unless she's here, I don't see a problem."

"The problem is—and I can't believe I'm saying this—I'd be using you. And that would be—what's the word I'm searching for? Oh yeah: wrong."

I may have heard the slightest sound next door. Alison definitely heard it. She moved closer and whispered, "Cosmo, what you just said—it's so respectful. Maybe you didn't mean to, but you've gotten me all worked up tonight. Can you just lay here with me a few minutes while I sort of solve my own problem?"

"I can do that," I said.

Over the next twenty minutes I forced myself not to laugh as Alison pinched, tugged and slapped various parts of her body while performing an over-the-top vocal medley from her sexual songbook: high-pitched, chirping sex sounds, throaty moans, and some sort of maniacal horse whinny toward the end that erupted into a crescendo of low-budget porn passion.

Which taught me that sex, when you're not a participant— can be hysterical. I've never been disinterested in sex before, so this was a ground-breaking experience for me. It gave me a sense of power I'd never felt before.

*So this is what it must feel like to be the woman,* I thought. *To have all the sexual power in the relationship.*

When Alison's last gasps and spasms had subsided, I said, "I need to make a quick call."

I brightened the light, lifted her phone from the cradle and dialed my room number. Alison heard the phone ringing next door.

"What the—"

I held up a finger to silence her. Quinn answered, said a few words, and I said "Okay."

I hung up the phone and said, "Alison, we need to talk."

She sat up in the bed and covered her breasts with her arms, a gesture that seemed odd, considering what we'd just been through.

154

"What's going on?" she said, trying to keep her voice steady, but failing miserably.

"There are two dead bodies next door."

Her eyes grew wide. She instinctively looked at the door that adjoined my room, then back at me.

"What are you talking about?" she said.

I looked at her. "Alison, I genuinely like you, but you've stumbled into something far more dangerous than you think. But I'm going to try hard to keep you from getting killed, because I have a job waiting for you when this is all over."

Something in my voice gave her the reassurance to say, "If you think I'm going to sell jewelry for a living—"

"Alison, listen up. I'm not a jewelry salesman."

I let that sink in for a minute before continuing. "I'm an assassin for the government. I kill terrorists."

She started laughing.

"I admire the fact that you can laugh at me when there are two dead men lying on the floor next door, men that are dead because you and the bellman tried to rob me tonight."

She stopped laughing.

"You know the big, scary guy that was following you tonight?"

She tried to speak, but the words didn't make it out of her throat. She swallowed and nodded her head slowly, not wanting to hear about the big, scary guy.

"His name is Augustus Quinn," I said. "He works for me."

There was a long pause. When she finally spoke, her voice had lost most of its power.

"What's going to happen now?" she said.

"You're going to get dressed and then we're going next door and see if you can identify the two goons on the floor. Then we're going to have a little chat about the bellman and your boyfriend."

"What boyfriend?"

"The guy in Denver. Adnan Afaya."

"Who?"

"Maybe you know him by a different name. But the guy you're dating in Denver is Adnan Afaya, a known terrorist."

Alison let out a gasp that sounded much more convincing than the sexual sounds she'd made a few moments earlier. Her face went pale and she seemed about to faint. Either she was the best actress in the world or she was genuinely frightened.

Again it took a little time before she was able to speak.

"Would you be a gentleman and turn your head while I put on my clothes?" she said.

"No."

She did a double take. "Why not?"

"I turned down enough action tonight to make me eligible for sainthood. This might be the last opportunity I'll ever have to see you naked."

"I can guarantee it," she said.

I gestured toward her open suitcase on the floor.

She stared at me with a blank expression, trying to read me, but that was getting her nowhere. I've made a career out of not being predictable. I tilted my head toward her suitcase. "This would be a good time to get moving, Alison."

"Fine," she huffed. "Knock yourself out, then."

She slid out of the bed and began pulling an outfit together: clean underwear, pink tank top, gray sweat suit, socks, jogging shoes. As she stepped into her panties she said, "I knew your name wasn't Cosmo Burlap."

"It's that type of perception that makes you a good job candidate," I said.

"What type of work do you have in mind," she said.

"Killing people? Because I don't think I can do that."

"We can talk about it later. Right now there's work to do. You ready?"

She laced up her jogging shoes and nodded.

We crossed the floor to the connecting door. I turned the lock and put my hand on the doorknob and paused.

"You need to prepare yourself for what you're going to see in here," I said. "Try not to scream."

"I've seen dead bodies before," she said.

"I'm talking about Quinn," I said.

# 31.

ENTERING THE ROOM, this is what we saw: Quinn, sitting at the table with a Diet Coke, finishing a phone call, two guys laid out peacefully on one of the queensized beds. One of the robbers was weasel-faced, with thick black hair slicked straight back. The other had a shaved head and a Fu Manchu mustache. Both were big and covered with prison tats. I made my voice as eerie as possible and whispered, "I see dead people."

Quinn said, "*Sixth Sense*, 1999."

Alison surprised me by walking straight up to Quinn with her hand extended.

"I'm Alison," she said.

Quinn looked at me before responding. I nodded, and he got to his feet. Alison took a step back to accommodate his size, but never took her eyes off him. He placed her hand in his and studied it, as if it were a plaything and he was a gorilla. He lifted her fingertips to the area of his face where lips are normally found, and made a kissing sound.

"I already like you better than your friends," he said, gesturing toward the bodies.

Alison looked them over carefully. They were dead, with no visible injuries.

"How'd they die?" she said.

Quinn looked at me. I nodded again.

"I Pronged 'em," he said.

It was Alison's turn to look at me.

I said, "Robert Pronge was a fearsome psychopath who discovered a way to mix cyanide with dimethyl sulfoxide, which he used to put in spray bottles. He sprayed his victims in the face like they were bugs, and like bugs, they died within seconds."

To Quinn I said, "These guys are big. How'd you manage to spray both of them?"

"One came in while the other stood guard in the hall. The first guy kept the door cracked so he could leave quietly after robbing you."

He glanced at Alison, and she dropped her eyes and looked away.

"The guy searching the room finally opened the bathroom door. When he did, I sprayed him and grabbed him by the shirt to keep him from falling. Son of a bitch was heavy, and hard to maneuver onto the bed, but I managed. Couple minutes later the other one's getting antsy, puts his face near the open part of the door and whispers to his partner, 'You need help? I whisper back, "Yeah! He comes in and I Pronge him and lay him next to the first guy."

"Alison," I said. "You know these guys?"

She looked at me through eyes of sincerity. "I've never seen them before. But Hector knows them."

"Hector the bellman?"

She nodded. "This whole thing was Hector's idea."

"You'll only get this one warning," I said.

Alison looked at Quinn.

"You'd kill me?" she said.

"At first I would," he said.

Alison said, "I'm not sure what that means, but it's so

creepy I want to amend what I said just now. Okay, so yes, I planned the robbery. But it was Hector's idea to use these guys. He was supposed to rob you."

We were silent a moment, and Alison said, "You understand, none of this was planned with you specifically in mind, right?"

"You'd planned it beforehand, and I happened to be the mark."

"Right."

"But I'm not the first."

"At this hotel you would have been the first."

"So you've done this elsewhere."

"Couple of places."

"Denver?"

"Not yet, but I was hoping to talk to Adam about it."

Quinn said, "Adam?"

"Adnan Afaya, the terrorist," I said.

Alison said, "Guys, I swear to God I didn't know he was a terrorist. He approached me last time I was here. He wanted to apply for a driving job. I told him we didn't have anything. He said the job wasn't for him, said he was rich and the job was for his cousin, trying to get a work visa. He offered me a thousand dollars to get his cousin a job."

"You took the money?"

"Yes. But I told him his cousin had to go through all the proper channels. He'd have to start cleaning cars, work his way up."

"When was he going to start?"

"He started last month. When Adam—or whatever his name is—picked me up at the airport, he gave me some more money to get his cousin pushed up to driver."

"You give him a time frame?"

"I said I'd do my best."

160

"And he said?"

"I'd get a thousand dollar bonus if his cousin was driving a van by the first of December."

I fished out my cell phone. "You guys chat a minute," I said, punching in Darwin's number. I went into Alison's room, closing the door behind me. My new information had Darwin concerned. This was either the very beginning of a major attack, or closer to the end stage, and we had to find out which it was. I completed my call and opened the door. Quinn and Alison both looked up.

I said, "Alison, how would you like to make some *real* money?"

"It's all I ever wanted," she said.

"Then, lucky day." To Quinn I said, "You packed and ready to roll?"

He nodded. We moved our suitcases to Alison's room and watched her finish packing. Then we went back into the room with the dead guys, or as we say, "the Bernies."

"Can I ask you a question?" Alison said.

I waited.

"What are you going to do with the dead guys? And when can we get out of here?"

"That's two questions. But the answer's the same: we wait for the door knock."

Alison said, "I'm new here, remember?"

"What I mean is our cleanup crew is on the way. In addition to the bodies, they'll eliminate all trace evidence. When they get here the three of us will move to your room and leave with our luggage."

"No offense," she said, "but you can't possibly get away with this."

"Why not?"

"Umm, gee, I don't know," she said sarcastically. "Dead bodies? Security cameras?" She tilted her head, spread her palms out, gave me a you-can't-be-serious look.

"The clean-up crew will disable the cameras when they get here," I said, "and confiscate all tapes of the last twenty-four hours."

She closed her eyes a moment, thinking things through.

"If you're about to ask me how they do it, don't waste your time," I said, "Because I have no idea. I only know they're clean freaks—not like your Aunt Ethel, who doesn't like a messy home. No, these guys want to clean a crime scene like Rainman wants to see Judge Wapner. They're abnormal, they're sick, and look about as professional as Nick Nolte and Mel Gibson after a hard night on the town."

Alison looked as though her mind was unable to process the thought. "Two guys are going to remove two bodies and clean this room of all evidence?"

"They're really unusual guys," I said. "I could write a book about them. Maybe I will, after I retire."

Quinn laughed.

"What?" she said.

"I was just thinking about something that happened one time." He chuckled again.

"Do I want to hear this story?" she said. I looked at Quinn. "This the one about the new guy and the maggot trail?"

"Jesus, guys," Alison said.

Quinn laughed again, harder. "That one's a classic," he said. "No, I was talking about the 400-pound naked fat guy they couldn't push out the window."

"The one they had on his knees, belly stuck in the window frame, butt hanging out facing the door? That guy?"

"Yeah. And every time they pushed his ass—what'd they

say? Sounded like the attack on Baghdad?"

I grinned. "Shock and awe."

"Right. So they get a can of Crisco, then the new guy calls from the lobby, and they decide to play a prank on him?"

"The initiation ceremony prank."

Alison held up both hands. "Please. This might be funnier in another setting, like—oh, I don't know—the boy's bathroom in junior high school?"

Quinn threw his head back and roared. It was good to see him happy; though I worried that hotel guests might report the unusual sounds.

After the laughter subsided, Quinn and I exchanged a silent conversation wherein I looked at him and raised my eyebrows and he shrugged in response. Which meant, "Do you think she'll ask about Hector?" and his shrug meant that he wasn't sure. Or didn't care.

Alison opened her eyes. "What am I supposed to tell Hector? He'll be calling me any minute now."

"I think not," I said.

She gave Quinn a look of disbelief. "You killed him, too?"

Quinn shrugged.

"I need a drink," she said.

I went to her room and brought her a miniature bottle of vodka.

She took it, saying, "I may have touched some of the stuff in the fridge."

"The cleaners will take care of it."

"They'll still have a record of us being here. You may have checked in with a phony credit card, but I didn't. They'll find me and question me."

"You're staying somewhere else."

"Oh really? And where might that be?"

163

"Don't know yet. The cleaning crew will bring your key. Your credit card history will show you checked into that hotel today instead of this one."

She looked at the door, as if mentally calculating her odds of escape. "Who *are* you people?" she said.

Quinn said, "It's complicated."

Alison finished her drink and placed it on the table. I said, "Augustus, tell me what you can about the Bernies."

Still looking at Augustus Quinn, Alison mouthed the word "Bernies?"

Quinn said, "You know the show? *Weekend at Bernie's*?"

She nodded.

"When we're stuck babysitting dead guys, we call them Bernies."

"Of course you do," she said.

While Augustus picked up one of the Bernie's forearms and studied it, Alison asked, "Why would Mr. Quinn know anything about these men?"

"They're ex-cons."

"So?"

"Prison tats."

# 32.

HERE'S WHAT I know about prison tattoos: they're almost always blue or black, since those are the easiest colors to make. The prison tattoo artist fashions a needle from whatever type of scrap metal is on hand: a paper clip, nail file, staple, nail, a bit of coat hanger, a piece of steel guitar string. Ink is usually fountain pen or ballpoint ink, but it can also be melted plastic. The artist usually puts the sharpened metal in a plastic holder like a ballpoint pen cylinder and attaches it to a small motor that causes the needle to move up and down. Once started, a hundred things can go wrong, ranging from misspelled words to hepatitis or AIDS.

On the bed in front of us, both Bernies had the letters T and S on their forearms.

"What's the T and S stand for?" I said.

"Texas Syndicate."

"You know anything about them?"

"One of the oldest prison gangs in Texas."

"Hard core?"

"Very."

Beyond the classic teardrops below the eyes, I wasn't skilled at reading tats. Quinn, on the other hand, was fluent. I said, "What else they have to say?"

Quinn ripped their shirts off and studied the markings like an Indian scout reading a trail.

"See the fine lines and shading on the drawings of the women? Tells me these guys were inked by an expert. In the prison world, no one gets more respect than a skilled tattoo artist.

"Big deal," I said. "What's this other stuff?"

"Prison tats are the first line of communication between inmates. A guy's tattoos tell you the gang he's affiliated with, his status in prison, the number of people he's killed, the city or country he's from, his marital status, number of children he's fathered, the tragedies he's suffered, his religious and political views."

"Thanks for the lecture," I said. "What are all these numbers?"

"The first part says they're local," he said. "Guy on the left claims he's killed three people, guy on the right claims two. I believe them."

"Why's that?"

"You don't want to lie with your skin," he said. "Too many people want to kill you for it."

"What's the thirteen mean?"

"They use marijuana."

"And you know that because?"

"The number thirteen stands for the letter M, thirteenth letter of the alphabet." He pointed to the guy on the left. See the eight on this one? Stands for the letter H. Means he uses, or has used, heroin. Sometimes you'll see a guy with an eighty-eight, which means 'Heil Hitler'."

"Why do they want people to know they use drugs?" Alison said.

"It tells drug dealers that they're buyers," Quinn said.

"What are those numbers on their shoulders?" Alison asked, getting into it.

"Their prison ID's."

"That's how we find out who they are?" she said.

Quinn smiled. "Exactly."

I called Darwin, rattled off the prison ID numbers for him. After hanging up I said, "Darwin's going to run the numbers and find out if there's any connection between the Bernies and bombers."

"And if there is?" Alison said.

"There won't be. You approached Hector with this robbery scam, but Afaya approached you about getting his driv-er into your bus. My boss thought Afaya might be dealing with you here in Dallas, and in the other cities you work.

"Afaya did ask me about the other cities where I work. But he hasn't said anything about putting his other relatives to work as drivers."

"Not yet, but you can bet he will."

"So what are you going to do, kill Afaya?"

"Darwin gets to make that call. But he'll probably want you to go on about your work, business as usual, and he'll put some people into your companies to keep an eye on things."

"Am I supposed to help Afaya's people get hired?"

"Again, Darwin's call. But my guess is he'll want you to get close to Afaya, develop a relationship, let him talk you into putting someone at most of your Park 'N Fly's."

"What if I want to walk away?"

Quinn and I exchanged a glance.

"There's no walking away at this point," Quinn said.

Alison folded her arms across her chest. "I'm not going to sleep with a terrorist," she said, indignantly.

"You will if you have to," I said. "And you'll give him the full treatment."

"Once you guys leave, you won't be able to make me do

anything. I'll get a new identity, go into hiding."

"Alison, you're in this up to your eyeballs. You're going to help us bring down the biggest terror cell in America, and you're going to do it for all the right reasons."

"What," she sneered, "Patriotism? A sense of duty?"

"That, and two hundred thousand dollars, tax free."

"You'll put that in writing?" she said.

"We don't put anything in writing. But we'll put the money in a locker for you and give you the key."

"What stops me from taking the money before you kill the terrorists?"

"You won't know the location of the locker until the job is finished."

"What, I'm just supposed to trust you?"

Quinn said, "If you like, we could just kill you instead."

"What a charmer," she said.

Quinn bowed.

"There's a more immediate problem," I said. "The Texas Syndicate. When they find out what happened they'll want to make an example of you."

Alison's face tightened. "This wasn't my fault," she said. "Hector's the one that got them involved."

"That's not how they're going to see it, Hector being dead and all."

She looked around, started to panic. "I can't stay here," she said.

We were silent awhile, Quinn and I thinking it through, Alison waiting to hear something reassuring. Finally I said, "When Darwin calls to ID the Bernies, I'll have him find out who's the head of the Syndicate. I'll arrange a meeting and see if I can keep you alive awhile."

Alison had used many voices in the short time I'd known

her. The one she used now told me she finally understood the danger she was in: "If you keep me alive and give me two hundred grand, I'll do my part." She thought a moment about what she'd just said, set her jaw, and nodded once, firmly. "I will. I'll do whatever you say."

"That's my girl," I said.

Alison pursed her lips. "Since we're going to work together, I don't have to keep calling you Cosmo, do I?"

Quinn laughed. "Far as I'm concerned, that's his new nickname."

I frowned.

"My name is Donovan Creed," I said to Alison.

"I like Cosmo Burlap better," she said.

"Of course you do."

# 33.

THE CONTROL UNIT of the maximum security prison at Lofton, Texas, was built four years ago, in response to the riot that ended the lives of four guards and twelve inmates. The unit houses 320 male prisoners under six different levels of security. The worst offenders are locked in solitary confinement twenty-three hours each day. Their cells are concrete chambers, with steel doors and a steel grate. Cell furniture, including the bed, desk, and chair, are comprised of poured concrete. The top of each cell contains a four-inch high by four foot long window that allows prisoners a view of sky and nothing else. This design has a purpose: without landmarks, inmates can't discern their specific location within the building. Their one hour per day outside solitary gives them an opportunity to exercise alone in a concrete bunker. Each month they're allowed one family and one attorney visitation. My visit was an exception, courtesy of Darwin's connections.

Roy "Wolf" Williams had recently bought three years at Level Six security for attempting to kill a guard. Now that Roy was removed from the general prison population, I had no doubt that some other maggot would soon step up to head the Texas Syndicate. Until then, Wolf Williams was the man.

"I don't give a shit how they died," Williams said. "It's on her, now."

"Alison didn't even know those guys. Hector's the one that

brought them in."

"Yeah, well Hector's dead. So that leaves the girl." He sneered. "Tell her it's gonna be ugly." He licked his lips. "Real ugly."

Wolf Williams knew all about ugly. He was a six-five, 350-pound turd, with vacant eyes, a puffy, pock-marked face, and cruel Joker-type lips that exposed a mouthful of tiny teeth in various shades of yellow, brown and black. Prison regulations ensured his hair was shaved short in a buzz, but you look at him and know he'd wear it long and filthy if he had the choice. Like the way he wore his greasy, scraggly beard.

"I'm going to ask you nicely not to kill her."

"Fuck you."

Visitors and inmates are separated by thick, floor-to-ceiling bullet-proof glass.

Lucky for him.

"Look," I said. "You want to go after someone for killing those pukes, go after me."

"We plan to. You're a dead man walking."

"Fine. So leave Alison alone."

"No way. She suffers. It's part of the code, man."

We looked at each other through the glass. "I'm willing to barter," I said.

"You wanna barter? Get me out of here."

"It doesn't work that way."

"Then no deal. I got little to gain and nothing to lose. I got no family, nothing to live for when I get out."

"You could have had family waiting if you hadn't killed them."

He shrugged his shoulders and stroked his wormy beard. I kept quiet, waiting for him to get to the question I knew he had to ask.

"What's she look like?" he said. "She hot?"

I took a plastic baggie from my pocket, held it up to the glass. Inside the baggie was a picture of Alison, fully dressed.

"Not bad," he said. "Tell you what: you get me a hundred grand and a conjugal visit with her once a month, and I'll let her live for a year."

I'd have bet a grand he couldn't have pronounced the word "conjugal."

"I can do the hundred grand," I said. "Not the sex."

"No deal, then."

"Look. They're not going to let you anywhere near a woman for the next three years. Surely they explained that when they put you in the hole."

"You're a big shot with the government, otherwise you wouldn't be here. So make them do it."

"Doesn't work that way unless you've got something huge to bargain. And we both know you don't."

"Which is why she's gonna die."

"I'd rather she live. And what's more, she'd prefer not to die. Let's wrap this up, Gumby. Here's the best I can do: a hundred grand and a hundred naked pictures of Alison."

"They won't let me have naked pictures in here."

"They'll never know." I showed him Alison's picture again. "The reason this is in plastic, it's a rub off. You give me the name of your guard, I'll make sure he sneaks you the pictures a few at a time. The way it works, you rub the picture with your finger. There's a totally naked photograph of Alison under this coating."

"Bullshit."

I held the photo at an angle so he could see the raised portion above her clothing.

"How long they been doing that?" he said.

172

"The technology is new, but the idea goes back to Leonardo Da Vinci. If you take an x-ray of the Mona Lisa, you'll find two other paintings beneath it. Back in those days canvases were hard to come by. If you wanted to paint something new, you painted over a used canvas."

"I look like I want a history lesson?"

"Rub the picture with your thumb or index finger just hard enough to make some heat. That's what melts the coating. I'll get you a hundred photos of Alison with clothes on. You can enjoy her that way or rub the pictures and make her nude, it's up to you."

"What kind of girl poses for a hundred naked pictures?"

"The kind who wants to live."

"She know about the hundred pictures yet?"

"Nope. She's only done this one."

"You seen it?"

"I have."

His face was flushed. He licked his lips. It was enough to make you sick. He said, "You're gonna bribe the guard, just give him the naked pictures in the first place."

"If I give him naked pictures, you think he'll pass them along to you?"

"Hell, no! Not that degenerate bastard."

"That's why I'm printing pictures on top of the naked ones."

I could see it in his pitted face: he was intrigued.

"She shaved?" he said.

"You want her shaved?"

"I want her shaved."

"Okay, well she's not shaved in this one, but I'll make that happen next time."

We worked out the logistics for getting him the money, and

he gave me the name of his guard.

"How did it go?" Alison said.

We were in my rental car, heading to our motel room at the Quality Inn.

"For now you should be safe. That'll change in a few days or weeks when he loses the power to decide."

"So what are we going to do?"

"Kill him."

She'd been looking out the window, but when I said that, her head spun back to face me.

"Why? How?"

"Why? Because it'll send a message to whoever takes his place in the gang. How?" I smiled. "I'll tell you later."

"We still going back to Dallas tonight?"

"Soon as I finish talking to Wolf's guard."

"What time's the meeting?"

"The guards get off at eight, so I'm hoping around eight-thirty. Wolf says his guard likes to have a few drinks at the titty bar on Euclid before going home to beat his wife."

She looked at her watch. "That's like, six hours. What are we going to do till then?"

"Nap. It's a long drive back to Dallas, and neither of us got any sleep last night."

"You only got the one room today."

"One room, two beds."

"What, you think I'll run away if I have my own room?"

"I think it would be harder for me to protect you."

"But I'm safe for now. You said so yourself."

"I said you *should* be safe for now. You want to take a chance?"

## 34.

FOR FIVE HUNDRED dollars and the promise of more to come, the guard was glad to smuggle Alison's photo into Wolf Williams' cell. I gave him the picture and cash in the parking lot behind the titty bar, and Alison and I were finally flying back down the highway to Dallas.

"I didn't pose for any nude photo," Alison said.

"It's only important that Wolf thinks you did," I said.

"I still don't understand. He's going to get the picture, he's going to rub it with his finger, then what?"

"The reason the picture is in the plastic baggie, there's a coating on it, made out of snake venom. There are hundreds of microscopic glass shards imbedded in the coating. When Wolf starts rubbing the photo, he'll cut his finger and create an entry for the venom."

"You're insane," she said.

"Probably."

She gave me a look of exasperation. "I'm supposed to hang my life on that ridiculous plan?"

"Trust me, he'll be dead fifteen minutes after getting the picture."

"You've done this before?"

"I have."

"What kind of person imbeds broken glass and snake venom onto a photograph in two hours'time?"

"Say it."

"What."

"You're glad you're on my side."

She shook her head. "You are seriously fucked up, Creed."

"And you're noisy in bed."

She looked at me. "Are you talking about last night? For your information, that was an act."

I didn't say anything.

"What, you think I actually *wanted* you?"

I didn't respond.

"Someone sure has a high opinion of himself," she said.

I sighed.

"Touching you last night gave me the creeps," she said, and she was just getting started.

It was a long ride back to Dallas.

## 35

I'VE LIVED MY entire adult life by what I call the phone call theory.

The way my theory goes, you can be good, bad, or somewhere in between. You can be rich, poor, or middle class. A winner or loser, a builder or breaker, a giver or taker, makes no difference: we're all just a phone call away from a life-changing event.

I've seen it a thousand times: you can abuse your body or nurture it. You can be the most honest, loving, generous person on earth—or the worst. You can live your life by strategy or pure chance, run with gangs or walk with kings, it doesn't matter. We're all hostage to the phone call. And if there's one thing in life you can count on, it's that at some point in your life, you're going to get one of these calls.

Like Ronald Goldman, a waiter, Mezzaluna Restaurant, LA: June 13, 1994, he got a call that Nicole Simpson's mother, Juditha, left her glasses at the restaurant. It was a call that changed his life.

Not all calls are bad.

Herbert Plant, former homeless guy, Worcester, England: got a call he'd won five million dollars playing the Lucky Dip Lottery.

Happens to someone every day. A guy with a perfect life gets a call. His white blood cell count is off the charts. A woman with a perfect life gets a call. Her husband is cheating on her. Or he just died in a car wreck.

Want to live like me? Every time the phone rings I wonder if this is the call that shatters my life or saves it. Not saying my life needs saving. I'm just saying.

So I'm in the Dallas-Fort Worth airport, waiting to catch a light to Nashville, when my cell phone rang. I looked at the caller ID and saw Kathleen was trying to reach me.

"What time does your plane get in?" she said.

"My plane?"

"Don't tell me you're still in Dallas."

"Sorry." I wondered what she was expecting me to do that day.

She sighed heavily. "You'll at least be here by dinner, right?"

"In New York City? By dinner?"

"Oh. My. God, Donovan. Please tell me you didn't forget." She sounded heartbroken.

Of course I forgot. My life was running at warp speed. Until that very moment I was planning to hit Nashville running, kill Trish and Rob to satisfy the requirements of Victor's creepy social experiment, then rush to Boston to start hunting Tara Siegel, to talk her out of using Callie's girlfriend for her body double.

"Of course I haven't forgotten. How could you possibly think that?" I said, stalling while forcing my brain to rewind.

"Thank God. You had me scared there for a minute."

Something big was happening today with Kathleen and I needed to figure out what it was. "Just a sec," I said, "I've got to give my credit card to the counter lady."

I covered the mouthpiece and started a brain back-track. The day before, Alison and I had driven to Lofton, where I'd met Wolf at the prison. Later that night I'd bribed his guard to deliver the death picture. Then we drove back to Dallas, where I helped Alison get settled into her new hotel room. I spent the next four hours giving her a crash course in how to help Darwin set up the terrorists. Afaya should be contacting Alison soon. Until then, she'd continue her Dallas audit of the local Park 'N Fly as though nothing unusual happened the past two days. Wolf Wil-liams'body had been discovered, and Augustus Quinn was guarding Alison until I could work a deal with whoever wound up replacing Wolf as head of the Texas Syndicate. Darwin would let me know when that happened, and agreed to set up a meeting between me and the new boss.

"Any clue who's first in line for the job?" I had asked Darwin.

"Could be any of a half-dozen guys," he'd said. "It'll probably be a guy on the outside this time."

"Any guess how long we've got?"

"No, but shit eventually floats to the top."

The mind backtrack wasn't working. Maybe I should try current events featuring Kathleen.

*Let's see*, I thought. *Kathleen was planning to move to Virginia so she and Addie could be closer to me. Something about the move? Something about…Aw, shit. How could I have forgotten?*

"Today's the day you get Addie," I said. "Of course I'm planning to be there."

"In time to go with me to pick her up, or in time for dinner?"

I looked at my watch. "In between those. With any luck, I'll be at your house before you get her home."

"I wish you were here already. I could sure use the emotional support."

"I know, baby. I'm sorry."

She sighed. "I know it's all part of the job. Maybe we ought to re-think that job. It sure keeps us apart a lot."

I didn't respond to that. But I was beginning to see why a bright, beautiful girl like Kathleen was still on the market. In the few months we'd been dating, she'd added a child to our romantic dynamic, had plans to move closer to my work, disapproved of my traveling lifestyle, and wanted me to change professions.

"I know about the big dinner at Serendipity tonight," I said. "But do you want me to arrange something special for afterward?"

"It's already taken care of. After dinner we're going back home. We're going to get on the computer and go video house-hunting until it's time to put her to bed."

"Sounds great!" I said, putting what I hoped was the precise amount of enthusiasm into the response.

She paused. "You're still all for this, aren't you?"

"Of course."

"I don't want to push you," she said. "I want you to want this as much as me and Addie."

"I do," I said, wondering if I was being honest.

"You sure?"

"Of course." Still wondering.

"You promise?"

*Jesus*, I thought. *Is this how normal people talk? No wonder there's so much drug use in the suburbs!*

"Donovan?"

"Huh? Oh. Yes, of course I promise I'm sure!" At least that's what I think she was asking me to say.

She kissed the air on her end of the line and giggled when

I didn't kiss her back.

"What," I said.

"You always try to act so tough. It's adorable."

I couldn't wait to tell Quinn how adorable I was.

After we hung up I sat in my chair by the gate that would have taken me to Nashville. Now I'd have to go all the way back to the main terminal, cancel the Nashville flight, and book the twelve-fifteen to New York City—which boards from the gate directly opposite the Nashville gate. On the bright side, I didn't have to get any suitcases off the plane. The phony jewelry suitcase I'd booked on the trip down had long since been discarded.

I took a deep, cleansing breath and closed my eyes. When I opened them I saw a well-dressed guy, late-forties, checking into first class astride a stunning, long-legged beauty, roughly half his age. She was toned and tanned and ponytailed, with shiny pink lipstick and perfect white teeth, and that effusive, self-confident-yet-naïve, perky quality that reminds every guy of the cheerleader from high school he loved from afar but could never approach.

In other words, she looked like half the hookers I'd taken on similar trips.

All of us in the waiting area stared at her like a kid trying to find Waldo in a picture book. Speaking only for myself, if Waldo had been hidden anywhere near her denim miniskirt or the pale pink panties we'd gotten a glimpse of, I'd have found him twenty times. I felt a tug of desire and realized I'd just gotten the phone call—the one that would either save my life, or destroy it. I might have been sitting at a gate in an airport at the time, but I was literally at a crossroads. Nashville loomed to the left, representing the status quo, my comfort zone, and the known.

The door to Nashville offered a future filled with hookers and free time, travel, excitement, bullets and danger.

The door to my right led to New York and Kathleen, who seemed to be moving me at breakneck speed toward monogamy, fatherhood, and the wedding altar. If I took that door, in three years the sex faucet will have slowed to a drip and the arguments will take longer to quell. Routine things would start annoying us about each other, and resentments would build. Addie would steadily crowbar her way into our hearts and lives and it was only a matter of time before we'd lose the "us" that brought us together in the first place. There would be endless hours of babysitting, homework, tears, adolescent issues, sleepovers. There would be obligations to church, school, friends and sports, and all spontaneity would vanish from our lives.

I glanced at the gate to New York City and saw a future unfolding before me that made me question my commitment to Kathleen and Addie. Would I have to give up my job and don a suit and tie and work for some corporate schmuck? Would Kathleen expect me to get involved in her charity work? Could I ever see myself playing tennis or golf at some tight-assed country club or hosting mind-numbing cookouts for the neighbors, having to deal in a civilized way with the guy that drools over my wife's ass and comes on to her every time I'm looking the other way?

I looked at the babe, cooing in the middle-aged guy's ear. He said something and she giggled and gave his earlobe a gentle bite with those perfect, porcelain teeth. Both of them seemed completely oblivious to the glares and stares of the disgusted women and envious men watching their public show of affection. As they headed through the jet way, he cupped her ass in his hand. Did she scold him or call him a pervert? No. She rewarded him with a squeal of delight.

*It's not too late*, I thought. *I can still be that guy.*

# 36.

IN THE END, it wasn't such a hard decision. While it was clear Kathleen was leading me to the altar, she wasn't forcing me to take the plunge immediately. She'd let me enter the water an inch at a time. I knew what it was like to take a hooker to Nashville, but I didn't know what it was like to live with Kathleen and Addie. And I wanted to find out.

Hours later, in New York, I waited in Kathleen's duplex until I heard the taxi door slam shut. I raced outside like any other suburban goober and hugged Kathleen and Addie like the lifelines they were.

Addie said, "Me and Kathleen are BFF's!"

"Wow, BFF's!" I had no idea what that was, and Kathleen knew it.

She smiled and whispered, "Best friends forever."

I whispered back, "I knew that."

"Of course you did!"

I paid the cabbie, picked up Addie's suitcases, but paused at the front door landing when Kathleen said, "Wait. Let's take a moment to appreciate this. When we enter that door, our lives are going to change forever."

She beamed with happiness, and Addie smiled back at her. This little burn victim had lost her parents, her twin sister, and all her possessions in a ghastly fire six months ago, but you'd never know it today. I might test torture weapons for the military, but my strength and endurance is nothing compared to Addie's. Beyond her strength of will, she had a plucky optimism that was as inspiring as it was contagious. Addie was part Little Orphan Annie and part Superman.

They passed through the doorway and Addie squealed with delight and clapped her hands when she saw the cookies I'd baked and set out for them on the kitchen table. I could only imagine how excited they'd be to see the gifts I'd bought: a large wicker picnic basket and a blue checkerboard quilt. I wondered if we would someday remember these as the first things bought for our new family.

I lingered the slightest bit on the landing before joining them, giving extra weight to what Kathleen had said. She was right, of course. After today, my life would never be the same.

And that was a good thing.

Two hours later, celebration dinner.

I don't know any restaurants in New York City that are the exclusive domain of little girls, but Serendipity 3 comes close. With its giant clock, colorful Tiffany-style lamps, white tea party tables and chairs, the interior made me feel as though we'd fallen into a movie set of *Alice in Wonderland*. It wasn't all about the décor. I'd been told the deserts, especially the frozen hot chocolate—was to die for. Addie raced around the little restaurant store while Kathleen and I waited for a table. When we were seated, Kathleen looked at me and burst into laughter.

I raised my eyebrows. "What?"

"You sitting here," she said.

"Uh huh."

She laughed again. "It's so, I don't know…"

"Incongruous?"

She looked at me and mouthed the word and made a funny

185

face to express her disbelief.

"Okay," she said, "that settles it. You're the homework parent."

I nodded.

She cocked her head and peered at me curiously.

"What now?" I said.

She reached her hand across the table and took mine. "I love you, Donovan," she said, "and I'm looking forward to our first picnic together."

"You want to have one tomorrow?"

"I want to have one in six weeks."

"Why six weeks?"

"That's when Addie will be able to stay outside more than a few minutes at a time."

"Cool. Six weeks then."

"It's a date," Kathleen said.

Addie ran back to the table, took a seat, and told us about the treasures she'd discovered. Like a perfect BFF, Kathleen was enthralled listening to her, matching her new daughter's level of animation and enthusiasm. No doubt about it, Kathleen was going to be a great mom.

While they chatted, I couldn't help but notice the curious stares from the other kids in the restaurant as they took in Addie's horrific deformities. The house fire that killed her family had done a number on her face, neck and arms. But I was pleased to see that no one was pointing at or making fun of her.

I didn't envy what this plucky kid would have to go through in the years to come, though I'm sure she was depending on me to be there to help. Would I be part of her life? Part of her family?

At that moment, I believed I would.

## 37

THE FOUR DAYS and three nights I spent in New York City with Kathleen and Addie could not have been better. We hit the aquarium, the planetarium, and several museums, and Addie settled easily into her new life with Kathleen. Our evenings were spent on the internet. Addie loved virtually touring houses for sale near Bedford, Virginia, and we found several that we planned to visit as soon as my schedule permitted.

One happy surprise for me: Kathleen appeared totally content with our relationship such as it was, and never once mentioned or even alluded to marriage. It must have been obvious to her that I cherished my time with the two of them, but it was probably just as obvious that I wasn't ready for fulltime duty yet. I tried not to show it, but by the fourth morning together in that cramped little house I was starting to climb the walls.

I hadn't entirely ignored my work, I'd made some calls. Quinn was still with Alison. She'd finished her work in Dallas and the two of them were heading to Phoenix, where she'd be conducting next week's audit. She hadn't heard from Afaya yet, but Darwin was certain she would, and soon.

Speaking of Darwin, he called to tell me that the new head of the Texas Syndicate was a slime ball named Darryl Hobbs. Darwin was putting together a profile on him, but because

Hobbs would be paranoid these first weeks, we'd have to take extra precautions before arranging a sit down with him.

I'd also put together a plan for dealing with Tara Siegel, assuming I could locate her. I'd need Callie for backup, and at least one other soldier. My diminutive, power-crazed employer, Victor, claimed to have an army of little people scattered all over the country. I hesitatingly called to ask if he had any capable associates in Boston I could contact in case things got too hairy with Tara. Victor was less than enthusiastic when I explained what I had in mind, since he preferred that I go to Nashville to kill Rob and Trish. Nevertheless, he gave me the contact information for a little person named Curly.

"Watch out for Curly," Victor said.

"Why's that?"

"He's a real lady's man."

"Uh huh."

"You and Callie really can't handle this woman by yourselves?"

"Tara might have soldiers of her own," I said.

## 38

THE ODDS OF finding Tara my first night in Boston were less than zero, so I decided to let her find me.

The Life after Suicide Therapy class (LAST) meets weekly at Boston's Norton Community Center on Franklin Street, near Devonshire. I purposely walked in a few minutes late hoping to catch Tara by surprise, but she wasn't there. It had been nearly two years since I'd been to one of these sessions, and I didn't recognize any of the attendees. The instructor was the same, and he remembered me well enough to frown. I nodded at him and took a seat and he continued his lecture.

"More people commit suicide in New York City than are murdered," he said. "And it's the same here in Boston and most major cities in America. Suicide has become the third leading cause of death among adolescents and young adults between ages fifteen and twenty-four." He paused to let his words sink in.

Then he said, "What's going on, here, people?"

Then he proceeded to tell us.

I listened as long as I could, which was about twenty minutes, before making an early exit to avoid becoming thoroughly depressed. His words, as always, brought back the memories.

Tara and I had hooked up during my dark days, when Janet and I were first separated. We were brooding, depressed people with several things in common: we were both freshly abandoned by our significant others, both worked for Darwin as assassins, both orphaned at a young age, and both of us were the offspring of suicidal parents. Tara's parents committed suicide together. They tried to take Tara with them, but at the last minute, for reasons unknown, failed to follow through. Both my parents attempted suicide several times, but only my mother succeeded, and that didn't happen until my father died from a heart attack. Tara and I had gone to these sessions for a while, as well as the annual convention held at the Park Plaza Hotel.

Those who have been affected by a suicide in the family— five million of us in America—are called survivors. As a group we have a tendency to dwell on death, and because only twenty percent of suicides leave notes to explain their behavior, most of us spend an inordinate amount of our adult lives trying to divine some sort of meaning from our devastating losses.

Suicide affects the surviving family members in a unique way. Sure, it saddens, confuses and angers us. But more than anything else, it worries us, because we know our chances of cocking that trigger or stepping onto that ledge are much greater than it is for the general population.

Women are three times more likely than men to attempt suicide, but men are four times more likely to succeed. Women like Tara Siegel often go through life with an internal suicide bomb set to explode at any moment, and when some external factor comes along to light the fuse—they're sitting ducks. What I came to realize over time is that Tara had a death wish. But while the two of us and the rest of Darwin's monkeys were mentally unstable, Tara was hyper suicidal as well, and her selfdestructive behavior manifested itself whenever things appeared to be going smoothly in her life.

Like when we were at our best.

That night I left the Norton Community Center building and walked to a nearby diner for a cup of coffee. Then I caught a cab to my hotel and spent an hour sipping whiskey in the hotel bar, watching people come and go.

No Tara.

I paid my bill and loitered in the lobby a few minutes, and caught the elevator to the sixth floor. I stood in front of the door to my room, slipped in the key, and took a deep breath before pushing the door open and ducking to the side.

No gunshots fired by Tara.

I entered the room, checked the phone for messages, checked the room for booby traps, and finally undressed, turned out the lights and climbed into bed.

An hour later I awoke to the sound of a gun being cocked four inches from my face.

Tara said, "100 billion people have died since the dawn of the human race."

Morbid as it sounds, Tara and I always started our conversations by quoting trivia death facts to each other.

I said, "In Madagascar, families dig up the bones of dead relatives and parade them around the village, along with the shroud their loved ones were buried in. Then they bury the bones with a new shroud."

"What do they do with the original shroud?" she asked.

"They give it to a young, childless couple."

"Why?"

"They drape the shroud on their bed and have sex on it every night."

"Eew."

"Eew indeed."

"How've you been, Donovan?"

"Good, actually. Mind if I sit up?"

"Actually, I do mind. As you can imagine, I don't trust you. I think the safest thing would be for me to kill you."

"Wouldn't be the first time you tried."

"That's rather unfair, don't you think?"

"I'm carrying a scar, says I'm right."

During the time we were together, I'd always suspected that as long as she could kill other people, Tara Siegel wouldn't have to kill herself. But I was wrong. One night after sharing a bottle of Cakebread with her I awoke to a gurgling sound. I flipped on the light and was horrified to find Tara lying on the floor in a pool of blood.

"Goodbye, Donovan," she whispered.

I called 911 while rushing to her side. As I flipped her body toward me, she lashed out at my face with her weapon of choice, a 10-inch AGA Camploin Catalana switchblade, causing the scar I've worn ever since. Tara has always maintained she wasn't trying to kill me, just trying to prevent me from saving her life. Either way, it was the defining moment in our relationship, and the one that brought it to an end.

"If I wanted to kill you I would have done it that night," I said.

"Maybe you came to your decision recently."

"Actually, I came to ask you a favor."

"Sorry, Donovan. It's your own fault. You're too fucking dangerous."

I shouted, "Now, Curly!"

Tara was about to laugh at my feeble attempt to distract her, but Curly's Taser found her thigh before she could get it started. I burst upward from under the covers and pushed Tara backward. Though virtually incapacitated, she managed to squeeze off a shot, and her .45 caliber hollow point cut a hole in the ceiling.

I made a mental note to check if anyone had been sleeping in the bed in the room above me.

The Taser worked its magic, and Tara was unable to maintain her grip on the gun. I climbed out of bed, grabbed her gun, and placed it on the end table. I turned on the light. Curly and I watched her writhe helplessly on the bed a few seconds. I wrapped my belt around her neck and spun her face down and placed my knee in the small of her back.

"Good job, Curly," I said. "Can you hand me a zip tie?"

He tossed me one of the plastic twisttie handcuffs with his free hand, and I secured Tara's wrists behind her. Only then did he remove the Taser barb.

Tara had used a silencer, so we didn't have to worry about the gunshot waking anyone up. Curly and I got her onto a chair and hooked her arms over the back of it. He fastened her ankles to the chair legs with zip ties while I kept my belt tight around her neck. Then Curly cut the ties around her wrists and rezipped each of them to the arms of the chair. Then he walked over to the door that connected the adjoining room and opened it. I released the belt and came around to face her.

"Where'd you get the midget?" she said.

"Little person," I said.

"How long has he been hiding under the bed?"

I looked at Curly. "What, six hours?"

"Give or take," he said.

To Tara I said, "Who tipped you off I was in town, the lecturer?"

"Doesn't matter. You going to kill me, or what?"

"I told you. I just want to ask a favor. You look great, by

193

the way."

"Uh huh. What's the favor?"

"Have you ever seen your body double?"

"The little gymnast from Atlanta? Eva something?"

"Right."

"Yeah, I checked her out one time."

"You think she looks like you?"

"She doesn't look anything like me. You know how it works. She's close enough. What's this got to do with you being here? What's the favor?"

"I want you to tell Darwin you want a different body double."

She looked at me a moment before speaking, and something cagey showed in her eyes.

"And if I don't?" she said.

"You will."

She laughed. "Why's that?"

"Because she's become a talented trapeze artist. She's about to get her big break in life, and it's such a small thing to ask of you, and by doing it you and I will be allowing one perfect thing to survive out of all this madness in our lives."

"Uh huh. So how long have you been fucking her?"

"Hand to God," I said. "I've never even met her."

"He's doing it for me," Callie said, coming in from the adjoining room.

Curly saw her and said, "Jesus, take me now!"

"Ah," said Tara. "The pretty killer."

"How are you, Tara?" Callie said.

"I've been better. You?"

Callie said, "That sort of depends on you."

Tara nodded slowly, working it out in her head. "I see. So you're the one fucking Eva. But more than that, you're in love with her. How sad."

Tara didn't sound sad, but she'd said it, and that was something. Tara sighed.

"Okay," she said, "I'll tell Darwin."

"You will?"

"Sure. Why not."

I turned toward Callie, to see what she thought, but all I saw was the gun in her hand, pointed at Tara's face. She pumped two rounds into the space between Tara's eyes, and perhaps a third one into my heart because I felt a stabbing pain. I grabbed my chest and fell to the floor. Callie raced to my side.

"Are you okay?" she asked. "Is it your heart?"

Just before losing consciousness I heard Curly ask Callie, "You ever thought about doing it with a guy? 'Cause if you have, I'm available."

# 39.

I CAME TO after hearing my voice say, "I'm okay, it's all psychosomatic."

I opened my eyes, looking for Callie, but received the shock of my life when the person who came into view was a total stranger in a nurse's outfit.

"Oh, my God!" she screamed, and pressed the button hanging on the side rail of the hospital bed I was laying in.

Hospital bed?

The nurse raced out of the room, leaving me to wonder what the hell was going on. I tried to figure out what happened. I remembered Callie shooting Tara, and then the pain came. I know why Callie shot her. Tara wasn't the type to let things go. If we turned her loose she might track Eva down and kill her out of spite. At the very least she'd tell Darwin, and he'd have Eva killed. So Callie's actions made sense.

But I should have seen it coming.

I looked around the stark room, trying to get my bearings. I may have been in a hospital bed, but I wasn't in an actual hospital. I was in one of the hospital rooms at my headquarters at Sensory Resources. I wanted to think about how I got here, and if someone had contacted Kathleen yet. I wanted to think about Addie, wanted to worry if she was scared. The poor kid couldn't afford to lose someone else in her life. I wanted to think about settling down and becoming a family. I wanted to think about all those things, but they'd have to wait because all I could really focus on was what Darwin might do to Callie.

You just don't go around killing Darwin's people without repercussions. I had to find Callie and get her somewhere safe. I had to speak to Darwin, had to work this out. I tried to sit up, but found I was hooked up to a battery of machines.

That couldn't be good.

I reached my hands around my body, searching for my cell phone. Surely Callie had put it within arm's reach. No, I thought, she wouldn't have come here with me. She was probably in hiding, waiting for me to find a way to call her, so we could put together a plan to deal with Darwin. Or maybe she rushed back to Vegas to protect Eva.

Wait.

Tara Siegel had been in the room, dead, strapped to a chair when I went down with the chest pains. Callie couldn't have been there when the paramedics arrived. She and Curly would have had to clean the scene as best they could, and then run.

If that's the case, Darwin has every reason to believe I killed Tara.

Thinking about it now, I realized what caused the crushing pain in my chest was the same thing that caused it at the Peterson sisters' trailer, and the same thing that made me question my motives for killing all the Rumpelstiltskin Loan candidates before them. It's the same thing that made me put off killing Rob and Trish in Nashville, and the same thing that bothered me about every other person I'd killed for Victor going all the way back to my first job for him, when he hired me to kill Monica Childers last Valentine's Day. As it turned out, Monica didn't die by my hand, but Callie and I had done all we could to carry out the hit.

They were people who didn't deserve to die. I'm not saying they were innocent. When someone has a contract on his or her head, there's always a reason. They've been found guilty of something and sentenced to die by whoever employs me.

But that doesn't mean the punishment fits the crime.

In all the years I'd killed people before meeting Victor, I knew the world would be a better place without those people. Whether I was killing terrorists or spies for the government, or wise guys for Sal Bonadello, I never lost a moment of sleep over my job.

But then, less than a year ago, Victor came into my life.

My first contract for Victor was Monica Childers. I killed her the day after I met Kathleen. Victor had given me some story about how we all have at least two people in our lives that deserved to die because of the terrible things they did to us. That was easy for me to relate to, since I'd had a number of these types of people in my life and I'd done something about it.

Monica Childers may have done something bad enough to make one person wish her dead, but in the court of humanity and justice, she didn't deserve to die. I think I knew it at the time, but I was running on autopilot. I'd sold myself on the idea that a hit man shouldn't ask questions. I believed a hit man's job was to carry out executions, not weigh the merits of them.

But my conscience obviously felt different.

The reasons for Monica's execution didn't stand up. When she turned up alive, I felt relief. Then to learn she'd been raped to death by the terrorists I'd been hunting—it hit me hard.

The Rumpelstiltskin Loan recipients had certainly done a monstrous thing, allowing someone to die in exchange for receiving a loan, but they'd been told it was an unpunished murderer. I knew in my heart it was a major stretch to kill them for allowing other people to die. By the time I got to the Peterson sisters, my body decided to rebel.

So Victor's victims were responsible for my heart issue. That makes sense, except for one thing: I got the pain again when Callie killed Tara Siegel. And Tara was not one of Victor's lethal experiments.

I'm no psychiatrist, but I think Tara fit the pattern of a person who didn't deserve to die. Tara was certainly no innocent, and there were several circumstances under which I'd have killed her. But she was good for the country, in that she was working for the government, killing terrorists. Also, she and I had a history, and in this particular situation I hadn't intended her to die. When Callie shot her, I felt responsible for the death of an innocent person, a former friend—even though my "friend" tried to kill me moments earlier.

Looking around the hospital room, hooked up to various monitoring devices, I made the life changing decision to never again accept a contract from Victor. I wasn't worried about my ability to kill guilty people, or those who deserved to die. After all, I'd recently done it, with no repercussions.

Ned Denhollen had probably been a decent man, but I suffered no remorse for killing him. Was it because he'd been supplying those kids with date rape drugs? No. It was because I feared my daughter Kimberly was about to be dragged into it. So Ned had to die. The kid I shot the night they tried to rape Callie didn't affect me because he was already dying and I'd done nothing more than put him out of his misery. As for Wolf Williams, he deserved to die for a number of reasons, including his threat to kill my new employee, Alison.

The door burst open so suddenly it startled me. The nurse flew into the room, dragging a doctor behind her.

"Calling Doctor Howard," I said, "Doctor Howard, Doctor Howard—*The Three Stooges*, remember?"

Dr. Howard managed to repress a grin. "That wasn't funny the last time you were here, and it isn't funny now. Good to see you back with us, Mr. Creed."

Dr. Howard treated me years ago for a particularly nasty bullet I took from a Ukrainian enforcer. If the good doctor was treating me, that meant I was back at Sensory Resources, in the medical center. My office was a mere hundred feet from this very room. When we buy our new house, Kathleen, Addie and I will be living about twelve miles from here, in Bedford.

"Mr. Creed, I'm Carol," said the nurse.

I lifted my arm and gave her a small wave. "Nice to meet you, Nurse Carol."

Dr. Howard assaulted me with questions and annoyed my eyes with his pen-light. Ignoring him for the moment, I turned to Nurse Carol.

"I need my cell phone," I said.

She opened the drawer by my bed, moved some items around, then she tried the closet, where she searched through the clothes someone had hung there.

She handed it to me. I pressed the power button.

Nothing.

I looked at her. "The battery's dead? How's that possible?"

Dr. Howard said, "Mr. Creed, there'll be plenty of time for questions later on. In the meantime I really must insist you cooperate with me."

"That would be easy to do if my life weren't at stake." To Carol I said, "Can you call Lou Kelly for me?" Lou was my right-hand man. His office was on the other end of the building.

"Why don't you go get him in person, Carol," Dr. Howard

said. "It's probably a good idea you leave us alone a few minutes."

She hooked the door to the wall so it would stay open, and headed down the corridor to fetch Lou.

Dr. Howard tried to beat McCauley Culkin's question record in the movie *Uncle Buck*, and I answered them the same way. Yes, I felt that, yes, I can focus; no, not dizzy, yes, I'm thirsty, yes, yes, yes.

I had to know something. "Doc, what kind of machines have you got me hooked up to? I know I came in with a chest pain, but that's psychosomatic. You can call my shrink on that, you don't believe me."

"Mr. Creed," he said. "You're hooked up to these machines because you've been in a coma for the past three years."

# 40.

IN A COMA? Three years?

I was, as the British say, gobsmacked.

Gobsmacked is much stronger than being surprised. It's a term used to describe something that stuns you speechless and stops you dead in your tracks.

That's what I was, gobsmacked.

I thought about eating live scorpions, or smearing cattle dung all over my body. Maybe I'll become a Whig, I thought, or take up phrenology. Every one of those things made more sense than what he'd said to me.

"Could you repeat that?" I said.

"You've been lying in this bed, unresponsive, for…" he consulted a chart. "Three years, two months and five days."

"You're shitting me."

"You know me better than that."

I did. But it still didn't make any sense.

"Why am I so lucid?" I asked.

"Psychosomatic comas are different than those caused by direct physical injury."

"Come again?"

"You didn't suffer any physical trauma to the brain or brain stem. Basically, your brain took a three-year vacation."

The room seemed to swirl around me as the significance of my situation hit home. There were a million questions I probably should have asked. But the first thing that popped out of my mouth was "When can I get up?"

In the movies, when the beautiful starlet opens her eyes and comes out of her coma, she does so in full make-up, with every hair in place. By the end of the scene she's out of bed, drinking champagne, dancing, and lives happily ever after. In real life it's not as easy as you think to get out of a hospital bed after three years of hibernation.

While Dr. Howard explained all this, he addressed some other aspects of my medical condition. He said there'd be weeks of tests and physical therapy before I could safely be released. He said I could get off the feeding tube, and they would gradually introduce real food into my diet, and see how I responded.

*Three years?*

That means Kimberly was half-way through college! Afaya could have blown up the airports years ago. Callie, Quinn, Alison...could all be dead by now. And what had happened to Kathleen? I must have scared her to death be-ing unconscious all this time. And Addie must be what, eight years old?

And Darwin. Why hadn't he killed me already? His people could have waltzed into this cracker box medical room and snuffed me faster than Monika Lewinski blowing out the candle on a one-candle cake. *Wait*, I thought. *Is that reference dated now?*

I had to get up and out of here before Darwin got the news of my resurrection. I had to get my cell phone working, had to make some calls and get some help. I didn't want to involve Kathleen in all this, but I had no choice. Unless the world had turned completely upside down during the past three years, Darwin would know my condition within hours, and my life expectancy would be about as long as a Twinkie in Kirstie

Alley's pantry. *Wait. Three years has passed. Maybe she's lost the weight again.* I made a note to catch up on my pop culture first thing.

"Donovan, thank God!"

I looked up and saw Lou Kelly entering the room, followed closely by Nurse Carol.

"Nice haircut," I said.

"Wait till you see yours!" he said.

"Lou. Turn your back to the doctor and look at me."

He shrugged. "Okay…"

"Have I been in a coma?"

He nodded.

"How long?"

"Three years, give or take."

The nurse joined us. Lou said, "Right. Carol, could you get me a newspaper and a magazine and anything else you can find with a recent date on it?"

"How about a movie ticket stub?" she said.

"Perfect."

"Lou, this is crazy," I said.

"I know, buddy. But it is what it is. At least you're back with us. How do you feel?"

"Pissed."

He laughed. "Same old Creed," he said.

Dr. Howard continued his examination. The thermo-meter went in, then out. The little thing with the light went in my ears. Then he felt my lymph nodes, checked my pulse, pushed on my stomach, looked up my nose and in my mouth.

Nurse Carol returned with enough evidence to convince me I'd been Rip Van Winkled for more than three years. I tried to get to my feet.

"Whoa," said the doctor. "You're still on life support. You

can't get up yet."

Lou moved to hold me down, but I waved him off.

"Can I at least sit up?"

Lou and the doctor exchanged a look. Lou nodded.

"Lie still a minute," he said. The nurse helped the doc-tor remove several tubes. She held some gauze against the wounds to stop the bleeding.

"I think you're out of the woods," my doctor said, "but I'll need to keep the rest of the equipment hooked up for twenty-four hours. It'll help us monitor your brain activity and let us know if you start experiencing seizures."

"Why am I still alive?" I said.

"Because you're receiving the best medical care in the world," Lou said.

"That's not what I mean."

"I'm not sure what you're asking."

"Why hasn't Darwin killed me yet?"

Dr. Howard said, "Let us finish up so you can speak freely. Carol and I don't want to hear anything that's unrelated to Mr. Creed's treatment."

Five minutes later it was just Lou and me, with the door closed.

"Catch me up," I said, "starting with last night."

"You mean—"

"Yeah, I mean the last night I can remember. The night Tara got shot."

Lou took a deep breath. "Okay. Look, I'll try to keep everything in chronological order, but I might miss a detail here and there."

"Just do your best. We can fill in later."

"Okay."

"Wait a minute," I said. "Before you start, tell me this: is

205

Kathleen okay?"

"She is."

"Addie?"

"Yes, she's fine. She's winding up second grade."

"Shit. I can't believe I've missed her formative years. She and Kathleen must be devastated. What about Kimberly?"

"Let me save you some time," he said. "Kimberly, Janet, Callie, Quinn—they're all alive and well. You want me to go into detail about them now, or you want to hear about that night?"

"Both. But let's start with Afaya. Did Darwin get him?"

"No, he never showed."

"Alison?"

"I never thought to ask," Lou said, "but I'll find out and let you know."

"Okay, so tell me about that night. I need to know if my life is in danger."

Lou said, "I'm the one Callie called when you had the heart thing that night. She told me she'd just shot Tara, and you were having a heart attack."

"She tell you the details about shooting Tara?"

"Later on, yes, but at that moment she was in a panic. She thought you were dying, but she couldn't call 911 because there was no time to hide Tara's body or clean up the crime scene. Blood spatter was everywhere, including your clothes."

"Makes sense. The EMS guys find blood, they'd have to call the cops."

"Exactly. Plus, all this happened in your hotel room, a room filled with your fingerprints, and—well, you get the picture."

"She had to move fast."

He nodded. "We were lucky this happened in Boston,

where we're thick with support. I called two cleaning crews and caught one of our doctors at home. At the time, I didn't know about your psychosomatic thing, you'd never shared that with me. So we thought you were in the middle of a full-fledged heart attack. Since we didn't have time to get our doctors to your hotel room, I told Callie to go up one floor and check for cameras in the hallway. If she didn't find any, she was to set off a fire alarm." That's what she did. Then I told her to get the midget Victor sent to help you—"

"Curly."

"You remember that?"

"Like it was minutes ago," I said. "I'm still not convinced it wasn't."

"Let's stay on track. Okay, so Callie stood watch in the hall, waiting until someone exited the room next to you on the far side. When the guy ran out to join the re-drill evacuees, Curly broke in, dragged you into that room and called 911. While waiting for EMS, he got your clothes and luggage and put them in the new room. We were lucky, turns out the guy next door to you was alone, a businessman."

I could see where this was going and didn't like it.

"What happened to the businessman?"

"Callie needed his ID and other information for the preliminary report. So she followed him down the steps. When they got outside she struck up a conversation with him."

Lou paused to make sure I caught the implication.

"When was his body found?"

"Sometime the next day."

I shifted my body in the bed and thought about the way I plow through life, the wake of bodies I leave behind. I instinctively touched my hand to my chest.

"You okay?" Lou said.

"Surprisingly, yes."

Lou continued: "EMS got to the hotel about the same time as the firemen, and put you on a gurney. By then, Callie was back in the room and she followed along and climbed into the ambulance with you. Curly was in his car by then, following you. Callie let them drive a few minutes, pulled a gun on the EMS guy in the back and made them stop the truck. Curly pulled up, got out of his car, put a gun on the driver, and Callie made the EMS guys load you into Curly's car. He drove you to the air ambulance while Callie shot the EMS guys. She ditched their bodies and drove their vehicle to the airport, where she was met by the second cleaning crew. They did their magic on the EMS truck, drove Callie to the FBO, where she boarded our jet to fly here. She beat you here by half an hour, but you were in the medical chopper getting the best care possible. The Chopper landed, and you've been here ever since."

I said, "I assume the first cleaning crew did a good job on the hotel?"

"By the time they finished, you couldn't prove humans had ever entered it."

"Where did Darwin fit in all this?"

"See, that's the thing. Callie called me because she was afraid Darwin would blame you for Tara's death. She wanted me to arrange a meeting so she could tell Darwin what really happened, and why."

"And you said?"

"I told her she and Curly were never there."

"So Darwin thinks I killed Tara?"

Lou nodded. "He thought you killed her and then got the heart thing because you'd been close to her in the past. Remorse, or whatever."

"So why didn't Darwin have me killed?"

"See, Darwin was getting ready to kill Tara anyway."

"What are you talking about?"

"He had already approached me about having you do it."

*All this could have been avoided*, I thought.

"What stopped him from giving me the hit?" I said.

"He thought you might be too close to her. He wanted to try someone else."

"There was no one else capable of killing Tara."

"That's what he found out."

"Who'd he send?"

"A couple of mafia guys. After that didn't work, I told him I'd talk to you about doing it."

"Why didn't you?"

"I was about to, but that whole thing came up with Afaya, and he told me to wait until you got back from Dallas. Then you wanted to spend a few days with Kathleen and Addie, so I put it off."

Timing is a funny thing. But this explained why Tara wanted to kill me. She thought I'd been sent to finish the job the mafia guys botched.

"So Darwin thinks you told me to kill Tara, and I did. So he's happy?"

"In general," Lou said, turning to open the door.

"What does that mean?"

Lou turned back to face me.

"He didn't like the part about you being out of commission all these years."

No surprise there.

"What does Darwin know about my heart issue?"

"He backtracked. He found the doctor that treated you after the Camptown incident…"

"Dr. Hedgepeth."

"Right. And Hedgepeth led Darwin to the psychiatrist…"

"Nadine Crouch."

"Right, and, if you'll raise up and look over my shoulder…"

"That's not necessary," Dr. Nadine Crouch said, enter-ing the room. "I'll come closer."

# 41.

"WHAT ARE *YOU* doing here?" I said.

"This might come as a surprise to you, Donovan, but I've worked for Homeland Security longer than you have."

"What?"

"I was on the payroll before the helicopter brought you from Camptown."

"Dr. Hedgepeth personally recommended you. Are you saying he's with Homeland too?"

"No. When you arrived at the hospital, Darwin was in close contact with Dr. Hedgepeth. He got the results of your tests before you did. When Hedgepeth decided you might require psychiatric evaluation, Darwin told him to recommend me. He felt it was best to use an inhouse psychiatrist."

"Your practice just happened to be in Newark?"

"Philadelphia. We had to move my practice to Newark to accommodate you. We worked a deal with Agnes Battle, the child psychologist, to sublease her back office.

My mind was swimming, but I'm a great detail guy. "The antique coat rack in the office seemed out of place. Was that yours?"

Dr. Crouch laughed. "Funny you should notice that. Homeland gave the office a complete makeover. When Agnes realized the coat rack didn't go with it, she gave it to me as a present. I felt obligated to keep it."

"So you've known all along what I did for Homeland?"

"Not specifically. Darwin told me almost nothing at first. He wanted me to report your comments to him. But he filled me in just before your last visit."

"I remember thinking at the time that you were awfully astute, for having known me such a short time."

"I'm still astute. For example, I can see that you're handling your current situation with an amazing degree of calm."

"How did you know I'd be conscious today?"

"I didn't. I've been waiting a long time for you to wake up."

"How long have you been here?"

"I arrived a month after you did."

I laughed. "They paid you all this time to wait for me to wake up? That's hard to believe."

"I'm stationed here because of you, but remember, I work for Homeland, so I've got other duties and responsibilities. Of course, you're quite an asset to them, and now that you're awake, you're my main concern."

"How much have they told you?"

She looked at Lou. "As far as I know, everything."

Lou said, "She knows most of what you've done for us. She's got a general understanding about your work with Sal. She has specific knowledge about the contracts you fulfilled for Victor, and the thing with Tara."

"Well, that's all in the past," I said.

"Is it?" Nadine said.

"According to you guys, I've just lost three years of my life. Three years I could've been with Kathleen and Addie. Three years I could've spent building my relationship with Kimberly. Yeah, I'm done. I'm done with *all* this bullshit. I'm going to get out of this nuthouse, marry Kathleen, and be a proper father to Addie."

Dr. Crouch looked at Lou. "Should I leave?" she said.

Lou frowned. "I'm going all in. You definitely need to stay."

"Lou?" I said. "What do you mean, 'all in?' Talk to me."

Lou asked Nadine if she had a mirror in her purse. She produced a compact and gave it to him.

"Lou..." I said, warily.

"Donovan, you may want to brace yourself," Lou said. He handed me Nadine's compact. I looked at both of them carefully before opening it, but none of us said anything. I closed my eyes a second, shook my head.

"This sucks," I said.

Lou nodded.

"I'm so very sorry," Dr. Crouch said.

I opened the compact and looked into the mirror.

# 42.

THEY'D GIVEN ME a new face.

Not a normal face, like I'd had before, but a Hollywood, movie star-type face.

Without the scar.

I closed the compact and handed it back to Nadine.

"I need a drink," I said.

Lou hesitated. "That's probably a bad idea."

"Bottom left-hand drawer of my desk," I said.

"I can ask the doctor, if you want," Lou said.

"Next to the bourbon you'll find four Glencairn glasses. Feel free to join me."

"Twenty-year Pappy?"

"It was when I bought it."

"I'll join you," he said.

We looked at Nadine.

"I'll pass," she said.

Lou called his assistant and placed the order.

While waiting, I touched my fingers to my face. Nadine handed me back the compact. I snuck up on the mirror this time, peering at myself from different angles. In every case it was like I was looking at someone else.

"Nice work," I said. "But it's too nice."

"I know it's quite a shock," Nadine said, "But you're gorgeous—not that I place a lot of value on a person's exterior."

"Lou? This is crazy. I mean, I know our guys are good, but I've seen their work before, lots of times. No one comes out of surgery looking better than they started."

"You did."

"How's that possible?"

"Our guys never had this much time before, or such a perfect environment for healing. We knew our surgeons were exceptional, but none of us knew they were *this* good. You know who you look like?" Lou said, getting into it.

I held up a hand. "Please. Don't tell me."

Lou nodded. His assistant showed up with a bottle of Pappy and two glasses.

"Mr. Creed!" she yelped. "I thought we'd never see you again. You look great!"

"Thanks, Linda. Nice to see you, too. Want a drink?"

She looked at Lou hopefully. He shook his head. "Another time, perhaps," Linda said.

Nadine moved some things off the end table to accommodate the glasses. As Linda placed them on the table, she said, "What's it like, waking up after all this time?"

"Surreal. For you it's been years. But in my mind, I saw you less than two weeks ago."

"That is so weird," she said.

Linda left the room, Lou poured the drinks.

"You sure you don't want a pull, Nadine?"

She gave me a world-class frown. "I think it's a dreadful idea. As for you, Mr. Kelly…"

Nadine abandoned the rest of the sentence, but shook her head with disgust, leaving no doubt where she stood on the subject of Lou's behavior.

I held up my glass as if making a toast. "Bourbon," I said,

"Is cheaper than therapy."

Lou grinned. We clinked glasses and began sipping.

"Like heaven in a bottle," I said.

We were quiet awhile before I broke the silence.

"Why'd they do it, Lou?"

He sipped again, took a deep breath, let it out very slowly. He bit the side of his lip before speaking.

"A lot of decisions had to be made in a short period of time."

I wasn't going to second-guess at this point. These decisions had been made years ago, so there was nothing I could do about the time I'd lost or the new face. There was only one thing that mattered.

"Has Kathleen seen me...like this?"

They looked at each other, silently trying to decide who should do the talking. Lou took the lead.

"There's a lot I need to tell you. But before I say anything, keep in mind, I'm the messenger. I was involved in the discussions, but I didn't make the decisions."

"Noted. So what are you saying?"

"I'm saying everything that happened was done because it made the most sense at the time."

I passed my glass to Nadine. Two sips of whiskey had left my head swimming.

"Serves you right," she sniffed.

Like all the rooms at Sensory Resources, the one that held me was windowless. It could have been noon outside, or midnight, I'd have never known the difference. A person could be wide awake in here for two weeks and not be able to give a proper accounting of the time he'd spent, so it made sense there would be a period of disorientation. But I was more than disoriented, I was in shock. Based on my timeline, in a

216

handful of minutes I'd lost the face I was born with, and more than three years of my life! There were no instruction books to tell me how I was supposed to react.

But it's not what I'd seen and heard that led me to the bourbon. Bad as it was, I knew things were about to get much worse. The proof was in Nadine's eyes and Lou Kelly's voice. And the fact that Darwin kept Nadine working here at Sensory all these years just to prepare me for what Lou was about to say.

# 43.

"YOU DIED," LOU said.

I paused a moment. "You mean I died on the table and they brought me back to life?"

He shook his head. "No, I mean we killed Harry."

Harry Weathers had been my body double.

"We didn't have a choice," Lou said.

I said nothing.

He continued, "You were here, completely unresponsive, barely alive. Days went by. The doctors *hoped* you'd be okay, but stopped *believing* it."

A thousand thoughts raced through my brain, competing to make sense.

Lou continued: "Tara Siegel had a lot of friends who heard you came to Boston looking for her. A few hours later she went missing, and no one ever heard from her again."

I shouldn't have had the drink. Or maybe I should have had more. I had to force my mind not to get too far ahead of his words. Otherwise it would take longer to find out what I needed to know about Kathleen and Addie, and where things stood in the present.

"Go on," I finally heard myself say.

"Well, there were two problems. First, Tara's friends—picture what Callie and Quinn would do if Tara showed up and you'd gone missing. Anyway, her friends demanded answers from Darwin, said if he didn't tell them, they'd beat the truth out of Kathleen."

I set my new jaw, clenched my fists, but said nothing.

"The second problem, quite frankly, was Kathleen."

"How so?"

"When she didn't hear from you, didn't get her calls returned, she went into a panic. She knew just enough to be dangerous."

"That's ridiculous," I said. "She knows—*knew* nothing."

"She knew Sal Bonadello," Lou said, "and Victor."

"So?"

"She also knew—or thought she knew—that you worked for Homeland Security."

"She started making calls?"

"She did."

"And?"

"She got stonewalled. And didn't like it."

I let a small, proud smile play around the corners of my mouth.

Lou saw it, said, "Yeah, I know. But she contacted the press, started demanding an inquiry."

"Oh shit."

"Exactly. So Darwin created a phony mission and produced enough of Harry's body to convince everyone you'd been killed."

My heart sank.

I said, "And this was more than three years ago, and no one ever told Kathleen any different."

Lou remained silent.

"And Kimberly and Addie—they watched my burial."

"I'm sorry, Donovan," Lou said.

Nadine moved to my side, placed a reassuring hand on my

arm. She said, "As they explained it to me, it was the only way to protect Kathleen and Addie."

"Not to mention Sensory Resources," I said.

"That too," Lou said.

I rolled it around in my head a few minutes, trying to find a way to make it work for me. Of course they had to kill me off. In their shoes, I'd have done the same. Okay, so I'd lost three years. No problem, I'd just have to come back from the dead. I could kill Tara's friends before they knew I was alive, then break the good news to my loved ones. Nadine could be helpful with that part. I'd tell Kathleen and Kimberly everything, make a full confession. Then I'd retire. It could work, I reasoned. I could still salvage my relationship with Kathleen.

"How did I die?" I said.

"Excuse me?" Nadine said.

"Harry's body wouldn't have fooled the people that knew me well. They couldn't say I had a heart attack."

Lou sighed. "This sounds so much worse when I say it out loud," he said.

I waited.

"Aw Christ, Donovan," Lou said. "Harry got thrown off a highrise."

No one spoke for a long time. We didn't need to; Nadine's expression said it all.

"On the bright side," I said, "I look like a movie star."

Nadine said, "You're taking this awfully well. Are you sure you understand the complexity of the situation?"

"Pardon the pun, but I'm trying to put my best face forward."

"He's facing his fears," Lou said, "putting on a brave face."

"Well," said Nadine, flashing a smile, "I think it's time to face the facts."

I returned the smile. "Good one," I said. "For a shrink."

"We can start with your new name," she said.

That wiped the smile off my face. "My what?"

# 44.

"CONNER PAYNE," LOU said.

"A sissy name."

"Blame Darwin," he said. "Still, it's better than the last one he gave you."

"Cosmo Burlap?"

Lou chuckled.

Nadine said, "This just occurred to me, but what about all your bank accounts, investments, legal papers, and so forth?"

"Everything is in my legal name."

"Your legal name. So Donovan Creed—"

"Was my third name."

"You people are insane," Nadine said.

"That your professional opinion?"

"Don't start with me," she said.

Dr. Howard entered the room and injected something into my IV.

"Did you just give me a sedative?"

"You've been through a lot today," he said.

"You're at least going to let me try to walk..."

He sighed. "The natural tendency with these things is to try to make up the time you've lost right away. But it's much more complicated than that. Your brain shut down for a reason, and we need to find out what it was, so we can prevent a recurrence. In the meantime, relax, take it easy, and understand you've got all the time in the world."

"That's easy for you to say."

"Look, we're trying to avoid a blood clot here," he said, "or worse. Don't worry, I've been ordered to get you moving as fast as possible, so your rehab is going to be supervised by the best in the business. You've waited this long, what's another day?"

"You contact them yet?"

"They're on their way."

"Okay." I gave him a mock salute.

Nadine said, "How is it you're completely lucid after being knocked out with a sedative?"

"I test weapons for the military."

"So?"

"Sedatives are like candy to me."

"Wait. You test *weapons*?"

"Uh huh."

"What sort of weapons?"

"Death rays, psychotic drugs, torture devices, live viruses, that sort of thing."

She gave Lou an exasperated look. "I can't believe I wasn't told this before. How do you expect me to do my job if you won't tell me what I need to know?"

"You're the psychiatrist," Lou said. "How would we know what you need to know?"

"To think that fourteen years ago I had a legitimate practice," she mumbled.

"Why'd you give it up?" I said.

She shook her head. "When your government calls you into service, you tend to believe they can't save the world without your help."

"I've heard that lecture myself. Many times."

# 45.

"THE DIFFERENCE BETWEEN a good man and a bad one," Nadine said, "has nothing to do with their jobs or the choices they make. What matters is the motivation—why they do what they do."

"You are so in the tank for Sensory," I said. "They must have paid you a queen's ransom."

"I won't deny the paycheck, and I'll leave it to you whether I sold out. But I've spent a lot of years learning about this agency, and I have to say, I believe in what you're doing."

"What I used to do."

"What you were born to do."

Dr. Nadine Crouch had been trying to reprogram me for days. Today she wore an ebony jacket and matching skirt over a white crepe blouse.

"You're wearing long sleeves again," I said. "Is it winter?"

She pursed her lips. "I must try to keep in mind how difficult this is for you. No, it's spring," she said, "and I always wear long sleeves. When you're my age, the arms have a tendency to sag."

"You've got bingo arms?" I said.

"I beg your pardon?"

I laughed, thinking about it. "Like when the old ladies at the bingo parlor hold their cards over their heads and yell 'Bingo!'"

"That's a harsh observation."

"Oh, please."

"You'll be old someday. See how funny it is then," she snapped.

"Hey, I was just kidding around. There's nothing wrong with your arms." I grinned. "Or your legs, for that matter."

"Let's just get back to the topic at hand," she said, trying not to smile.

She'd been showing me dozens of news articles depicting senseless, tragic deaths, in an attempt to convince me that innocent people die every day, and they're going to die whether I kill them or not.

"I'm done with this," I said.

"This is who you are," she said. "You're a tragic hero."

"Me? A hero? You mean, like Superman?"

"Like Joan of Arc."

"I remind you of a chick? Must be my sissy new name."

"Fine, forget Joan. A tragic hero is an inherently noble, extraordinary person. He has a greatness about him that makes him seem almost super-human to others, and a purpose that serves mankind. He sacrifices his life for a great cause or principle."

"I sense a however coming."

"However, he has a fatal flaw that ultimately brings about his destruction."

"And mine is?"

"Somewhere along the way, you've lost your ability to remain detached."

"Have you met Callie?"

"I have, many times. She visits you regularly."

"And Quinn?"

"Not so regularly."

I nodded. "Quinn is very detached," I said.

"I know you consider him a friend, so I'll refrain from criticism."

"I can't believe Darwin hired you to reprogram me. Wait—yes I can. But how does that sit with you? I mean, you treated me as a patient. Do you really feel it's ethical to brainwash me into killing people?"

"I'll say it's appropriate. As for your use of the word 'brainwashing,' I'm not going to split hairs over terminology."

I'd used the term on purpose, trying to get a rise out of her. But she didn't bite. I said, "Nadine, you're the most honest professional person I've ever met."

"It helps to believe in the cause."

"You know about Monica Childers?"

"I do. She was the catalyst, the one that put the wedge of doubt in your mind."

"You're very good at what you do, Nadine."

"Not as good as you," she said.

I kept my eyes fixed on hers until she blinked. "You're a psychiatrist," I said. You're supposed to stand for something. You seriously expect me to believe you want me to keep killing innocent people?"

"Your issues with innocence started with Victor, and they'll end the moment you stop working for him."

"It's good money," I said, though I had already made the decision to stop.

"You took the work for one reason. And I'll wait for you to tell me what it is."

I already knew. "There was too much hang time," I said, "between the killings."

Nadine's eyes misted briefly. She patted my hand. "This is one of the three reasons it's worth giving up my practice to

226

work with people like you."

"What are the other two?"

"Money and Joan."

"Joan of Arc again?"

"You remember the first time we met, the pictures on my desk?"

"The two Japanese-American boys your sister adopted?"

"You have a prodigious memory," she said.

"For me it was a month ago."

"Joan was my sister. On the morning of September 11, 2001, she worked on the top floor of the World Trade Center."

I winced. "I'm sorry," I said.

"She called her husband that morning, but he was busy with a client. She called me, terrified, but I was busy with a patient. She tried to leave me a message, but her phone went dead."

"You feel somehow responsible?"

"Of course not. But it shouldn't have happened. And when it did, I should have been there for her."

"And now you want revenge."

She shook her head. "Revenge is a waste of emotion."

"But you want me to prevent it from happening again, even though innocent people will die. Sounds to me like you have a fatal flaw. You can't remain detached from what happened to your sister."

"Let's keep this about you," she said. "You're a soldier, a man of action. You can't survive in captivity."

"By captivity you mean settling down, raising a family?"

"You tried it before, with Janet and Kimberly. Didn't you learn anything? Your domestication only served to torment the people you love."

"You think you know me—"

"We both know you. You're an eagle. Eagles don't flock. They can't be domesticated. They do not thrive in captivity."

"You must be the worst marriage counselor in the world," I said.

"Quit working for Victor. Get your mind back in the game."

"My country needs me, eh?"

"Not to make a cliché out of it, but yes, we do."

"What about Sal?"

"Sal Bonadello?"

"Do you object to my working for him?"

Nadine took some time to weigh the question. She sighed. "I suppose not." She saw my eyebrows rise in disbelief and added, "Sal's jobs keep you sharp. In the end, what's it to society if tomorrow morning we all wake up and find there's one less bit of scum on the pond?"

"Nadine, you're an astonishingly bad psychotherapist."

"That's entirely possible, but it doesn't change who you are, or what you were meant to do."

"Nevertheless," I said, "I aim to quit the business, marry Kathleen, and help her raise Addie."

She said nothing.

"You're disappointed in me," I said.

"Not true. As for marrying Kathleen, if that's your motivation for getting strong and healthy, it's as good as any."

# 46.

I'D BEEN WARNED that the physical therapy would be agonizing. Instead, it was thrilling. Every stabbing pain made me feel alive, eager for more. Dr. Howard kept trying to back me off the weights and leg machines, but I was relentless, having set a goal to be in Kathleen's arms within ten days. Nadine was just as relentless in her attempt to keep me out of "captivity," but what could she do? In a competition for my soul, Kathleen would always win.

One day Nadine walked into my room and turned off the CPM machine that had been flexing and extending my knees.

"Conner," she said, "there's someone here to see you."

My heart raced. "Kathleen?"

She shook her head. "If you choose Kathleen, you'll have to approach her on your own."

"So who's here?"

I heard the electric whir before I saw him.

"Good to...see you...Mr. Payne...you're...looking...well."

"Hello, Victor. Where's Hugo?"

"He's...in the...corridor...with...someone."

"You don't seem surprised to see me alive."

"Curly...told me...you were...alive."

"And you've not told anyone all this time? Not even Sal?"

"It was...not my...business...to tell...anyone."

"Who wound up killing the couple from Nashville?"

"No one...I termi...nated...the pro...ject...after you...got here."

"And you're here to talk me into coming back to work for you?"

"No, I'm...part of...your...therapy...Dr. Crouch... wanted ...me to...show you...something."

"Then do so."

Victor was a quadriplegic, which means his paralysis affects all four limbs. But like many quads, Victor's paralysis and loss of function was not complete. He still retained partial use of his hands. With them, he controlled an array of buttons and toggles, one of which he used to summon his general, Hugo, and his mystery guest.

Hugo walked into the room with a very attractive woman who seemed familiar to me.

"Creed," he said.

"Hi Hugo. These days I'm going by Conner Payne." I studied the woman standing next to him. I knew it would come to me. She had shoulder-length blonde hair. The eyes were a different color than the last time I'd seen her, but they were still deep set and expressive.

"Holy shit," I said. "Monica Childers. I thought you were dead."

"I wish *you'd* died," she said. "But I take comfort knowing you're going to suffer."

"Nice to see you, too," I said.

I glanced at my wheelchair-bound former employer. "Victor, you told me Monica had been fucked to death by the Fathis."

She gave him a hard look.

"That...was a...cover...story," he said.

I said, "Monica, you've got every reason to hate me, but

seriously, I'm glad to know you're alive."

"Fuck you," she said.

"It's a generous offer, but I'm already spoken for."

"Really? What's his name?"

"You're a saucy little thing," I said.

"And you tried to kill me."

I said, "Victor, what's the story here?"

Victor gave Hugo a single nod, and Hugo said, "Monica was married to Baxter Childers, the surgeon who botched Victor's operation and left him paralyzed."

"I remember," I said.

"Monica met Victor during the lawsuit. They kept in touch with throwaway phones. Baxter was a serial cheater, and a piece of shit human being," Hugo said. He looked at Monica, held his hands up as if asking her to take over. She did.

"Not that I give a rat's ass what you think," she said to me, "but I knew for years he'd been cheating. I forgave him twice. Then I opened my heart to another man and fell in love. During the trial, I shared information with Victor's people and they reciprocated. I found out Baxter had a child with one of his young lovers. He was getting ready to divorce me and marry her. I could go through an extended divorce, or I could see him put away for my murder."

"And you chose the latter."

Monica's eyes narrowed, causing her eyebrows to flare like the wingspan of a predatory bird. "Victor said he'd take care of everything." She turned to address him face-to-face: "You failed to mention I'd be beaten and murdered."

Victor grimaced. "I…believed…you would…live, but…if not, then…Doctor…Childers…would…lose his…wife… *and*…the case."

I said, "So one day you're jogging at Amelia Island, and I

kidnap you. Soon thereafter, you're with your lover, savoring your sweet revenge."

"Let's keep the story straight," she said. "You beat the shit out of me, injected me with a lethal poison, kicked me out of a moving truck, and left me to die."

I glanced over and saw Dr. Nadine Crouch holding her head with both hands.

"Bygones?" I said.

Hugo offered his version: "You killed Monica, our people brought her back to life, she's living on a plantation in Costa Rica, and Baxter's serving twenty to life."

"All's...well that...ends well," Victor said.

"You could have smuggled me out of the country," Monica said. "You didn't have to let him *kill* me!"

"We've...been...through this...many...times," Victor said.

"Right. You were testing your anti-serum on me, killing two birds with one stone."

"But you're happy now," I said.

"Eat shit and die," she said. "It took four surgeries to repair my ear. The pain was excruciating."

"You keep dwelling on the bad parts," I said. I looked at Victor. "Is she always like this?"

"In my...experience...she is."

"Fuck you both!" she said.

Dr. Crouch said, "Monica, I want to thank you for coming today. Though you can't imagine it, or care to, your presence here has been meaningful."

"I only came so I could look this bastard in the face and tell him about Kathleen."

"What about her?" I said.

Monica's eyes grew ice cold. Her mouth curled into a smug smile. You could tell she'd rehearsed this scene many times. I think she planned to say more, but changed her mind at the last minute, realizing the faster you say it, the quicker it hurts. She'd come all the way from Costa Rica to get this out, so I waited as she paused to gather the proper venom in her voice. When she was ready, she lifted her chin defiantly, and spit two poisonous words at me: "Kathleen's engaged."

# 47.

MONICA'S WORDS SENT my heart into freefall. I blinked, forcing my brain to accept what I'd heard. Nausea flooded through me in that terrible way you feel when you can't quite vomit. You know you'll feel better if you do, but your body won't cooperate. I took a deep breath. I should have stayed in the coma. This was too much to deal with all at once. When I let the breath out it felt as though my life force went with it.

Nadine broke the silence: "How nice for you to take this opportunity to tell him that."

"No man ever deserved it more," Monica said. "I bet her fiancé is fucking her right now, making her say his name."

Hugo shook his head. Victor lowered his eyes in embarrassment. Monica kept the smug look on her face, and I thought, revenge agrees with her. *She's probably never looked more beautiful than she looks at this moment.*

I wanted to scream, but I found myself smiling. I mean, you have to smile, right? During the past week I learned I'd lost three years of my life, lost my face, lost my name. And now, hearing I may have lost the love of my life, well, what else are you going to do?

Monica sneered. "How does it make you feel to know another man has taken over your life? A man who at this very moment is screwing your lover, spending your millions, and raising your little match girl."

"How does it make me feel?" I repeated.

*Like I'd been tied to a whipping post*, I thought. But what I said was, "I feel like thanking God."

"What?"

"No matter how much I love Kathleen and Addie, I can't live like that. Dr. Crouch spent the past week helping me understand that, and what you've told me just makes it a lot easier to leave them behind. I'm glad they've found someone special to take my place."

"Bullshit," she said.

"I'll miss the sex," I said. "And Addie."

"And the money?"

I laughed. "I've got as much as I need and I can always get more."

"So your story is that you're fine with all this," Monica said.

"It's true," said Nadine, "though I wouldn't have chosen you, or this time and place, to tell him about Kathleen."

"Well I think he's bluffing," she said. "He won't admit it, but I think I hurt him worse than he hurt me."

"And I think you look sensational," I said.

"What?"

"I like the whole package. You've got a kickass little body, and I bet you're a wildcat in the sack."

Her face smoldered like a live coal. "From what hellish pit have you summoned the gall to talk to me like that?"

"What do you expect me to say? I haven't been laid in three years. Suddenly you waltz in here all worked up, wearing those 'check-out-my-tight-ass'pants!'"

"How dare you!"

I shrugged. "A kind word never broke a tooth."

"What the fuck is that supposed to mean?" Monica said,

235

but stormed out before I had a chance to answer.

"Guess you'd better chase after her," I said to Hugo. "She won't like it when security pins her against the wall."

He left, and Victor said, "It...was all...about you."

"What was?"

"The...experi...ment."

"The experiment," I repeated.

"We...wanted...to see...how far...you'd...go."

I thought about the seven loans Victor had Callie make to four couples and three individuals, loans that represented eleven lives and seven hundred thousand dollars—loans made and lives taken for nothing more than a bet between two midgets.

"You had me kill all those people just to see how long I'd do it? Why?"

"You...ever see...that...movie...*Trading...Places*?"

"Yeah..."

"Well...we had...a bet...Hugo...and me."

"Who won?"

"He did."

I stared at him blankly. "How much did he win?"

"Like...the movie."

"One dollar?"

"Yes but...it's the...principle...not the...money."

Hugo made a bow, reached into his pocket, pulled out a single dollar bill, held it up, and performed a strange little victory dance.

Victor said, "He's...very proud...of his...victory."

Nadine and I looked at each other.

"I think we're done here," she said.

When it was just me and her in the room I said, "When were you going to tell me?"

"I was working up to it."

"You and Lou let me believe everything was fine with Kathleen and Addie."

She looked at me awhile before speaking. "You want the truth?"

"Tease me with it. We can always default to your bullshit later."

"Dr. Howard asked us not to say anything that might interfere with your recovery."

"She's engaged," I said.

"She is."

This, along with all the rest, was almost too much to bear. "I guess Kathleen's had it pretty rough," I said, "Addie too."

"And Kathleen had every reason to believe you were dead. She attended your funeral, don't forget."

"Did she seem pretty broken up at the time?"

"I wasn't there, but I understand she took it hard."

"You think she brought a date?"

"That sort of talk is destructive, don't you think?"

"You really want to know what I think?"

"I do," she said. "It's my job, after all."

"I know she wants to be married, and it's certainly better for Addie. Still, I think it's pretty quick on her part. Don't you agree?"

"I try to avoid judgment," Nadine said.

# 48.

"HELLO, SAL," I said.

"What? Who is this? How'd you get this number?"

"Listen to my voice. You know who it is."

"The fuck?"

"You got some work for me?"

From the dead silence on the other end of the line I could practically hear the wheels turning.

"What is this, a—whatcha call—previous recording? Someone trying to be funny? Trying to play a bad joke?"

"It's me. Creed."

"Bullshit."

"Go ahead," I said. "Ask me something only I would know."

"Holy shit, it is you!"

"You didn't ask me anything."

"Only you woulda said something like that. Jesus H. The friggin'attic dweller comes back from the grave."

Then, as if something just struck him, Sal said, "I want my money back for the—whatcha call—funeral wreath."

I laughed. "Take it out of my next job."

"Don't think I won't. So who got killed and passed off as you? And where the hell you been, anyway?"

"You know how it works. That's classified."

"And you government fuckers wonder why I have—

whatcha call—trust issues."

"So, you got any work for me, or not?"

"I could give you ten jobs today."

"Give me an easy one to start. I'm at half strength right now."

"Which means you're still the best I ever seen."

"Stop," I said. "You're making me blush."

"You want easy?" he said. "I was gonna do this one myself."

"What, some girl scout forgot to deliver your cookies?"

"After all these years you're still a wise guy," Sal said.

"I didn't know wise guys called other people wise guys."

"I could write a book on what you don't know. You want this candy job or what?"

"Feed me, Seymour."

"The fuck you talkin'about?"

"I want the easy hit first. Then we can talk about the others."

"That's my boy."

"So," I said, "what makes this hit so easy?"

"The fucker *wants* to die."

I didn't know the fucker, but I knew how he felt.

# 49.

"CALLIE, IT'S ME."

There was the briefest silence, and then an explosion took place on the other end of the line.

"Oh my God, Oh, my GOD, OH MY GOD!" Callie shrieked.

"I'm back."

"Oh, Donovan. Thank God!"

We went through all the questions as if checking them off a list, and set a date to have dinner.

"I'm looking forward to meeting Eva," I said.

She laughed. "There may be some gay girl stuff going on. Think you can handle it?"

"Let me think a minute. Yes."

"Good. I can't wait for you to meet her. Did you hear? She's the lead now."

"I never doubted for a minute that she would be. But here's the real question: have you told her what you do?"

"Of course. I'm a decorator, all A-list clients."

"A job that requires extended travel."

"Exactly."

We were silent awhile.

"How are you with explosives?"

"Pretty current. Why, you've got a job for me already?"

"I do."

I went through the details of what I needed from her, and she had a number of questions about that. When at last all her questions were answered, some more silence passed between us.

"You ever think about quitting?" I said.

"Every day. But then I come to my senses. You?"

"Same."

Callie and I are alike in more ways than not. We both believe that the killing we do for the government is necessary, and we both love the danger rush. At the same time, we both long to be normal someday, with normal lives, surrounded by people who care about us.

Oh, and we both love beautiful women.

"Good to have you back, Donovan. I thought I'd lost you. I can't wait to see you."

I closed the phone as Lou came into my office with a folder.

"We've played this scene before," I said.

"With different results," Lou said.

"So, the new boyfriend is clean?"

"Like an eagle scout. Sorry, Conner."

I stared straight ahead at nothing in particular. "It's for the best," I said. "And Lou?"

He looked at me.

"Stop calling me Conner. I'm sticking with Creed."

He frowned. "Darwin's not going to like it."

"Fuck Darwin."

"Always an option, I suppose." Lou's frown deepened. "What about Tara's people—aren't you afraid they'll come after Kathleen?"

"Why should they? We're not together anymore."

"What if Kathleen finds out Donovan Creed is still walking around?"

"There's no reason for that to happen. If it does, I'm just another guy with the same name. Other than size, as long as I wear phony contacts, there's no way to recognize me."

"I have to confess, I hated the name Conner Payne."

"Keep the ID's, though, in case I want to use the name on a job."

"What about Joe Leslie?"

"We'll keep that one alive as well."

"I'll tell Darwin," he said. He started to leave.

"Lou—wait up a minute."

He stopped and turned.

I said, "There's something I want from Darwin. It's important."

He cocked his head in an *I-can't-wait-to-hear-this* kind of way.

I said, "This face job I got, it's amazing, yes?"

"It's a work of art," he said.

"I want Addie to get one. And I want all the charred skin removed from her body as well."

Lou said, "No way. Darwin would never authorize that."

"Tell him I'll pay every dime."

"Donovan, look at me. To do what they did for you? That would cost millions."

"I'll pay every dime."

"I don't know…"

"It's a deal breaker," I said.

He paused a bit, thinking it through. "You'll pay up front?"

"Whatever it costs."

"I'll set it up."

"What about Darwin?"

"Better he finds out after we start, than before."

I grinned at my friend. "Thanks, Lou."

# 50.

I CAUGHT HIM at 38th and Walnut.

Augustus Quinn—pro that he is—picked up the tail immediately, slammed on the brakes, and threw his car into reverse, trying to hit me. I slipped lanes and passed him, then jerked my car into reverse and pulled alongside him. We continued lying backwards down Walnut several blocks, side by side, staring at each other, until it hit him. He mouthed the word "Creed." I gave him a thumbs up. Then we both had to swerve in opposite directions to let the angry black pickup pass safely between us. I motioned Quinn to follow me, and we continued driving in reverse down Walnut until we hit Rittenhouse Square. We screeched to a stop in front of the hotel and tossed the be-wildered valet our keys.

"You ever try their crackling pork shank?" I said, pointing to the sign.

"With firecracker applesauce? They don't serve that here."

"Pity. In that case, I'll have a strip steak."

"I look like a waiter to you?"

"Not so much," I said. "Want to join me for a steak?"

"I'd join you for rooster knees!"

"Well, who the hell wouldn't?"

Smith and Wollensky was still the premier steakhouse in Philly. Like its cousins in South Beach and New York, the restaurant has a bank of windows that offers great people watching. We sipped some bourbon in the main bar and rated the women. It was mostly sevens and eights until we saw a Megan Fox lookalike who had it all going for her: high cheekbones, sultry smile, the impossibly toned abdo-men she bared for those of us who appreciate such things. She wore designer jeans with rhinestone-studded back pockets. Every now and then we caught a fleeting glimpse of thong when she set her purse down or picked it up, which by my count happened twice. At one point, while I was distracted by the soulless bartender, Quinn caught a down-blouse.

"Real or fake?" he said.

"I missed the defining moment," I said, "but you date enough strippers you get a feel for these things, pun intended."

"So your answer is?"

"Definitely real. Without question, you are looking at a gift from God."

"I agree. What do you give her?"

"For me it's an eleven."

"There are no elevens," he said.

"Look again."

He did.

"You're right. We need to create a new category."

I said, "Must have been a perfect day in heaven, what, twenty years ago? This girl comes down the assembly line, God's in the best possible mood, and, there you go."

"So for you it's a religious experience."

"Some people see God in a potato chip."

"How do you rank her against Callie?"

"Callie's a twelve."

Quinn was about to argue for a higher score, but two Asian girls walked past us wearing cut off jeans that showed half their backsides.

"Look at that ass," Augustus said.

"Which one?"

"Both."

"Okay," I said, "but just long enough to make sure I can identify them in case someone called the cops."

"You're a good citizen, Donovan."

The hostess brought out our waiter to us, and we fol-lowed him to our seats. Of course, everyone in the bar and restaurant gave Quinn a wide berth. As we walked past him, a drunk guy said to a friend, "Gimme your cell phone, I think I just sighted Bigfoot," but instead of laughing, his drinking buddy moved away. Quinn seemed not to notice. He was actually chuckling.

"What are you laughing at?" I said.

"I just remembered the name of the movie star you look like."

"Stop!" I said, "don't tell me."

"Fine. But you know who I'm talking about."

"I feel like an idiot, taking this face out in public."

"The chicks seem to like it," he said. "You're getting more fingers pointed at you than William Shatner at a Star Trek convention."

Although I felt it was more likely the fingers were be-ing pointed at Quinn, I said, "This is my test drive. So far so good, meaning, you're the only one who's laughed."

"I'm not used to you with—what is it, sandy blond hair?"

"Light brown."

"How often you have to dye that?"

"Regularly."

"And the eyebrows?"

"Let's change the subject," I said. "How's Alison these days?"

"Ouch. How would I know? I haven't seen her in years.

How's Kathleen?"

"The same. What happened with Afaya?"

"He never showed up. One morning his 'cousin' was at work in Denver, took his usual lunch break, never came back."

"Someone tip him off?"

"That's what Darwin thinks, but it doesn't matter. The threat went away."

"How'd you and Alison start dating?"

"Who said we did?"

"Lou Kelly."

Quinn stared at me a moment. "I guess you could call it dating. It lasted a couple of weeks, is all."

I nodded, took a sip of my drink. He knew I was waiting for him to tell me how he and Alison got together sexually, when he was supposed to be training her to kill people. He finally did.

"She thought with you dead, maybe I'd give her the high-paying job you promised. I didn't discourage her from thinking that."

"You dog."

"Woof. So anyway, when she realized that wasn't gonna happen, she bolted."

"You never heard from her again?"

Quinn laughed. "I know. You'd think, sensitive guy like me, she'd call whenever it rains or when she's feeling blue, right?"

I smiled at the thought. "What about the guy from the Texas Syndicate?" I said.

"He didn't follow up on her, far as I know. I think he had enough problems of his own, trying to stay in power."

We were quiet a minute, and then I chuckled.

"What," he said.

"She ever do that love song for you while in the throes of passion?"

"Which one—the asthmatic alley cat, or the singing horse?"

"The horse is the one I remember."

Quinn gave a sudden imitation of her that made all the surrounding tables take notice. I laughed like I hadn't laughed since the days of Kathleen.

Quinn said, "Alison was really something, she was."

"So was Kathleen," I said.

Quinn nodded. "So when do you want me to kill her fiancé?"

# 51.

OF COURSE I didn't want Quinn to kill Kathleen's fiancé, but I appreciated the gesture. Hell, I'd thought of killing him myself and starting over with Kathleen, but like Callie said about quitting the business, each time I thought about it, I came to my senses.

Quinn and I had our steaks and split an order of truffled mac and cheese. During dinner we drank an outstanding cabernet, the 2004 Oracle, from Miner Family Vineyards.

"I only eat like this when I'm alone or with somebody," I said.

"You were due," he said. "Keep working out and eating like this and you'll be back to normal strength before you know it."

I almost told Augustus how much I'd missed him, but changed my mind at the last second. It wouldn't have been worth all the shit he'd give me for saying it.

"What brings you to Philly?" he said.

"I came to see you."

He twisted his face in the manner I've come to recognize as his signature smile. "That's nice," he said.

"People like us," I said, "can't afford to have many friends. I like to think of you and Callie as people I can count on."

Quinn said, "I feel the same way. They'd have to pay me a lot to kill you or Callie."

Coming from Quinn, that was quite a compliment. On the other hand, it was scary to think that this monstrous man who would kill me for the right price was the closest I had to a guy friend.

I looked at him as he stared at the women coming and going on the sidewalk in front of the restaurant, and wondered if our team of surgeons could do anything about his extreme deformities. I decided they could not.

Quinn wasn't as ugly as Joseph Merrick, the Elephant man, but at least Merrick enjoyed two years on earth as a normal human being before the growths began forming on his face and head. Quinn was born this way, and his world view was formed in response to the reactions he got from others.

Doctors couldn't agree on the source of Quinn's particular malady, but the consensus pointed to a form of Proteus Syndrome, a condition so rare that less than a hundred cases have been documented worldwide.

Proteus would explain the deformed facial features on one side of Quinn's head and face, but none of the reported cases shared the strange, multicolored striations that covered the left side of his face and neck. It wasn't a skin disease, and there was no odor to his skin, so one theory was that the splotches were a giant, multi-colored birthmark.

Bottom line, Quinn's poster boy looks were closer to Joseph Merrick than Brad Pitt. As you might imagine, there were gaping vacancies on Quinn's social calendar, a situation that afforded him plenty of time to ogle the women that entered his field of vision.

A model-thin stunner entered the main dining room at Smith & Wollensky's and took a seat at a table where three suits had been waiting. Her glimmering platinum hair was chopped shoulder length, and she had on some sort of purple make-up that looked like war paint.

"Oh Mama," Quinn said. "What would you do to that one?"

"How long do I get?"

"Thirty minutes."

"I'd turn her more ways than a monkey can turn a coconut."

He looked at me. "Can I make an observation?"

"Please do."

"You're saying all the right things about these chicks, but your heart's not in it."

"Like I said, tonight's more of a test drive."

"You know what you need? You need to get your pipes cleaned. You're in my town, let me make a call. Right now you're sitting in a steakhouse, but you're only thirty minutes away from the best night of your life."

"What's her name?"

"Her *name*? Jesus, you really *are* a mess," he said.

I shrugged. "I'm a detail guy."

"You are that," he said. "Her name is Heavenly."

"What makes this hooker better than all the rest?"

He did that smile thing with his face, and when he did it, I smiled too.

"She got a friend for you?" I said.

"Her roommate's Delight."

"Heavenly Delight, huh? What are they, a tag team?

He cuffed me on the arm. "I won't pretend I don't know," he said.

We sat in silence awhile, me thinking again about how we're all just a phone call away from a life-changing event. Quinn's eyes fairly danced with anticipation, like a kid hoping I'd take him to get ice cream.

"What the hell," I said. "Make the call."

"Really? That's great! You won't be sorry!"

He stepped away from the table. A moment later he returned, still on the phone, but didn't sit down. I heard a click.

"Tell me you didn't just take my picture," I said. He pointed behind me. "Chick with the boobs." He pressed a few buttons, ended his call.

We finished our fine dinner with a sauterne as rich and thick on the tongue as syrup.

"That some kind of wine?" Quinn said. "Are you kidding me?"

"It is and I'm not."

"Tastes more like dessert. What is it?"

"Lafaurie Peyraguey," I said, showing off my French accent.

"Those words could never come out of this fucked-up mouth of mine," he said, "but I can see why it's your favorite."

"Actually, purists prefer Chateau d'Yquem."

"What do they know," he said.

His phone buzzed and he checked the text. He winked at me.

"We're on! The girls are excited."

"Excited hookers?"

"I told them I was bringing a movie star."

"You didn't!"

"I had to, they were already booked."

"Let me guess: they didn't believe you, so you took my picture and forwarded it to them."

"Well, what was I gonna do," he said, "send her a picture of the chick with the boobs?"

"You took a picture of her too?"

251

He did that grinning thing again. "You want to ride with me or follow me there?"

I thought a moment. "I'd better follow you. We'll probably be there awhile; the restaurant might be closed by the time we're done with the girls."

"That's what *I'm* talkin' bout!" Quinn said, cuffing my arm again.

The valet guys retrieved our cars. Quinn rolled out and I followed from a short distance. I reached under my seat and found the small box Callie had put there while Augustus and I were in the restaurant. I placed it on the seat beside me.

Car bombs are as diverse as the people they kill. They can be wired to ignition systems, set to timing devices, attached to tilt fuses that detonate when the car hits a bump in the road, or detonated wirelessly from a distance. The payload can be placed under the driver's seat, dash, or attached magnetically to the underside of the car, or, as in this case, inside the wheel well. The detonator on the seat beside me was good for a distance of at least a hundred yards line-of-sight, or fifty if obstructed.

Quinn was my best guy friend, and one of the last people I'd ever want to kill. But he was also the guy who'd kidnapped Alison Cilice and held her captive in his warehouse for the past three years. I knew this as well as I knew my name. Well, scratch that. I knew it as well as I knew anything. It began as a hunch, and became a near certainty after having Lou Kelly's geeks run a full-out search on Alison. When they found that her trail dried up less than a month after I went into my coma, I measured her disappearance against my in-depth knowledge of Quinn. I'd been ninety-nine percent sure before talking to Quinn at the restaurant. By the time we'd gotten our cars, I had no doubts at all.

If Quinn had told me Alison was dead and buried in a specific place, or that she'd taken up with someone or changed her name, or given me any plausible explanation for her current whereabouts, I could have Lou follow up on it. But Quinn said all the wrong things.

He admitted to dating Alison. He also said she bolted after a few weeks, and I believed him. But I had entrusted Quinn with Alison's care and well-being, and whether she wanted anything to do with him or not, he'd have kept tabs on her these three years.

Because he'd still be guarding her, would in fact have guarded her for the rest of her life, since that had been my last request, just as I would, had our positions been reversed. It's how we're wired. We keep track of the people we guard, period. So his claim that he hadn't heard from her in three years was preposterous.

My guess is that after being spurned, Quinn tracked her down and tried to get her back. She would have refused, and he would have kidnapped her. Like *Beauty and the Beast*, he probably hoped in time she'd grow to love him. But of course, Beauty and the Beast were from a time and place where women had fewer options.

And it was a fairy tale.

And Augustus Quinn was a real life monster.

Quinn turned left on Clancy, and as I followed him I glanced at the compact rectangular box with the toggle that meant life and death for Augustus Quinn.

Did I have to kill him?

I could pretend I didn't know about Alison, and hope Augustus would release her someday. Except that I knew Quinn well enough to know that the only way he'd let her go is if he killed her. Which he wasn't likely to do, because as his captive, she'd represent everything he wants in a woman: she'd be subservient, faithful, always available, and grateful to see him return. By that I mean he held the key to her survival. If he failed to return, she'd starve to death, so of course she'd be relieved and grateful when he returned to the warehouse.

I didn't want to kill Augustus. We'd worked together so long I could hardly imagine going after the bad guys without him. Of all my assassins, Quinn and Callie were the only ones I trusted with my life. To a point. But I needed to save Alison, and there's no way I could save her if Quinn was alive. I've seen his warehouse, and I knew the room he'd be using to hold her, and it was virtually impenetrable. I'd need a great deal of time to bust her out, whether it was through the steel door or one of the reinforced walls that held her.

If I did manage to distract Quinn long enough to break Alison out of the warehouse, Quinn would make it his mission in life to kill both of us. On my own, I could probably handle Augustus, or at least stay ahead of him. But I'd have to protect Alison, and she'd slow me down in short order. We'd be sitting ducks for a guy with Quinn's killing ability. It made no sense to rescue Alison if Quinn was going to hunt us down and kill us anyway.

Quinn stopped at a red light at Clancy and Olmstead. I could see his monstrous form silhouetted by the headlights of the cars facing us. I wondered if he suspected I knew about Alison. If so, was he already plotting my death?

I sighed. In the end it came down to this: Alison was innocent. She was being held captive because of the decision I'd made to place her in his care. That made me responsible for her, and I take my responsibilities seriously. Always have. Besides, I don't like the idea of her being at Quinn's grisly mercy these many years. It's the fatal flaw part of the heroic code Nadine had spoken about, my inability to remain detached. I simply could not ignore Alison's situation, much as I'd love to. And Quinn would never allow her to leave.

The light turned green and Quinn released his foot from the brake. When he did so, the brake light went dark and the car moved forward. I placed my thumb on the toggle switch and followed him.

Maybe I could hold off. We could bang the hookers, make a great night of it, and maybe afterward he and I could talk about Alison.

But what would we say? If he agreed to release her, and I agreed to forgive and forget, we'd still have the problem of her going to the police. Quinn would never allow himself to be a fugitive. He'd either commit suicide or die in a fight after killing a dozen members of a SWAT team.

There was no getting around it, Augustus had to die.

But did he have to die right now?

He's already had his last meal, why not let him have one last fling with these first rate whores? It could be sort of a gift from me to him, for old times' sake. I could always kill him afterward, maybe come up with a more peaceful way to take my friend out of this world.

The more I thought about it, the more I decided this was the way to go. Let him enjoy Delight's full menu of services first. Then I'd give him a lethal dose from my syringe before the smile has time to fade from his face. While waiting for the perfect opportunity to strike, I could even spend a little time getting to know Heavenly.

The night was clear and clean and we headed east under a thick canopy of stars that seemed bright enough to drive by if we wanted to turn off our headlights. I thought about Kathleen and Addie a mere ninety-five miles away and felt connected, wondering if they were looking into the same sky.

I shook my head. Who was I kidding? I wasn't ready to jump into the sack with anyone, let alone a hooker named Heavenly. And anyway, the moment you know a damsel is in distress, you save her. It's rule number one in the *Hero Handbook*, no exceptions. I backed off the gas and let Augustus get fifty yards ahead of me. Then I made a sudden left turn. As I did, I flipped the switch on the detonator box and blew my best friend, Augustus Quinn, to hell.

# 52.

I CIRCLED THE block from the other direction and did a drive by, inspecting my work. My friend was in a more peaceful place now, and yes, I'm referring to hell. Because hell would be a picnic compared to the torments of Quinn's life.

I drove two more blocks and picked up Callie. She gave me a huge hug and said, "It's so great to see you!"

"You too, I only wish the circumstances were better."

"I wish we could have met before all this happened," she said. "But you're right, it would have been too risky."

She settled into her seat and I put the car in gear.

"I heard the explosion," she said. "I assume everything went according to plan."

"It did."

"Okay, then."

She grew quiet as I picked my way through the down-town streets. Knowing where the explosion occurred helped me avoid the police cars and ambulances converging on the scene. Once we were past that, I stole a glance at Callie and saw her staring straight ahead with vacant eyes.

"You okay?" I said.

Her lip trembled. When she spoke her voice sounded spent, like it had traveled a long way to get here.

"I feel dirty," she said. She turned and watched my face as I drove. "I can't even imagine how you must feel."

"No," I said, "you probably can't."

Most people would consider Callie and me to be stone-cold killers. But we're not killers, we're assassins. Maybe I'm splitting hairs here, but to me the distinction is we don't get a high from killing. To us it's a job, like working in an ice cream store or delivering the mail. You don't get emotionally attached to the ice cream or the mail. You just scoop or deliver it. But Quinn had been a friend to both of us, and while I'd known him many years longer than Callie, she had considered him to be trustworthy in all the ways that count.

Until the thing with Alison.

I wondered about the repercussions I might experience from killing Augustus, and subconsciously touched my chest. No pain is good. I hadn't expected the symptoms to return, due to my counseling sessions with Nadine, but after going through what I did, I suppose there will always be a small wedge of doubt in the back of my mind when I take lives in the future.

For now it was working. Nadine helped me understand it was a question of degree. Everyone is guilty of something, but not everyone can agree on the severity of a crime. And everyone has a different yardstick for what warrants the death penalty.

For me, according to Nadine, the killing has to either benefit the victim or society. For example, I had no problem putting Robbie out of his misery after Callie dealt him a mortal wound. That benefitted the victim. When I kill terrorists for Homeland, I'm benefitting society.

In preparation for killing Quinn, I'd asked Nadine if I would have been able to kill Tara Siegel. She said, "You could have killed Tara without batting an eye as long as it benefited her or society. If Tara had turned against Homeland Security, or if she had violated your moral code by threatening to kill Kathleen or Addie, it wouldn't have the slightest psychosomatic effect. That's why Callie had no problem pulling the trigger. Callie perceived Tara as a serious threat to her life with Eva. But you weren't convinced of that at the time. When Callie shot her, you were still trying to work out an agreement with Tara. When Callie took matters into her own hands, your brain perceived a senseless killing."

I'd asked Nadine if that wasn't just so much psycho babble.

She said, "Your body reacts to things that appear to be real, whether real or not. For example, if I were to punch Nurse Carol in the stomach, totally unprovoked, she'd double over in pain. If tomorrow I started to punch her in the stomach, but stopped my fist just short of the target, she'd probably still double over to protect herself from the perceived blow."

"So it's not the actual violence, but my perception of it that counts."

"As long as you're in charge of the killing, and you know the killing has nothing to do with someone's idea of entertainment, you'll be fine."

I'd said, "Nadine, what happens to you when I leave here?"

"I'll go home and learn how to have some fun in my life. I plan to dote on my nephews and make friends in my neighborhood."

"You've earned enough to retire?"

"Yes, with the money I've saved and the fortune Darwin has paid me to nursemaid you, I'm set for life."

"So you and I are done?"

"For you I'll come out of retirement any time."

"You'll talk to me as a friend? Help me through the hard times?"

"Don't be ridiculous. Once you leave, if you want to talk

to me, you'll have to reach into your pocket."

"Your words sound harsh," I said, "but I see a smile on your face."

"Well, don't tell anyone," Nadine said.

That was a week ago. Now, with Callie beside me, mourning Quinn's death in her own, quiet way, I thought of the effect Quinn had on the other people in my life. Kathleen and Addie had taken to Augustus, had accepted him with open arms. He'd protected Addie day and night at the burn center when Joe DeMeo's goons wanted to kill her. He'd said nice things about me to Kathleen the first time I thought I had lost her. By her own account, it was the comment Quinn made that helped her see me in a different light.

I continued putting miles between us and the body of our good friend.

"So what happens now?" Callie said.

"Now we rescue Alison."

## 53

QUINN'S TORTURE CHAMBER was the basement of an abandoned building in an isolated part of the city. He actually owned the building, so there was no danger of losing the sweat equity he'd put into renovating it. I'd been inside before, and remembered he'd put drains in the floor, reinforced the walls, and soundproofed them with the same material used in upscale movie theaters.

As I pulled into the parking area, a random thought crossed my mind, something I remembered from a previous visit: in addition to being an excellent saxophone player, Quinn had been an accomplished chef. He used to blister the skin of his torture victims with the same small handheld butane torch he used to caramelize the surface sugar on his crème brulees.

There were no parking lot lights, so I left the car headlights on to get a good look at the exterior of the building. I removed a bag of tools from the trunk and slung them over my shoulder. Callie got out and we stood next to the car and looked at the gray, rundown building. To be precise, the overall color was gray, but there were faded and peeled areas that revealed former colors. I'd say the bricks had been painted at least three times over the decades. Two feet from the top of the building, a series of rusted pipes ran horizontally across the back and disappeared around the side.

"I don't see any wires," Callie said. "You think he's got an alarm?"

"No way." Last thing in the world he'd want would be to lead people to his workplace."

"His workplace," she said.

Standing there quietly for a moment felt right, somehow. Callie finally spoke. "I felt a bit sick tonight, setting the charge."

"Augustus always lived on the edge," I said, "but this time he crossed the line."

Callie studied the building some more. "It would have been tough saving Alison if he were alive."

"He'd be a tough adversary."

Callie said, "You really think she'll be sane enough to work for Sensory after this?"

I said, "Are any of us sane? Hell, this experience might make her a better agent."

Callie nodded. "You ready?"

I put my hand in my pocket and felt the silver dollar, felt the satisfying heft of it, like I'd done ten thousand times before.

"Let's get her out of here," I said. "Assuming she's alive."

"Let's get her out either way," Callie said.

# 54.

IF YOU BROKE in through the front door like we did, you'd find yourself standing in a small entry office, with reinforced glass walls that offered a view of the huge room beyond. We clicked on our penlights, opened the door and walked into the dank old warehouse, where I was immediately struck by the immaculately clean concrete floor. I wondered how many times a month Quinn had to scrub it to keep it completely free from dust and dirt and blood.

We moved slowly and steadily through the open space until we came to the little concrete room where I believed Alison was being held captive. I called out her name, but heard no response.

"Help me find an electrical outlet," I said.

"The power's not on," she said, "and I doubt you want to flip the main circuit breaker and light the whole place up."

"He keeps the lights off, but the outlets work."

We found one close enough to reach with an extension cord. Callie held the flashlight beam on my bag while I opened it and selected the proper tools for the job.

"You're never going to get through that door," she said.

She was right. The door and frame were made of thirty-gauge, cold rolled steel. Quinn had told me that every twelve inches of it was reinforced with a checkerboard of steel columns, and that the gaps between the columns were filled

263

with hardened concrete. The door was secured by three kick-proof, pick-proof locks, and a hardened steel security bar.

"I'm going through the concrete wall," I said.

Callie swept this part of the warehouse with her flash-light.

"What's that room over there?" she said.

"That's the torture room. If you want, you can drag a chair out of there and bring it over to sit on. You may as well, this is going to take awhile."

"Will the car be safe where it is?"

"Probably. People around here have seen Quinn. I doubt they'd want to make him an enemy."

While Callie left to get a chair, I positioned a drill against the center of the wall about three feet above the floor, and started the process.

When Callie returned she sat in her chair and said, "Did Augustus really think you wanted to tag team the hookers?"

"I believe he did."

"You boys ever do that before?"

"Nope."

"Never got drunk, decided what the hell?"

"Never did," I said.

"You remember your first time?"

"With a hooker?"

"Uh huh."

"You never forget your first," I said.

"I suppose."

I reversed the drill bit out of the hole to inspect my progress.

Callie said, "Tell me about it."

I turned to look at her. "What, the first time I slept with a hooker?"

She nodded.

"On purpose?"

She laughed, and I resumed working on the wall while I thought about it.

"I can't guarantee she was a hooker," I said. "But she was certainly a stripper."

It was summer and I was just out of high school. In a few months I'd be a sniper for the army, but that night I was in Bossier City, Louisiana, where I'd planned to go gutter-sniping with a buddy at a club on the Bossier strip. He never showed, so I picked up a skinny, thatch-haired stripper an hour before closing time and took her to the little fleabag motel across the four-lane highway where we did a couple of lines off a stained, wood veneer table. She peeled down to her panties and we sat on the edge of the bed and started making out.

Someone kicked the door open, startling us. Her hus-band, one of the bouncers from the lounge, the one she hadn't mentioned—aimed a .38 snub at my face, cocked the trigger and told me to start praying.

In real life you're not going to have the stones to walk up to a total stranger and blow his brains out, even if you're a badass, and yes, even if the stranger happens to be in a hotel room groping your semi-naked wife. I didn't have any real-world experience at the time to help me know this, but it was something I understood on a gut level.

I said, "I don't know any prayers, but you know what kind of woman you married. Killing me won't change her behavior."

The big man stood just inside the room with the door propped open behind his back. The door was splintered around the lock but it was still on its hinges and the frame was intact. We looked at each other in that way men do when they're sizing each other up, just before a fight. In the background I could hear his wife selling me out enthusiastically. She used a lot of words to say she'd been high as a kite and I'd taken advantage of her. Not wanting to give him too much time to focus on that viewpoint, I headed for the door. I knew he'd try to sucker punch me as I walked by, so I ducked when I felt it coming. I did a good job of it, but he had the angle on me and the butt of his gun grazed the side of my head and spun me around. I lurched out the door and slid a bit on the gravel in the parking lot before gaining enough traction to start sprinting. I heard him coming after me but he didn't have the legs. Twenty yards into it he gave up and shouted, "Get the fuck outta here! You ever come back, you're a dead man! You hear me?"

Yeah, I heard him.

I was half a block away, crossing the highway, backtracking toward my car and I could still hear him. Only what I heard now was the sound of him beating her. I heard her screaming above the traffic noise, begging him to stop. I was closer to the bar than I was to them but I still heard his yelling and her screaming over the muted roar of the band inside. I doubled back to check on her, but the noise had stopped. I crept up to the room, peeked through the broken door.

"What did you see?"

"Two stoners having make-up sex."

"Women," Callie said. "Can't live with 'em—"

"What about you?" I said, "Your first time with a john."

"I might be splitting hairs here, but I wasn't an authen-tic hooker."

The drill bit finally burst through the wall. I reversed the direction and retracted the drill, leaving a quarter-inch hole. I cupped my hands around the opening and shouted, "Alison!" Then I put my ear up to it and heard a muted re-sponse that sounded like someone saying the letter "M" over and over.

"Yeah," I said to Callie.

"Yeah, what?"

"You might be splitting hairs when you say you weren't an authentic hooker."

"Kiss my ass," she said.

"I'd be delighted to. And while we're on the subject…"

"Of my ass?"

"Of johns. You ever have any issues with violence?"

"One time a sweet old gentleman enjoyed my company for about four minutes before smacking me in the back of the head with brass knuckles, knocking me out, and robbing me."

"See, that's the problem with civilians. They're emotional, unpredictable, and they come at you from all the wrong angles. By the way, Alison's alive. She's got her mouth taped up."

"Well that's good news. How long till we're in?"

"Let's put it this way. Have you had dinner yet?"

"I don't eat much."

"Good thing."

I started drilling the second hole.

# 55.

WHEN THE DRILL started smoking, I stopped a few minutes to let it cool. Callie took the opportunity to say, "The first time you put your life in danger."

"What about it?"

"How old were you?"

I thought a minute.

"Ten."

"Early bloomer," she said.

I'd just finished fourth grade. Summer break, my grandfather took me on a camping trip in the Colorado foothills. We spent the second night in a little cabin in a roadside campground, and the next morning I got up early and went for a hike. I'd probably gone two miles when I realized all the pines started looking alike. I stopped and made a slow, complete turn, searching for a trail. But there was none. I wasn't exactly afraid, but I wasn't exactly fearless either. I closed my eyes and took a step in the direction I assumed would take me back to the campground. No, that step was slightly higher. I took a step in the opposite direction. Slightly lower. Funny how sometimes you can figure things out with your eyes closed that you'd never know by looking.

The drill had cooled off enough to continue my assault on the wall. I went at it with gusto. While I worked, I thought about that morning, thirty years ago, when I was lost in the

Colorado foothills.

It took twice as long to get back that morning, and my route wasn't a direct one, so I wound up approaching the campsite from the opposite way I'd started. There was a fenced-in corral I hadn't seen the night before, and a couple of fleabitten horses picking at the sparse grass. A good sized kid, maybe thirteen, with strawberry hair and freckles—saw me coming out of the woods. He pointed to the fence and giggled the laugh all childhood bullies have in common. He was older and bigger than me and I wanted to avoid confrontation. I was also dying of thirst and wanted to let my grandfather know I was safe. Nevertheless, I allowed my eyes to follow the direction the big kid was pointing.

There was something moving on top of a fence post. I walked over for a closer look and saw that the little bastard had stuck a box turtle on top of the fence post. He'd centered it in such a way that the bottom of the turtle's shell was perched on the post but its head, feet and tail dangled in the air on all sides. The turtle's feet moved furiously in a futile effort to make contact with something solid. It was apparent the kid intended the turtle to die this way, either from thirst, exhaustion, or maybe he expected it to boil to death as the day wore on. The kid didn't care, he thought it was hilarious. He kept grinning and pointed to the line of fence posts behind me, where I saw a dozen more turtles lined up as motionless as any group of sports trophies.

Callie said, "What did you do?"

That morning in Colorado after the big, strawberry blond-haired kid showed me his turtle graveyard, I took the silver dollar out of my pocket, the one I'd carried all these years, and flipped it in the air. It flew maybe twenty feet high before starting its descent. When the turtle killer looked up to catch my coin I punched him on the side of the head, exploding my fist into his jaw the way my grandfather had taught me, turning into the punch, putting everything I had into it. The bully and the silver dollar hit the ground at the same time. I rescued the live turtle, picked the dead ones off their perches, and left the big, strawberry-haired kid laying there, his legs twitching like a turtle on a fence post.

"Did he die?" Callie asked.

"From a skinny ten-year-old's punch? No way. I hadn't gone twenty yards when I heard the rocks whizzing past my ears. The son-of-a-bitch tried to kill me!"

"What did you do?"

"Ran like hell!"

Callie laughed.

"You put your life on the line for a turtle."

I laughed. "I guess."

"I think it's noble."

"Uh huh."

"Donovan Creed, Ninja Turtle."

The drill burst through the wall, leaving a second hole, about an inch from the first one. From the bag I got a hammer and chisel and started banging away. The chisel made short work of the area between the holes, and left an opening I could have gotten two fingers through.

I put my mouth to the new opening and said, "Alison, this is Donovan Creed. I know they told you I was dead, but I'm very much alive and I'm going to get you out of there. I've got a friend with me. Her name is Callie Carpenter, and she's going to rescue you."

"MMM...MMMM" Alison said.

"Save your strength," I said through the opening.

Callie said, "How much longer?"

270

"Fifteen minutes, tops."

"How's that possible?"

"The wall is weakening," I said.

I got the concrete saw and started cutting a vertical line from the center of the hole. When I'd made a two-foot cut I turned to Callie and said, "See? We're practically in."

"That was more than a half hour," Callie said.

I gave her a look that said I was doing all the work, and followed it up by asking, "That chair comfy enough for you?"

"Depends how long I've got to sit here."

"Five minutes, tops."

Then I got out the sledge hammer.

# 56.

FORTY MINUTES LATER I gave Callie the concrete saw and directed her to start a horizontal cut from both sides of the twelve-inch opening I'd managed to create. Between the drinks, the big dinner and the physical labor, I was beat. Though it was cool in the building, I was drenched with sweat. My back, neck and shoulders ached. I took her place in the chair and hoped my strength would return.

I sat there holding the flashlight on the wall as she'd been doing for me. The penlight threw off enough light to perfectly silhouette her body. Because the line she was cutting was about two feet above the floor, she had to squat and perch herself on one knee while she worked. Did I mention I'd had a few drinks and been looking at women earlier that night? Somehow the flashlight's beam moved away from the hole in the wall and found a home on Callie's perfect backside.

"Do you mind?" she said.

"Not at all."

"Dude!" she said. "We're trying to save a life here."

"Spoilsport."

I reluctantly moved the beam back to the wall where it belonged. Twenty minutes later I began the final assault with the sledge hammer. Twenty minutes after that, I'd created an opening large enough for Callie to slip through, and she did. She took a flashlight with her and I placed mine on the floor of the room to add some light.

I was only able to fit my head and neck into the opening, but that was enough to see that Alison's room was small, with a bed, a TV, a toilet, sink, and a mini fridge that probably held water and food. But Alison was enjoying none of these comforts. She was completely naked, chained to the wall. Her mouth was covered in tape that encircled her head. Above and below the tape I could see the top and bottom of a red bondage ball Quinn had forced into her mouth.

I had no idea how long she'd been chained to the wall like that, but she was at least thirty pounds thinner than the last time I'd seen her. She was also clearly in agony, and there was a large puddle of urine beneath her. Callie turned to me and said, "What now?"

I backed out of the opening and retrieved a pair of heavy-duty bolt cutters from my equipment bag. I passed the cutters through the hole to Callie. It took her a minute to cut the cuffs, then she said, "Donovan, give us a little privacy."

I backed out of the opening again and waited while Alison used the toilet. I heard Callie say, "This will hurt less if I go slowly." Then I heard the tape coming off Alison's mouth. She gagged and coughed and sputtered. Callie kept saying, "It's okay, Quinn's dead, everything's going to be all right."

Callie got her cleaned up and dressed and helped her through the wall. When Alison emerged she gave me a cold look. Her eyes narrowed and her nostrils flared.

"Your fault," she said.

"My fault?"

"That's right," she said, launching the words aggressively. "It's your fault. All of this."

Callie said, "Donovan's the only one in the world who figured out what happened to you. You're safe because of

# 57.

WE GOT THE hugely ungrateful Alison out of there, checked her into the hotel room between mine and Callie's, got her fed, and got her story.

After I was declared dead, Alison had indeed entered into a romantic relationship with Quinn, hoping to cash in on the work I'd promised her. Like Quinn said, when Alison realized it wasn't going to happen, she took off. Unfortunately for her, Quinn was the best guard in the business, and she didn't get far. When he caught her they had some words and he kidnapped her and brought her to the warehouse.

When he was home, which was most of the time—Quinn doted on her. But whenever he left, he chained her to the wall, his way of making sure she was glad to see him when he came home. If he planned to be gone more than a few hours, he'd use a longer chain, one that allowed her access to all her comforts. Quinn had been gone about three hours and was on his way home when I caught up to him on Walnut Street.

So again, according to Alison, my fault.

"Did he beat you?" Callie asked.

"Occasionally," Alison said.

"Did he force himself on you?"

"At least twice a day."

"You ever put up a fight?"

"The times I did, that's when he'd beat me."

Here in the welllit room she looked white as a ghost. I said, "Before tonight, how long had it been since you've been outdoors?"

"More than three years," she said. "And the only reason I know that is that I had a TV."

Callie gave her a sleeping pill and sat up with her until she fell asleep. Then she joined me in my room and we broke the seal on a bottle of mini bar wine and drank it while working out Alison's training schedule.

I said, "I'll give Lou the second and third weeks, you get the next three, and I'll take the next two. Then she can shadow you on a couple of jobs. After that we'll test her out on something easy, see how she handles it."

"What's the going rate for nurse maids these days?"

"Twenty grand a week, plus whatever you make on jobs."

"Works for me," Callie said. "Who gets her the first week?"

"Dr. Crouch. Because if Nadine doesn't think she's ready, we pass on the project, and try to help Alison get her old life back."

I punched a key on my cell phone and winked at Callie. "Listen to this," I said, pressing the speaker button.

Dr. Nadine Crouch answered by shouting, "Unacceptable!"

I said, "I've got a patient for you."

"What's the matter with you? Do you have any idea what time it is?"

"This is a good gig," I said. "It will appeal to your avarice."

"I'm trying to sleep, Donovan. Don't ever call me in the middle of the night like this again. Unacceptable!"

"How's twenty-five hundred a day sound?"

"I'm sure it will sound a lot better when I wake up in a couple of hours. Call me then," she said, and hung up.

"She's a bitter old bitch," Callie said. "Don't you think?"

"Yeah, she doesn't care much for people, though she seems to like me."

Callie shook her head. "You ever hear yourself talk?"

# 58.

MYRON GOLDSTEIN WAS already parked at the rest stop at mile marker 177 just outside his hometown of Cincinnati when I pulled up. I got out of my car and made a wide circle around his, checking for possible snipers. As I approached his passenger door, he unlocked it, and I got in.

"Sal says you want to die," I said.

"You're Creed?"

"I am."

"I thought you'd be younger."

"I thought you'd be older."

Myron Goldstein nodded. He was a gaunt, sadfaced man with thick lips and sagging jowls. A thatch of wiry black hair protruded from each of his nostrils. He kept a wet, mu-cus-soaked handkerchief in one of his shaky hands, and used it to dab at the slimy fluid that steadily dripped from his nose. He wore thick hornrimmed glasses.

I said, "The way this works, you tell me what's on your mind and I'll tell you what I think."

"Have you always been a healthy man, Mr. Creed?"

"Can we just get to it?"

He smiled a thick-lipped smile. "Yes, of course," he said. He paused for a moment to dab at his nose, and then said, "Are you familiar with ALS?"

"Lou Gehrig's Disease?"

"Yes, that's the one. ALS is a progressive, fatal, neuro-degenerative disease that slowly but steadily robs your body of voluntary movement. The disorder causes your muscles to weaken, day by day, until they are unable to function. You can see it already in my hands. That's not Parkinson's, it's called fasciculation, and it signals the beginning of the end."

"I'm sorry to hear it," I said, and meant it. Looking at Myron Goldstein made me ashamed of myself. For the past seven weeks I'd been hosting a pity party over losing Kathleen and Addie, while this poor son of a bitch has been dying by inches. Of course it hurt to lose the people I'd wanted to grow old with—but Myron Goldstein wasn't going to grow old at all. Maybe Kathleen and her fiancé would someday break up, allowing me to slip back into her life. Or maybe not. But at least I had a future to dream about, which was a hell of a lot more than Myron Goldstein was going to get.

"So what you're saying, you want me to kill you, put you out of your misery."

"Yes."

"Why not just commit suicide? You'd save fifty grand."

"I have insurance policies worth much more. But they don't pay for suicide."

"I have to say no," I said.

"Why not?"

"This money, fifty thousand dollars. It's money your wife and kids should have."

He tapped the envelope on the console between us. Beyond this, I have no other money," he said. "The insurance will pay off most of my debts and allow my wife to keep the house, the car, and have a comfortable life. It may not be enough to put my kids through Dartmouth, but there are state schools available if they can't qualify for scholarships. More than anything, if I go now it will spare my family having to care for me the last year of my life. I don't want them to go into debt, have to put their dreams on hold, watching me die a slow and horrible death."

"What's so great about Dartmouth?" I said. "Their football program sucks."

"Don't get me started," he said, laughing. "I might wind up killing *you*!"

I couldn't help but like the man. When Callie put a bullet in Robbie, I finished him off, to end his suffering. Myron was suffering too, but—

"Killing you," I said, "It doesn't seem right, somehow."

Myron laughed hard enough to start coughing, which caused him to hack up all sorts of disgusting elements.

"What's so funny?" I asked.

"No offense, but you kill people for a living. Does that seem right?"

"The people I kill, they don't have a choice. You do."

"And I've made it. So which is the better kill?"

We went silent a minute, me thinking about it, him giving me time to do so.

"Put yourself in my shoes," he said. "What would you do?"

I thought about my heart, wondered if there was any way to fulfill this contract without causing a relapse.

"You ever kill a man?" I said.

"Heavens no!"

"Ever cheat on your wife, beat your kids, anything along those lines?"

"No." He saw where this was going. "I've yelled at my kids a lot, and scolded my dog."

"Scolded your dog?"

"More than once."

"You bastard!" I said.
He smiled.
I smiled.
Then I slit his throat.

# 59.

IT WAS ABOUT four in the afternoon when the dry wall guys finished laying their last coat of mud. A bunch of them planned to meet up afterward at a nearby tavern, but I said they'd have to celebrate without me this time.

The temperature was mild, and several hours of day-light remained. I loitered around the lot of the newly constructed 8,500 square-foot home, picking up trash until the last worker drove away. Then I set to work.

The house at 2010 Dunvegan sat on the cul-de-sac of a new development called Rock Hill Gardens. Several homes in the neighborhood had already made it to closing, but none were inhabited yet. When seeking an attic to live in I prefer high income spec homes like these in new, protected neighborhoods. I cordon off a cubicle in a strategic gable of a house like this and use it as a safe house. I had a number of these safe houses scattered in major cities throughout the country, but this would be my first in Atlanta.

This particular lot was just under an acre, and featured a steep, wooded fall-away that afforded me access to the rear of the house while being sheltered from the view of future neighbors. It would be ready for occupancy in a month, but probably wouldn't sell as quickly as the others because it didn't overlook the Rock Hill Country Club golf course.

I had come to Atlanta because the leaders of a local terror

cell had been identified and needed killing. Before I'd had a chance to get them, our informant learned that my old nemesis, Abdulazi Fathi, was coming to town in two weeks to give his people final instructions and a proper sendoff. Reasoning that killing Fathi along with the others would deal a severe blow to Al Qaida, Darwin decided to put my mission on hold until Fathi arrived. With two weeks to kill (pardon the pun), I decided I might as well establish a safe house, so I checked out the neighborhoods until I found an upscale one in the final stages of construction. Then I called the number on the builder's sign in front of the house and got myself hired on his construction crew.

For days I'd been hiding tools and wire and dry wall under rolls of insulation stacked in the attic above the garage. In a few minutes I'd start walling off the interior gable above the guest bedroom. I'd lay wire for electricity to run my computer and keep my cell phone charged. Then I'd tap into an HVAC vent for heat and air to keep me comfortable, and splice a line into the high-speed internet signal. Thirty days from now, give or take, I'd be living in a mini mansion with all the comforts of home.

Dry walling a gable is a simple way to steal part of a family's home without paying rent. All I need is a few square feet and a couple hours of uninterrupted time to nail it up. If the builder were to notice the dry wall in the attic, he'd just think his guys made a dumb mistake. But that hasn't happened yet, because in these late stages of new home construction, no one ever looks into the far ends of the attic. In older homes there's always a risk of detection because when homeowners decide to renovate, my gable might need to be accessed to run phone or cable wires or TV antennas for better reception. But new construction at this price point always pre-wires. If the particular gable I want has been pre-wired, I simply re-route the wires around my living space.

My early years as an army sniper required me to re-main perfectly still for hours at a time, useful training for my later years of living in the attics of occupied homes. To hedge my bet, I try to select an unused gable, located as far from the attic access doors as possible. I'm safest just off the far side of a rarely-used upstairs guest bedroom, in case an unexpected cough or snore might alert a family pet. Usually that isn't an issue, since most of my construction time is spent sound-proofing my living space. I lay a top-quality, non-squeak floor. Then I mix sawdust and baby powder into the caulk I lay between and below the floor joists and in the nail holes to keep the floor from squeaking. My access door is always located on the far side, indented a couple of feet into my living area to avoid detection. Several times a day I don a blindfold and practice escaping. The blindfold forces me to memorize the location of the floor joists in case I have to escape in pitch darkness.

Once completed, I move in and try to adapt to the rou-tines of my host family. When possible, I sleep when they sleep and remain quiet when they're active. I monitor their personal computers, their phone calls, and watch family interactions through pinhole cameras I've hidden throughout the house. Within weeks I'll know their habits and schedules better than they do, at which point living with them becomes more enjoyable. If they're going to be away a few hours I'll use their toilets, enjoy a hot bath or shower, nap in their beds, share their food and liquor, and use their computers instead of mine when sensitive work needs to be done without leaving an electronic trail.

The most fun I have is playing with their pets.

Dogs and most other pets are easy, but I can't live with a cat. Once a cat discovers me, things are never the same. It never stops looking up at the ceiling and always tries to find a way to get to me. It moans and fusses all night every night and never seems to get over it. I've got a soft spot for all types of pets, but when one of my families brings a cat into the house I have to find it a new home ASAP. Otherwise, the owners keep sending exterminators into the attic to check for mice.

# 60.

IT TOOK FOUR evenings to complete my living space on Dunvegan, and wouldn't you know it, Fathi never made it to Atlanta. That's the problem working with informants: they're usually worker bees who have access to little more than rumors. But I was content to kill the two local leaders, and did so with ease.

I'd followed them to a lively nightspot in downtown Atlanta. The place was so jammed it took me ten minutes just to find them. They were part of a crowd that was watching two hard-bodied women dancing to the loudest music I'd ever heard. Every thirty seconds the cavernous room went dark, and strobes and laser lights flashed from all directions.

It was a perfect killing field.

I positioned myself behind the terrorists, put a syringe in each hand, and waited for the strobes. When they flashed, I plunged the needles into their lower backs and stepped aside as they fell to the floor. A couple of people shouted, but the dancers kept dancing, the music kept blaring and I was out of there before anyone figured out what happened.

My new living quarters were complete, but because the construction crew was still on site, it would be weeks before I could move in. The two weeks I planned to spend training Alison were still in the future. My dinner with Callie and Eva had been postponed twice due to Eva's tireless rehearsal and performance schedules, but I had a firm commitment from them for Sunday night.

Finding myself with three days of free time, I decided to meet Dr. Nadine Crouch in Jacksonville, Florida. For five thousand dollars and a beach vacation, Nadine agreed to help prepare my daughter Kimberly for the news that I was alive.

I could have contacted Kimberly sooner, of course, but I wanted to wait until I was certain I wouldn't have a relapse. Now I'd killed a dying man and two terrorists without incident, so I figured to be okay from this point on. Since I'd missed a big part of Kimberly's life, I planned to make up for it, starting now. But first I had to pave the way. I couldn't just walk up to her with this new face and say, "Hey, Kim, it's me, your dead Daddy!"

Kimberly had inherited my entire estate—or to be more precise, the entire estate identified in my will and supporting documents. Naturally I had secret stashes of money tucked away in case I needed to fake my own death.

Lou Kelly had spoken to Kimberly a few times over the years, but my funeral was their first face-to-face meeting. Since then, he'd called every month to see how she was doing. It was Lou who presented my "Last Will and Testament" to the attorneys settling the estate, so it seemed natural to have Lou phone Kimberly about this. He taped the exchange and emailed it to me in an audio file.

"I want you to meet someone," Lou said. "Her name is Dr. Nadine Crouch. She was your father's therapist."

"There must be some mistake, Mr. Kelly," Kimberly said. "There's no way my father would ever see a therapist."

"She only saw your dad a few times that last year. But she has some information you'll want to hear."

She went silent a moment, then sighed. "I'm not so sure I

287

want to hear it, Mr. Kelly."

"Kimberly, you're just going to have to trust me on this."

"You obviously know what it is," she said. "Just tell me now."

"Nadine's going to be in Jacksonville this week anyway. Plus, the type of news she's got for you—well, let's just say she's better trained to deliver it."

Kimberly agreed to meet Nadine in the lobby of the hotel where Nadine was staying. Kimberly showed up, the two exchanged pleasantries. After a while Nadine said, "It's a beautiful day. Can we walk on the beach while we talk?"

I'd never been to Jacksonville Beach, but I was mildly surprised to find it as nice as it was. Located on a barrier island east of the city, Jax Beach had plenty of sand, decent but not overwhelming surf, and was relatively uncrowded. Nadine, Kimberly and I walked north along the beach, though I remained fifty yards back. If you saw the big guy in the Penn State ball cap, sunglasses and earbuds, that was me. The earbuds allowed me to listen to their conversation.

Nadine said, "Your father and I spoke about you many times."

Kimberly said, "Can we just skip to the part where you tell me he's alive?"

"Excuse me?"

"My father. Donovan Creed. He's alive. You know it and I know it. So where is he and why hasn't he contacted me before this?"

I couldn't believe what I was hearing. Kimberly *knew*?

Nadine was speechless as well. Kimberly started looking around the beach. It took her all of five seconds to spot me. "What a ridiculous disguise," she said, laughing. She and I ran toward each other like actors in the worst forties movie ever made. When we got close, she leapt up in the air and I caught her in my arms. I spun her in circles as I'd done when she was four, and she hugged me like a long-lost teddy bear she'd rediscovered.

I placed her gently back on her feet and looked at her. She was older, more mature, but she was still Kimberly. She slapped my face.

"I can't believe you'd do this to me!" she said. "You don't trust me enough to call or send a message? What the hell kind of father *are* you?"

"The kind who was in a coma for more than three years," Nadine said, catching up to us, out of breath.

Kimberly looked into my eyes. "I believe it."

"You do?" I said.

"Yes. If you'd been conscious, you wouldn't have chosen *that* face!"

I laughed. "It's so great to see you!"

"You too," she said. "But you've got a lot of explaining to do."

"I'll tell you everything. But first, you've got to tell me how you knew I was alive."

She reached into my pants pocket and pulled out my silver dollar, the one my grandfather gave me all those years ago. "This was not among the personal effects they gave me."

I grinned proudly. Nadine said, "Well, you are certainly your father's daughter." To me she said, "Just so we're clear, I still get to keep the money, and the vacation."

"You're the most mercenary shrink I've ever known," I said.

"It's always nice to be number one," she said.

I gave her a hug.

"Unacceptable," she said, pulling away.

"Thanks for trying to help," I said. "I think I can take it from here. Have a great vacation."

"I plan to." She headed back toward her hotel.

The next three days were the best Kimberly and I ever spent together. Hours into the reunion, when the subject of Kathleen and Addie came up, I told her everything and she said, "If Kathleen made you that happy you need to tell her you're alive. More importantly, she deserves the right to choose what makes her happy."

"I'm afraid she might choose me out of guilt."

"And that bothers you because?"

"Tom's a good man, much better husband material than me."

"How can you say that?"

"I checked him out."

She shook her head. "Can you really know so little about women?"

"I can, and you know it."

"Dad, listen to me," she said, assuming the role of parent, a role that suited her better than me. "You need to tell her four things: you're alive, what happened, why it happened, and how you feel."

Sure, I could tell Kathleen those things, but I felt she'd have a better chance at happiness with a steady, normal guy like Tom. Addie was also a major part of the equation. Addie had lost her first family, then, three years ago, she'd lost me. Then Tom came into her life, and I had no doubt that she loved him and accepted him as a father figure. If I came back into Kathleen's life Addie would be forced to lose either me or Tom. The poor kid had been through enough, she didn't deserve to lose a third father figure. To further complicate things, I still wasn't certain that life in the suburbs would suit

290

me. Last but not least, if Kathleen chose me, she'd always wonder if I was the right choice. If she rejected me, she'd always wonder if Tom was the right choice. It wasn't fair to put her in that situation.

But I did love Kathleen, and wished things had turned out differently.

"Dad?" Kimberly said, bringing me back to the present. "Will you tell her the four things?"

I sighed. "It's not that simple."

"Is it simpler than losing her?"

# 61.

EVA LESAGE WAS a doll.

Maybe five feet tall, she weighed about the same as my left arm. Her face and everything else about her was delicate to the point of seeming fragile. She had almond, cat-like eyes, frosted hair, and a young girl's voice that still retained the slightest hint of a Russian accent. Looking at her up close, it was hard to find any similarity between her and Tara Siegel, other than height and general facial resemblance. If Darwin had truly intended to cover Tara's death with Eva's body, our people would have had an uphill battle convincing anyone they were even related. All I could think was that Eva must have changed dramatically over the past few years, and no one told Darwin.

I wondered if Callie had done something to alter Eva's weight or features. A half drop of arsenic taken once a week might keep the weight off and produce a complexion similar to Eva's.

Callie, watching me like a hawk, caught me staring, probably understood what I was thinking. She shook her head at me, a subtle reminder that I was on her turf, and therefore my life was in her hands. I nodded back, hoping to send the signal: okay, none of my business, everything's cool.

We were in Callie and Eva's luxury high rise condo, overlooking the Vegas strip. These types of units start above two million dollars, and from the looks of the upgrades, the furniture and wall coverings, I'd say this one was somewhere north of three.

Eva turned out to be a gourmet cook. She prepared a wonderful four-course dinner, one that partnered different wines with each course. Whenever I complimented Eva, Callie beamed. It was clear that Eva was her treasure.

My cell phone rang. I checked the caller ID and excused myself to the foyer.

"What's up, Sal?"

"You see the paper today?"

"Which one?"

"Cincinnati."

"I'm in Vegas, Sal."

"Yeah, whatever. Anyway, paper says some-one—whatcha call—anonymously donated two hundred thousand dollars scholarship money for Myron Goldstein's kids to go to Dartmouth."

"So?"

"Goldstein was a guy got his throat slit at a rest stop here a few days ago, as if you didn't know."

"So?"

"So what do you think about that?"

"I think his kids would rather have their father alive."

"My kids wouldn't," he said.

"Don't sell yourself short, Sal. I'm sure your kids love you."

"They love money, sex and drugs more."

"But you're still on the list, right?"

He thought about it a minute. "Yeah. I'm still on there somewhere."

"Stay on the list, Sal. That's what it's all about."

We hung up and I found the girls in the kitchen.

"Let me help you with the dishes," I said.

"No, please," Eva said. "You and Cal go in the den and visit. I'll finish up and join you in a few minutes."

Callie escorted me to the den.

"Well?" she said.

"She's a doll."

"I told you."

"You did. And listen, Callie, if you girls want to make out in front of me, or play a little slap and tickle, I hope you know I'm cool with it."

"Slap and tickle? Oh. My. God!"

I looked at her. Eva might be adorable, but Callie was peerless. She was wearing high-waist, navy pinstripe pants and a white V-neck Tee with cap sleeves. Her hair was wild tonight, almost electric. Slung over one side of the armchair beside her was a navy leather Dior handbag with a buckled strap. A substantial diamond tennis bracelet graced her wrist.

"Looks like you've managed all right without me these past three years," I said.

"A girl's gotta do," she said. Then she fell silent. Something invisible came over her eyes and her expression changed the slightest bit.

I'd been out of commission for more than three years, and my reflexes were bound to be shot, and I'd probably lost a step or two since I was in peak shape. But my instincts were still sharp.

"There's something on your mind, something you're not telling me," I said.

"Yes."

She got up, took a few steps to the window and stood there a bit with her back to me. I gave her some time. From my vantage point I could only see the dark Vegas sky and a haze of casino color out the window, so I focused instead on Callie's perfect backside, which I knew to be eminently more interesting than whatever she was staring at. Three years ago she'd been a perfect ten. But somehow she'd gotten prettier.

She turned and faced me.

"It's Kathleen," she said.

"What about her?"

"They've set a date."

The news shouldn't have had a major effect on me. I mean, I knew they were engaged. But Kimberly's words suddenly started ringing in my ears. Kathleen did deserve to know. Maybe I'm not the best man she could have fallen in love with, but she chose me three years ago knowing there were better men in the world. Certainly Addie deserved a better father than me, but what if she didn't want the world's greatest father? Maybe Addie would rather have me in spite of my shortcomings. Bottom line: Kathleen had a right to choose.

The last thing Callie said to me before I left was this: "If you want Kathleen, you'd better hurry!"

"The last thing I said to Callie before I left was this: "You remember when you were a kid, after you were attacked, how you stared at that window for hours at a time?"

"Of course."

"You were trying to figure out something about the way the wooden pieces intersected, the wooden slats that frame the window panes."

She nodded.

"You said if you could figure that out, it would be something to hold on to, a place from which to reclaim your sanity."

"What are you getting at?"

"I'm not a spiritual guy."

"No shit."

"Hard to believe, right? Anyway, I was just wondering if you ever figured it out."

She frowned. "If I did I'm not conscious of it." She thought some more, shook her head. "Why are you bringing this up now?"

"You're happy," I said. "I've never seen you truly happy before."

"I am happy. But what does this have to do with the wooden slats and the way they intersected on the window pane?"

"It's like you were at a crossroad in your life. And you chose to move forward."

"And that's what you're going to do?"

"It is."

# 62.

I'VE ALWAYS LIVED my life by the theory that we're all just a phone call away from a life-changing event. It could be a phone call like the one Kathleen will get tomorrow morning, informing her that a man named Donovan Creed bequeathed an unusual gift to her adopted daughter. A financial gift that would make it possible for Addie to receive a new face and body, one that would be completely free of all scars caused by the fire that ravaged her.

We're all just a call away from a life-changing event. But it doesn't have to be a phone call.

It could be a guy like me, standing by an oak tree in the park, watching a little girl playing with the tiniest puppy, say, a Teacup Maltese. There might be something wrong with the little girl's skin. She might be a burn victim. Behind her, a man and woman might be enjoying a long-overdue picnic. They might be sitting on a large blue checkerboard quilt, removing food from a wicker basket. The woman might handle the basket tenderly, almost lovingly, as if it had been a gift from someone she'd loved and lost. The quilt and basket might appear unused, as if they'd been waiting a long time to be placed into service.

I pretended to go for a long, circular walk while Kathleen and Tom ate and played with Addie and the puppy. It was clear the three of them had the chemistry to be a perfect little family, and for a minute I thought about walking away. I mean, just walk away and never turn back. Because I hated the thought of destroying Tom, hated destroying the foundation Kathleen had built these last three years.

But I hated to lose her and Addie even more.

I timed my loop to hit the ice cream stand at the same time they did, with the three of them in front of me. Addie held a tiny leash in her hand, tethered to her puppy. I wanted to wait before announcing myself, wanted to step into their world a minute, smell Kathleen's hair, her perfume, hear her voice.

I stood motionless behind them. Addie turned and smiled at me, and my knees nearly gave out.

I smiled back.

I wanted to say something, like, "that's an adorable little puppy you've got there, Miss"—but I knew Kathleen would recognize my voice, and I hadn't heard hers yet.

Now that I was standing here I didn't mind breaking Tom's heart. He was young, he'd get over it. And he'd know it was for the best, he'd be able to see it in Kathleen's eyes: she and I were meant to be together.

I stepped closer, positioning myself directly behind Kathleen. I closed my eyes and inhaled her fresh-scrubbed scent and remembered the day I snuck into her home in North Bergen and waited on her bed while she showered. On that occasion, just before making love, I thought to myself, *when I look at her I am reminded of all that matters*. It was the day of Sal's party in Cincinnati, and we hadn't left New York yet. That day she came out of the bathroom, smelling the same way, pretending not to notice me. Then she jumped into bed and practically devoured me.

Addie turned back to me for a second look. Not because she recognized me, but because most people are so shocked by her face, their first reaction is to look away. I didn't. Instead, I lifted my hand and mouthed the word, "Hi." She gave me her full-wattage smile and I almost choked on the lump in my throat.

For a tough guy I was having a lot of trouble with this.

I felt a tear collect in my eye, wimp that I am. It slid down my cheek, where my scar used to be, the one Addie and the other burn kids traced with their fingertips the day I met her, the same day I met Kathleen. See? Like I said, the three of us were meant to be together.

I wiped the tear from my cheek. I'd wait until they ordered their ice cream before saying anything. That way I'd get to hear Kathleen's voice. I knew if I could hear her voice just once, everything would be all right.

At that moment Kathleen turned to face Tom, leaned her body into his, and said, "I love you so much."

# EPILOGUE

I've always lived my life by the theory we're all just a phone call away from a life-changing event.

But it doesn't have to be a phone call.

It could be a guy like me, standing in an ice cream line, a guy who suddenly gives up his place in line and starts walking away, a guy who hears a small, raspy voice say, "Good-bye," and knows that voice will stay with him the rest of his life.

You can choose between your
wife, or your lover, but one
of them has to die...

DONOVAN
CREED

SAVING
RACHEL

1.75 MILLION COPIES AND COUNTING...

JOHN LOCKE

# 1.

MAYBE IT ISN'T fair, but I blame Karen Vogel for what just happened.

I mean, sure, I'd made the first move, and true, I'd plotted her seduction with all the precision of the Normandy invasion. I baited the hook with romantic candlelit dinners, private dining rooms, and elegant wines. I'm the one who made all the promises, bought the clothes, the mushy cards, and glittering jewelry.

But none of this would have happened if Karen Vogel hadn't been so...gorgeous.

We're in Room 413, Brown Hotel, Louisville, Kentucky, 10:15 a.m. My twenty-something-year-old conquest lies on the bed watching me through eyes like aquamarine crystals. I'm scrambling into my pants, tucking in my shirt, but those piercing eyes freeze me in place, and I'm like a deer caught in the headlights.

Karen rolls onto her side, props her chin on her fist, and says, "You meant what you said, right, Sam?"

Her toned, athletic body features long legs and a belly so flat I can see two inches down the front of her panties, elevated as they are between two perfect hips. It's a good view, the kind you never get tired of, and I get that feeling again, like I'm riding a lucky wave. I mean, *I just banged Karen Vogel!*

"I meant every last word," I say.

1

"It was just three words," she laughs, flashing her dazzling white-cliffs-of-Dover smile, and I'm thinking, *If I couldn't bang Karen, I'd pay serious coin just to watch her brush her teeth!*

Yeah, I know what you're thinking. Go ahead, tell me I'm pathetic. I won't deny it. But I'm the one standing in a hotel room with the semi-naked and infinitely beautiful Karen Vogel, not you. And of course, I'm the one she loves. What? You don't believe me?

Keep reading. I'll prove it.

"I love you, too, Sam," she says. "That's why I did this."

See?

She could have asked me to free Charlie Manson, watch an Oprah film festival, or swim up a ninety-mile-an-hour river of shit to Spain, and I'd have done it. But all I had to do to get in her pants was say, "I love you."

I won't lie. I could tell you I've had my share of beautiful women, and I'd be telling the truth—provided my share is equal to one. So yeah, if I'm brutally honest, I've slept with one beautiful woman before today. And her name is…

Her name is Rachel.

I don't really want to talk about Rachel right now, but I'll give you a promo and you can be the judge. It's been years since we dated, but in those days, Rachel was coltishly beautiful. She had long brown hair with blonde highlights and eyes the color of tupelo honey. Her face was unique, a fabulous contradiction for a young computer geek like me. Angular and beautiful, her face suggested a sophisticated bearing. But her ever-present, enigmatic smile identified her as a keeper of naughty secrets.

At her best, Rachel wasn't in Karen Vogel's league, but honestly, who is? No one I've ever seen. Karen is superstar

2

gorgeous, a French Riviera head-turning, jaw-dropping beauty. So if you're saying Karen's the measuring stick, then Rachel, along with the rest of the planet's women, can't reach it. But with Rachel's looks, you take it all in and maybe you decide the word you're searching for isn't *beautiful*, but something even more special.

She had been adorable.

I see Karen watching me from her perch on the bed. I know I'm supposed to say something to her now, something reassuring, but there's a disconnect between my brain and mouth. So I just keep staring at her, freezing the moment in time, wondering what's going to happen between us from here on out, and realizing we've both upped the ante in our relationship.

I zip my pants, notch my belt, step into my seam-stitched Prada loafers, and wonder if it's true. Do I really love her? *Perhaps not as much as she loves my money*, I think. Then again, it's hard to measure these things when you're only a month into the relationship.

I kiss her good-bye and take the elevator down to the hotel parking garage.

In case you care, I drive an Audi R8, red with a black vertical stripe just back of the cabin. This sexy, low-slung rocket runs a hundred thirty grand and turns heads faster than Paris Hilton crossing her legs in a biker bar.

So I'm in the parking garage, fishing in my pocket for the keyless remote when I hear a crackling sound and—*Christ!*—something zaps my calf muscle from behind. I turn to see what's happened, and the next thing I know, I'm rubbing the back of my neck where it feels like someone stuck me with a hypodermic needle.

I'm groggy, but I feel movement and realize I'm in the back

3

seat of a stretch limo with two guys. The one on the left is a muscle-head; looks like Mr. Clean on steroids. The other guy's a well-dressed older man with slicked-back gray hair. He's wearing a black silk suit with vertical white lines and a white tie. The voice in my head is saying, *Oh shit, this is the real deal*, and the voice is right. This is a full-fledged gangster sitting across from me, and he's just asked me something. Unfortunately, my head is in a fog and I'm still reeling, so I can't quite make out what he said.

Trying to buy time to get my bearings, I say, "I'm sorry. *Who* are you? What did you just say?"

"Your wife," he says.

I look around. *He's talking to me?* His words seem to be coming from deep in a well. *Did he just ask me about my wife?*

"What about her?" I ask.

"What's her bra size?"

"Her...*what*?" I ask. "Who *are* you? What the hell are you talking about?"

He sits there in silence, with no hint of a smile.

I pat my pocket instinctively, feeling for my cell phone. Then I remember I left it in the car so I wouldn't be disturbed while seducing Karen. Nothing kills the mood faster than a phone call, right?

*Unless you're interrupted by a gangster. That would be worse.*

I'm trying to remain calm, hoping to clear my head of this thick, fuzzy feeling. I look out the window and see we're only about eight blocks from the hotel. We're moving slowly, making our way down Liberty Street. I look out the window and see a homeless guy sitting on the curb, his back propped against a street lamp. He's wearing a red corduroy jacket and

4

holding a sign in his lap that says, "Stop Offering Me Work!" I wonder briefly if this is some sort of marketing ploy on his part, and it strikes me I've got more important things to worry about, like what the hell is going on. I'm afraid to stare at the gangster or Mr. Clean, so I continue looking out the window. We're picking up speed now. I watch us pass a heart rehab clinic, an office building with a Starbucks on the first floor, a Thornton's gas station, and then it's under the interstate and up the ramp onto the expressway, heading east.

"Where are you *taking* me?" I ask.

The well-dressed *Sopranos* wannabe waves his hand. "Here's your problem: you ask too many questions. I ask a simple question, you ask me two in return. So I'm gonna try again," he says. "What's Rachel's bra size?"

I go cold inside. *This mobster knows my wife's name?*

If we're being completely honest, I should admit that after dating Rachel six years ago, I married her. And while she's no longer coltish or enigmatic, I still love her very much. I know you'll find this hard to believe, given my recent activities with Karen Vogel and having heard me profess my love for her back in the hotel room. You need to understand—well, you don't need to understand it at all. But I'd like to explain. Wooing and bedding Karen has nothing to do with loving Rachel. I need—I *crave*—the attention, the...appreciation. It's been such a long time since Rachel was impressed by anything I'd accomplished. Do you have any idea what it's like to invent something no one has ever thought of before? Something only a handful of people in the world even *know* about?

No, of course you don't. No offense, but if you'd done that, you'd be telling your own story right now instead of reading mine.

What did I do that's so special?

Drum roll, please... I created a computer program that makes it impossible to track money. Bear with me, this is a bigger deal than you might think. If you deposit, say, a hundred million dollars in a checking account, my program splits that sum into a hundred different bundles and shoots them at bullet speed to different banks all over the world every twenty minutes. The only way to stop the transfers is to enter a sixteen-digit code into my Web site. When that happens, the bundles park themselves in their current location until a second code, known only to my clients, is entered. Then the bundles reassemble into the client's original checking account. I only have eighteen clients, but they each pay me ten thousand a month to keep their money safe from prying eyes.

We all sit and look at each other as the limo switches lanes and accelerates onto I-64. In the background, I hear the limo driver talking softly into a wireless phone device. "Four minutes," is the only thing I hear him say clearly.

*Four minutes? Till what?*